Copyright Page

Heir and the Shadows

Copyright © 2025 Nic Smurthwaite

For permission requests, contact:

Nic Smurthwaite

ISBN: 978-1-9193313-0-0

Cover design: Nic Smurthwaite Cover image: Licensed stock photography, edited by Nic Smurthwaite

Printed in the United Kingdom

THE HEIR
AND THE SHADOWS

THE DEEPER THE LEGACY,
THE DEADLIER THE ENEMY

BY

NIC SMURTHWAITE

Disclaimer

This is a work of fiction. Names, characters, places, businesses, organisations, institutions, events, and incidents are either products of the author's imagination or are used fictitiously.

Any resemblance to actual persons, living or dead, or to actual events is entirely coincidental. References to real locations, landmarks, or institutions are included for atmosphere only and are not intended to depict actual events or to suggest any endorsement or association.

All trademarks, service marks, product names, brands, and logos that appear in this book are used fictitiously and remain the property of their respective owners. The author makes no claim of ownership, endorsement, or affiliation with any trademarked entity.

Government agencies, departments, security services, and law-enforcement bodies referenced herein are portrayed fictitiously. Nothing in this book should be taken as a statement of their policies, practices, or operations.

This book is a work of entertainment. It should not be relied upon for legal, financial, or operational guidance in any context.

Dedication

This book is dedicated to my grandchildren —
you are the light in my life —
and to the generations that follow.
May it inspire you to chase your dreams,
no matter your age.
You are the future.

Epigraph

'We are all visitors to this time, this place.

We are just passing through.

Our purpose here is to observe, to learn, to grow, to love…

and then we return home'.

— Aboriginal proverb

Acknowledgments

My heartfelt thanks to my wife, Pat,

and my daughter, Helen,

whose love and encouragement have carried me through every page.

To my friends new & old — Donna, Ray, and Giulia —

for your help, support, and belief in this project,

your insights and steady presence made all the difference.

And to all my family and friends who cheered me on along the way:

I am deeply grateful.

Contents

Preamble

For centuries, wealth had been power, and power had always attracted shadows.

Behind the grandeur of empires and the marble façades of London banks, another current ran: quieter, older, and ruthless. Some called it the Syndicate. Others knew it by no name at all, only by its reach.

Its roots stretched back to the darkest trades of the Empire: sugar, opium, and slaves. Wherever fortunes were built, the Syndicate had been there, taking its share. Its genius was never to stand in the light. It worked through others' pliable heirs, compromised politicians, indebted merchants… always seeking a house strong enough to carry its wealth, yet pliable enough to bend to its will.

For generations, the Aldridge family had resisted that bend. Their bank had been courted, threatened, and undermined, yet the Aldridge name endured. Iron wills had held the line, and the Syndicate had seethed at the insult.

The Syndicate had time. It could wait years, decades, lifetimes. And if waiting failed, it would act.

Part I

The Ghost and the Vineyard

The past awakens in the scent of old vines, and one man follows a face across half the world to reclaim what time and lies have stolen.

Chapter 1: A Taste of the Past

The first week of January 2000 was hushed on Harley Street, the silence broken only by the tick of the old carriage clock on the mantel. The street itself had changed little since Lord Richard Aldridge first walked its length in his youth. The motorcars outside were faster now, the suits slimmer, the air perhaps a little less scented with pipe smoke.

He sat in the familiar leather chair, hands resting lightly on the silver head of his cane. This office had been a second home to him in times of injury and illness, and once, long ago, the place where his life had been saved and he had been nursed back to health.

The Aldridge name carried weight in England: centuries of titles, land, and an old and venerable institution, the Aldridge Merchant Bank, one of the oldest in the City of London. The title of Marquess, along with the estates and the bank, had always passed through the male line. That unyielding tradition had shaped his life before he was even born.

Richard had been the younger of two children. His elder sister, Lady Catherine, should have been the natural heir, but her gender excluded her from the succession. Before Richard's birth, Catherine had fallen for a man of questionable character and, to the dismay of the family, borne him a son, Edward. Upon the death of the old Lord Aldridge, Edward would have inherited everything: the title, the estate, and the bank.

But fate, or chance, had other plans. Two years after Edward's birth, Richard was born. As the first legitimate male in the direct line, he vaulted ahead of Edward in the order of succession. That single twist of bloodline law had ignited a rift between Catherine and Richard himself, a rift that had never healed. Over the decades, it had festered, becoming something colder, sharper, and more dangerous than mere resentment.

Edward himself had not gone to the war. A childhood injury, a badly broken leg that had never healed truly, had spared him the call-up.

Instead, the fourth Marquess, Richard's father, had found him a place in the family bank. It was meant as a kindness, but in time it proved a chink in the armour. Through Edward, outsiders found their way into the ledgers and corridors of Aldridge & Co., not outright control but a crack wide enough for influence to seep in.

Edward survived into middle age. He married late and, in 1950, became a father for the first and only time. The boy was named Jonathan. For a few years, Edward seemed almost to outpace the limp that had dogged him since childhood, but he never shook off the compromises that had been forced on him in the bank. When he died in the late sixties, Jonathan was still in his impressionable teens. Left fatherless so young, he was not without mentors; the very hands that had once guided Edward's pen in the ledgers soon shaped Jonathan's ambition.

Where Edward had been hesitant, Jonathan grew to be ambitious; where Edward had been compromised, Jonathan embraced those compromises as opportunities. And when Jonathan stepped into his father's place in the bank, the rivalry and resentment came with him. Where Edward had been the Syndicate's crack in the wall, Jonathan was the one who would prise it wide open.

The door opened and in stepped Dr Fiona Markham. Tall, poised, her dark hair pulled neatly back, she carried the brisk confidence of her profession, but her eyes softened when they met his. She had known him all her life; he had dangled her on his knee when she was a toddler. Her grandfather, the first Dr Markham, had been the man who'd brought Richard back from the brink after a mission in France went wrong. Fiona still reminded him of her grandmother, the same way of tilting her head when she was about to deliver bad news.

She closed the door gently behind her.

'Richard', she began, taking the seat opposite, 'I'll not dance around it. We've had the latest tests back, and… it's not good'.

He held her gaze, his expression unreadable.

'How long?'

'A few months, if we're lucky. The treatment options…' She paused, then added quietly, 'They'd do little but make you miserable'.

He nodded once, without flinching. 'Then we shan't bother with them'.

'Richard—'

'My dear girl', he said, with the faintest smile, 'I have been on borrowed time since 1944. This is no great surprise. Now, as I see it, we've both had a rather trying morning. You will come with me to the club for lunch'.

She gave a short laugh, shaking her head. 'Only you would receive a death sentence and respond with an invitation for lunch'.

The club was as it always had been: wood-panelled, quiet, its leather chairs worn smooth by generations of old soldiers, barristers, and merchant princes. It was not just another club, and Richard was not just another member. The first Marquis of Hunton had helped finance its founding, his father had chaired its committee, and Richard himself had grown up half in its dining room. The Aldridge connection was woven into the place as deeply as the brass nameplate on the door.

At their table by the window, Richard picked up the wine list, but before he could speak, the sommelier approached with a conspiratorial air.

'My Lord', he said, lowering his voice as though sharing state secrets, 'we've a bottle I'd like your opinion on. New World, I'm afraid, but reputedly rather exceptional. From Western Australia'.

Richard arched an eyebrow. 'Australia? And you wish to serve it here? The committee will have a fit'.

The sommelier grinned and set the bottle on the table.

'All the more reason to have your verdict. After all, it was your family's coin that helped found this place, and your lordship's word still carries the weight it always has'.

Richard reached for it and then, halfway through turning it in his hands, stopped dead.

The photograph on the back label leapt out at him like a ghost.

She was there.

Margaret O'Connell. His Maggie.

Not as she might look now, well into her nineties, but exactly as she had been when he'd last seen her: standing in the dappled light outside a little French church, a shy smile on her lips, her hair pinned back in that no-nonsense nurse's style. Her eyes were what stopped him cold: dark, steady, full of quiet fire.

The blurb beneath was a gut punch:

Margaret O'Connell, chief winemaker of O'Connell Estate, Margaret River, Western Australia.

Fiona's voice sounded distant, muffled, as though through water.

'Richard? Are you all right? You've gone white as a sheet'.

He set the bottle down with care, afraid that if he held it a moment longer, the truth might spill out for all the club to hear.

'Quite all right, my dear. Just… an unexpected memory'.

But inside, his heart was thundering. Maggie had been dead for decades; he had mourned her, grieved her, built a life without her. And yet here she was, impossibly preserved in glass and paper, staring back at him from a wine label on the far side of the world.

The sommelier hovered nearby, clearly pleased with the effect.

Richard forced himself to breathe. His throat was dry, his voice low.

'Tell me, would it be too great a nuisance to have this label removed for me? I've a… personal interest in it'.

The sommelier inclined his head, as if such odd requests were all in a day's work.

'Not at all, my Lord. I'll see to it at once'.

He whisked the bottle away, returning a few minutes later with the label dried flat between sheets of card, pressed and protected as if it were a collector's item.

Richard slipped it into the inside pocket of his jacket. His hand lingered there a moment longer than necessary, as though by touch alone he might reach across the gulf of years and hold her again.

After a lunch he'd barely touched, Richard rose, still lost in thought. Fiona insisted on walking him to the waiting Bentley, despite his protests that she had appointments to keep. As the two of them crossed the hall, the atmosphere shifted. A few of the older members glanced up from their papers and brandy glasses. No one spoke; they never did, but conversations paused, heads dipped in quiet acknowledgement. Lord Richard Aldridge was more than a patron here; he was part of the club's fabric, as enduring as the portraits that lined its walls.

Outside, the late afternoon light slanted across Pall Mall, gilding the club's brass railings and catching the deep claret paintwork of the Arnage RL waiting at the kerb.

Yet for the first time, those same eyes lingered. His step was measured, his expression composed, but his colour was a touch too pale, his jaw set a fraction too tightly. The shock of that wine label of Maggie's face staring back across the decades was still with him, and he wanted nothing more than the quiet of West Farleigh to order his thoughts. To others, though, it looked like age was catching up at last.

At a corner table, two younger men in well-cut suits set down their glasses almost in unison. They looked every inch the modern face of the club: discreet financiers, perhaps, or civil servants on the rise. To most, they were invisible. To those who needed to know, they were Syndicate. Their voices never broke from polite talk of the markets, yet one noted the stiffness of Richard's gait, the pallor beneath his old soldier's tan.

They did not see the sharpness in his eyes, the careful calculation behind his silence. They saw only an old man waning.

A folded crossword, a single pencilled mark in the margin, and the message was sent:

Lord Aldridge departing. Appears unwell.

Within the hour, it would be on a Syndicate desk.

'I'll have my secretary ring you tomorrow', she said, squeezing his hand. 'And Richard…' She hesitated, her voice lowering. 'Don't try to face all of this alone'.

'My dear girl', he replied, opening the heavy rear door for her, 'you forget I've had rather a lot of practice'.

The drive back to Harley Street was quiet. Fiona sat with her hands folded in her lap, her professional poise restored, though every now and then, he caught her studying him out of the corner of her eye. When they reached her surgery, he stepped out and escorted her up the steps. She paused in the doorway.

'You'll call me if…'

'I'll call', he promised, though both knew he likely wouldn't. She gave a brief nod, then disappeared inside, the door closing softly behind her.

Richard settled back into the Bentley's deep rear seat, the faint scent of Connolly leather and polished walnut reminding him of a time before the world had gone quite so fast.

'Not home, Mason', he told his driver. 'We're going to Kent. West Farleigh Manor'.

'Yes, my Lord'.

The Arnage eased into the late-day traffic, the muted rumble of its engine a comforting undertone. London's sprawl gave way to open countryside, the air sweeter, the light softer. The journey was long enough for his mind to think about the label, the photograph, the decades between them.

West Farleigh Manor appeared at last, rising from the green folds of the Medway Valley like a memory made stone. A large Georgian house, its red brick softened by centuries and half-draped in wisteria, stood with the quiet dignity of a place that had weathered wars, births, deaths, and scandal without ever bending to fashion. Not grand, never ostentatious, but elegant in the way of old things built to last.

The gardens ran down in gentle terraces to the river, where the Medway glimmered between willows and alder. At the far end, half-hidden by trees, stood the old boathouse. Its timbers were weathered to silver, but the slate roof remained sound, the slipway still clear. Once it had served for summer punts and fishing trips; in the war years, it had offered discretion, a quiet way in and out when the lanes above were watched too closely. Even now, though rarely visited, it was kept in careful repair.

The wrought-iron gates swung open at their approach, and the Bentley crunched up the gravel drive. Mason stopped before the wide steps, where tall sash windows mirrored the late evening sky and the sweep of the lawn. Behind the house, the River Medway curled past in silence. Here, on its banks, privacy was absolute. Richard stepped out, inhaling the scent of damp earth and clipped box hedges. The air here always seemed different, as if the river itself carried away the weight of London.

He had come here for one reason: to think and to plan. He needed to get to Margaret River; that was the only way he was going to solve the conundrum. And if the questions raised by that wine bottle had disturbed him in the club, here, in the silence of his study, they seemed louder still.

From his days with the Special Operations Executive, Churchill's secret army in WWII, he was adept at slipping in and slipping out of places unseen, and he now needed to call on these skills once again. A commercial flight to Perth was out of the question, too public, but he needed to get there quickly. Quietly, he formulated a plan. First, he called his driver into the study.

'I need you to take this down to the solicitors, Becket & Thomas in Canterbury, and, equally as important, drop this into Headcorn Aerodrome on your way', Richard said, holding out two sealed envelopes. 'They'll be expecting the Headcorn envelope tonight; ask for the flight desk. The one for the solicitors is for Michael O'Shea, first thing in the morning. Stay the night in Canterbury and see them as soon as they open. It is not to go by post; the contents are both sensitive and time-critical'.

'Yes, my Lord', Mason replied, taking the envelope without question. He had been with Richard long enough to know that some errands were never to be delegated, and never to be delayed.

Within the hour, the Bentley's deep exhaust note faded into the Kent evening, carrying the envelopes safely east.

Richard waited until the sound of the Bentley had faded before lifting the telephone.

His next call was to his London PA, Anna Hargraves, who had been with him for more than twenty years. 'I'll be unavailable for a few days', he told her. 'Can you clear my calendar of all engagements; tell anyone who asks that I'm under the weather. Nothing more than that. And inform my great-nephew Jonathan that he'll be overseeing the Bank in my absence'.

There was the briefest pause at the other end, the sort of silence born not of hesitation but of quiet concern. Anna had long since learned never to question his instructions, yet there was something in her tone, a softness, almost protective, when she replied:

'Of course, my Lord. Everything will be taken care of. I hope you feel better soon. Would you like me to put you through to your nephew?'

Richard allowed himself the faintest smile. She had always been more than efficient; loyal to a fault, and perhaps, though neither would ever admit it, a little too fond of the man behind the title.

'Please', he responded.

There was the faint scratch of a pen on paper, then a polite pause.

'I'll put you through now, my Lord'.

A moment later, Jonathan's voice came down the line, smooth and businesslike.

'You're not well, Uncle?' There was the slightest emphasis on the word, as if weighing it.

'Nothing serious', Richard said evenly. 'You'll be handling the Bank until I return. I trust you'll keep it standing'.

'Of course', Jonathan replied, his tone perfectly even, perhaps a shade too even. 'Rest well'.

Richard ended the call, satisfied that the necessary arrangements had been made. He replaced the receiver and, after a pause, dialled another number.

The line clicked, then a familiar voice answered in French.

'Bonsoir, Richard, mon marquis'.

Richard allowed himself the faintest smile. Luc was the son of the Resistance fighter who had spirited him out of France in 1944, when the Germans had left him for dead after an ambush. The bond between their families had never broken.

'I need to reach Western Australia—quickly, and without drawing notice. Can you arrange it?'

'But of course', Luc replied. 'The Gulfstream will be waiting at Dunkirk. Your papers will be in order'.

'Merci, mon ami'.

Richard set the receiver down, the link to his wartime past now secured, and reached again for the telephone.

'Hermes, Ben speaking'. The voice was brisk but warm, the easy assurance of someone who knew every lane between Maidstone and the Weald.

'This is Lord Aldridge. I'll need a car at West Farleigh Manor first thing tomorrow morning. To go to Headcorn Aerodrome, need your usual discretion'.

'Understood, my Lord. We'll have a silver saloon at your door by seven sharp'.

'Thank you, Ben'.

Hermes was a small, family-run firm, their cars a familiar sight across the Medway Valley. Richard had relied on them for years, not for their punctuality, though they were never late, but for their discretion. In his world, that counted for more than anything.

True to form, they arrived on time as arranged. The pre-dawn was black and windless when Richard stepped out onto the gravel sweep in front of West Farleigh Manor. Headlights picked out the wisteria on the façade as a silver Ford Mondeo rolled up the drive.

Ben climbed out, his easy manner unchanged since the first time Richard had used Hermes Cars twenty years ago. His lordship had asked for discretion, and so, after finishing his dispatcher's shift, Ben had decided to make the pick-up himself.

'Morning, my Lord', Ben said quietly, taking the single leather holdall Richard carried. 'Light packing, that's a good sign'.

'Let's hope so', Richard murmured.

The Ford slipped through the lanes towards Headcorn. By the time they passed through Staplehurst, a thin grey light was seeping into the eastern sky, hedgerows standing out sharply against it. Even at that hour, the little aerodrome was stirring a lone light in the clubhouse café, the smell of bacon and coffee drifting into the cold.

At the counter by the window, a uniformed officer glanced up as Richard stepped inside. Mason's discreet delivery to the Canterbury solicitors had included the necessary stop-off at Headcorn to deliver the required paperwork; the flight plan and customs notice were already in place. Here, passport control was little more than a desk and a rubber stamp.

The officer leafed through Richard's documents, gave a curt nod, and marked the page. Formalities complete, he was free to board.

The pilot stood by the steps, flight plan filed, everything ready. Ben carried the bag to the edge of the grass, then shook Richard's hand.

'Safe travels, sir. We've not had this conversation'.

'Quite right, Ben. You never do'.

Within minutes, the Cessna was skimming down the frost-hardened grass and lifting into the pale sky, banking south-east over the patchwork fields of Kent. Richard watched the Medway snake away beneath him and felt the old, familiar shift in his mind, the quiet narrowing of focus that had carried him in and out of places unseen, a skill he'd never truly lost.

Later that morning, Jonathan rang West Farleigh Manor.

It was Mrs Fletcher, the housekeeper, who answered.

'Lord Aldridge? No, sir, he's not here'.

Jonathan let a beat of silence hang. 'Not there?'

'No, sir. He left early this morning. He left no instructions as to where he was going, just took an overnight bag with him'.

Jonathan's jaw tightened around the receiver.

'Quiet', he said smoothly. 'If he contacts you, let me know at once'.

He replaced the phone with deliberate care. Across the desk, one of his Syndicate contacts raised an eyebrow. Jonathan's voice was calm, but the message was anything but:

'He's gone. Off the grid. And none of them know where'.

So, the old queen's off on a trip… what are you up to now?

But even as Jonathan allowed himself the thought, the news was already moving upward. Within the hour, Alpha had been briefed, and the weight of it was clear: this was not a matter to sit on. He requested an audience.

The ritual was familiar. A secure line, a series of numbers tapped in by hand, and then the sterile tone of an open conference bridge. He laid the handset beside the console, logged into the WebEx link, and waited.

The screen came alive with a shared whiteboard: blank at first, then populated by nothing more than a list of anonymous initials. No faces, no names. Just presence. The voices, when they spoke, were distorted, clipped, devoid of warmth.

Alpha reported crisply. 'Lord Richard Aldridge has informed Jonathan that he will be out of the office for a few days. Further enquiries confirm he left his house in Kent early this morning with an overnight bag. Destination: unconfirmed. Duration: unknown. Prior observation at his club suggests he may be in declining health'.

A pause, then a voice flattened by a scrambler: 'Inheritance?'

Alpha inclined his head, though they could not see it. 'Should Lord Richard die without issue, Jonathan inherits both the title and, through his existing control, the Bank. Our objective would be achieved in full'.

Another pause. Then the whiteboard refreshed, the words appearing one line at a time:

RISK?

Alpha flicked a chart onto the shared screen: exposures, family history, dormant assets. 'Potentially significant. The timing is… inconvenient'.

The whiteboard flickered, refreshed. One stark line appeared in black text, typed from nowhere:

GLOBAL ALERT: LOCATE LORD RICHARD ALDRIDGE. URGENT.

After Alpha left, the bridge should have gone dead, but one line stayed live.

A distorted voice broke the silence, its Scottish burr sharper than protocol allowed.

'Decades we've waited. Decades! We could have ended him in '45, '55, any year since. But no — patience, always patience'.

Another voice, lower, measured, cut in.

'And for good reason. A wartime accident was plausible. But a peacetime death of a Marquess? Questions would have been asked. Too much light on the Bank'.

'Light, we could have handled', the first snapped, sharp with fury. 'A banker found hanged beneath Blackfriars Bridge did not shake the system; it absorbed it, explained it away. But this man? We let him grow into a legend. Decorated soldier, pillar of the City, untouchable. And all the while, his sister's line was ready. Jonathan is ready. We should never have let it drag on this long'.

A third voice cut across them, distorted tones bristling with contempt — a woman's voice, clipped and precise.

'Do you forget the plan? Catherine's bloodline was always the answer. Groomed, indebted, inside the tent. When the old man died, succession would pass cleanly. The Bank would be ours without a shot fired'.

There was a pause, then the Scottish voice hissed again.

'I thought we closed this out'.

A fourth voice entered, rougher, the Russian accent flat and cold.

'We did'.

'Did we?' the first pressed. 'Are we absolutely sure we did?'

The pause that followed was heavier than any argument. Then the Russian spoke again, quiet and final.

'Find out where he is going'.

The line clicked out. Orders were already moving through the Syndicate's chain of command.

The Channel coast was clear that morning, the sea a dull steel-grey under the first sunlight. Within the hour, they were banking over the white curve of Cap Gris-Nez, then lining up on approach to Dunkirk.

Luc Moreau was waiting by a weathered hangar, his coat collar turned up against the wind. His handshake was firm, his eyes sharp as a hawk's.

He took in the man before him, now in his nineties yet carrying himself with a poise and vitality that belied both age and reputation. Luc had expected frailty; instead, he saw a spark, as if the mere act of leaving London had lifted a weight from Richard's shoulders.

'You haven't changed much', Luc said, eyes glinting. 'Or so my father used to say—the man who never stayed still long enough to be caught'.

Richard allowed himself a faint smile. 'Some habits', he said, 'are too useful to break'.

The Gulfstream IV sat ready on the apron, its polished silver fuselage gleaming in the morning light. No airline markings, no paperwork in Richard's name, just a discreet registry and a crew who knew better than to ask questions.

Once airborne, the long hours passed in the low hum of the engines. Richard dozed lightly, waking now and then, from dreams of Maggie, wine bottles, and his past life, to watch the thin cloud drifting over the vast, empty ocean. Somewhere south of Jakarta, they dropped down for a refuelling stop.

The strip was small; little more than a tarmac ribbon carved from scrub and heat-shimmer. The refuelling crew worked in silence, but Richard's instincts prickled. One man near the fuel truck looked away too quickly when their eyes met; another lingered at the foot of the airstairs a moment longer than necessary, his gaze flicking over the cabin interior.

Nothing overt. No threat he could name. But the old habits stirred that cold, coiling certainty in the gut that something might be wrong. The man at the airstairs touched his pocket as he turned away, a small, casual gesture that set Richard's nerves on edge.

When the tanks were full, they climbed back into the haze, the Indian Ocean stretching unbroken to the horizon. Hours later, the coastline of Western Australia rose from the sea—pale sand, turquoise water, and the dark fringe of forest beyond.

The Gulfstream banked low over Geographe Bay, its glassy curve catching the morning sun, and touched down on the runway at Busselton. Small, quiet, the sort of place where a man could come and go without making the society pages.

Richard stepped out into the dry warmth, the tang of eucalyptus sharp in the air. He took a slow breath. Whatever lay ahead—answers, danger, or both—it had begun.

Chapter 2: The Wedding, 1944

Richard had first met Maggie O'Connell in the canvas wards of a British field hospital not far from Caen. A bullet graze to his shoulder. 'Nothing serious', he insisted. But it had forced him from the line, though the fever that followed nearly undid him. Maggie, tall and sun-browned, with the clipped vowels of Western Australia, had tended him with brisk efficiency. She had the knack of making even stubborn soldiers obey, her hands gentle but her tone sharp enough to cut through morphine haze.

The young doctors deferred to her judgement, and even Richard, who had stared down Gestapo interrogators without blinking, found himself quietening when she ordered him to rest. One night, as the ward rattled under the drone of enemy bombers, she laughed and told him she had come 'half the world over just to keep pig-headed poms alive'. The sound carried like sunlight in the gloom.

When his convalescence dragged on longer than expected, she sometimes walked him down into the village where her unit was billeted. At first, it was just companionship: her steady arm on his, her bright chatter softening the dull ache of recovery. She teased him about his accent; he countered with mock-serious critiques of her French. Somewhere between the laughter and the silences, a closeness grew.

One evening, in the glow of the soft lamplight outside the café, he brushed an unruly strand of hair from her face. She didn't step back. The world beyond the square, the war, the losses, seemed to pause, just for a breath. After that, the idea of being apart felt unthinkable.

They took a small apartment above the café run by an elderly widow, Madame Rousseau, who pretended not to notice when Richard's boots were left by the door overnight. The room was cramped, one narrow bed, one warped wardrobe, a single window overlooking the square, but Maggie made it bright. She put flowers from the hedgerows in a chipped vase, spread her nurse's cloak over the chair, and laughed that it was 'home enough'.

The village itself bore the scars of war: shuttered shops, walls pocked with bullet marks, a square half-emptied of men. Yet life clung stubbornly on. Each morning, the smell of coffee and fresh bread rose from the bakery opposite; each evening, the clatter of cups in Madame Rousseau's café mingled with the hushed conversations of farmers and partisans. Sometimes Richard and Maggie sat in the shadows by the window, sharing a crust of bread and a bottle of vin ordinaire, listening to the curfew patrols tramp past. She would rest her head on his shoulder, and for a few stolen minutes, they lived as though the war had been banished from their door.

By the time his bandages came off, Richard knew two things with absolute certainty: that he owed his life to her, and that he could not imagine facing what came next without her.

One evening, in the dim light of their little apartment, he reached into the battered trunk at the foot of the bed. From a small leather case, he drew out a heavy gold ring, set with a single deep-blue sapphire.

Maggie stared. 'Richard… that looks like it belongs in a museum'.

'It belonged to my grandmother', he said softly. 'Passed down to the eldest son in every generation. I wasn't meant to carry it into the field, but I did. Something in me thought…' He broke off, unable to finish.

He slipped it onto her finger. 'Maggie O'Connell, will you marry me?'

Her laugh was half joy, half disbelief. 'Here? Now? In the middle of France?'

He smiled, a glint of mischief in his eyes. 'Yes. Here. Now. In the middle of France. If not now, when?'

The vineyard lay in the gentle curve of a sunlit valley, vines heavy with summer fruit. The chapel bell called softly across the fields as a handful of guests gathered. There was no grandeur, no pomp; war had stripped all that away, but dignity remained.

Richard stood beside the chaplain, boots polished, battledress pressed. His shoulder still ached beneath the tunic, but he stood straight, proud. Maggie wore a borrowed cream dress, the lace at the cuffs carefully mended. Wildflowers were pinned in her hair in place of her nurse's cap. She looked to Richard like hope itself.

A farmer and his wife acted as witnesses, the wife pressing a sprig of lavender into Maggie's palm. 'Pour la chance', she whispered for luck.

The other witness lingered at the vineyard's edge. Stocky, thickset, with the air of someone who didn't quite belong, he cradled a camera that gleamed too new for a farmhand's wages. Its heavy shutter snapped with mechanical precision, each frame measured and deliberate. Richard barely noticed his attention was fixed on the warmth of Maggie's hand and the way her lips curved when she said, 'I will'.

The vows were spoken, halting but strong. The kiss that sealed them was fierce, the claiming of joy in a world intent on crushing it. For a moment, even the birds hushed, as though the day itself had paused to honour them.

In the shadowed rows afterwards, Maggie laughed softly. 'You were trembling', she teased.

'Facing the Gestapo was easier', Richard admitted.

She touched her forehead to his. 'Then perhaps trembling suits you'.

They stole a moment among the vines. Maggie plucked a grape and pressed it to his lips, her free hand drifting, just briefly, to her stomach. Richard noticed but said nothing. The thought warmed him: perhaps their joy was already bearing fruit.

At the far end of the row, the man with the camera adjusted his lens. One last shutter click, and the moment was fixed forever—an image destined for hands neither bride nor groom could have imagined.

The chaplain made a careful note in his service book, signing it with the steadiness of a man who had performed too many funerals and too few weddings. 'It will be copied to Army records in London', he assured Richard. Maggie's name, her unit, and her country of origin were all set down in ink alongside his own. The farmer and his wife signed as witnesses; Maggie drew her name in a bold, looping hand.

It was official. A marriage recognised not only by God and the law of France, but by the British Army itself.

The photograph crossed borders more swiftly than soldiers could march. Hidden in a neutral embassy pouch, it passed through Lisbon, a city where whispers carried further than rifles. Too many hands brushed against it on its way, and not all of them belonged to friends.

At the Aldridge townhouse in Belgravia, Lady Catherine Aldridge studied it in silence. Her brother had married a colonial nurse. A child would follow, perhaps already on the way. And if that child were a boy, the Syndicate's careful plans for succession would unravel.

Catherine slid the photograph into a silver frame, admired it for a heartbeat, then locked it in her desk. Later that evening, a sealed envelope left the house. It bore no family crest, no military routing. Only a discreet cypher mark one Catherine had used before, not with ministers, nor generals, but with those who prided themselves on keeping awkward matters firmly… in hand.

At the War Office, a clerk later discovered that the official record of Lieutenant Aldridge's marriage had 'gone astray' in transit. The chaplain's duplicate copy had also been quietly redirected. On paper, no wedding had ever taken place.

A week later, Richard was cleared for a reconnaissance near Chartres. The ambush came suddenly and mercilessly, German fire tearing the hedgerows. Resistance fighters dragged him half-dead into the forest; he barely survived.

When he woke in England, weak but alive, they told him Maggie had been killed in an air raid.

In France, Maggie was told Richard had died of his wounds and been buried in an unmarked grave.

Both mourned the other. Both carried grief like a wound that would never close. And the war rolled on.

Chapter 3: WA

The jet touched down just before midday. Busselton was nothing like Perth International: no bustling concourses, no banks of CCTV cameras, no customs officials eyeing every passenger. Just a small, local terminal, a scattering of light aircraft, and the smell of aviation fuel drifting on the warm breeze.

It was exactly what Richard had wanted: anonymity.

Waiting in the small arrivals hall, little more than a shed, was Jack. His eyes swept the trickle of passengers from the tarmac until they settled on Lord Richard. He moved forward with easy confidence, hand outstretched, the picture of a man greeting an old friend or a business acquaintance down from Perth.

'G'day, name's Jacques, but everyone here calls me Jack or just Jac. Came out of France years ago. Old mate of Luc's'.

As they stepped out into the sunlight, Richard quietly thanked Luc in his mind, efficient as ever, just like his father, never leaving anything to chance.

Jack gave a wry smile as he opened the passenger door. 'Apologies, it's not the Jag today, she's in for a service. We'll have to rattle down there in the old Land Cruiser instead'.

Lord Richard glanced at the dust-caked Toyota and allowed himself a faint smile. 'After what I've driven in my time, Jack, a Land Cruiser will feel practically regal'.

The Land Cruiser rumbled out of the car park and onto the open road, heading south. As the kilometres rolled by, Busselton gave way to stretches of eucalyptus, vineyards, and open farmland, the scent of sun-warmed earth drifting through the open windows. Jack glanced sideways at his passenger and blinked. For someone in his nineties, Lord Richard looked almost ruddy with health, the warm sun on his face. Not the frail figure he had been led to expect.

Richard let the conversation wander easily, but in the back of his mind, the image of Maggie on that wine label burned as sharply as it had in the club. Somewhere in this vast country was the truth, and he was getting closer with every kilometre.

In a discreet office suite overlooking Collins Street, the regional Alpha adjusted his headset and keyed in the familiar sequence. Below, trams rattled along the boulevard, the gothic spires of St Patrick's rising over a city that thrived on respectability. Collins Street was Melbourne's answer to Wall Street and Pall Mall rolled into one: merchant banks, law firms, and insurance houses wearing discretion like armour, the perfect camouflage.

Inside the office, the disguise was complete: open-neck shirt, sleeves rolled against the heat, papers scattered in the manner of a mid-level consultant pushing through an afternoon call. To anyone passing, he was just another bloke in an anonymous tower. Only the multiple locks on the door and the faint hum of the noise-scrambler on the desk betrayed the truth.

The secure bridge came alive with its familiar ritual. A sterile whiteboard flickered into being, initials populating one by one, faceless as the city outside.

Alpha cleared his throat, voice level.

'Subject confirmed. Busselton arrival cross-checked against refuelling report. He's en route to Margaret River'.

He hesitated a beat, then added, quieter:

'That should not be possible. We closed that file years ago'.

The whiteboard pulsed once, waiting for a response. Outside, another tram clattered past, its bell ringing cheerfully against the silence.

'Margaret River...' One of them let the words hang, heavy. 'That is the last place in the world we would want him'.

Another voice, flatter: 'Exposure risk. If he reaches the O'Connell property...'

The whiteboard flickered, refreshed by unseen hands. Two stark lines appeared in black text:

REMOVE HIM.

MAKE IT LOOK LIKE AN ACCIDENT.

The Australian Alpha leaned back, thumbed his pen across the desk, and exhaled slowly as the whiteboard cleared to blank.

'Right', he muttered under his breath. 'Welcome to Australia, you old pommie bastard'.

By mid-afternoon, the Land Cruiser turned off the main road and onto a long gravel drive flanked by neat rows of vines. A tasteful wooden sign read: O'Connell Estate – Cellar Door & Visitor Centre.

Jack slowed the vehicle near the main building, a modern structure of timber and glass. The car park was empty, save for a single white Ute.

As they approached the main gate, a broad-shouldered security guard stepped forward, his expression stony.

'Sorry mate. Cellar door's closed today. Private business only'.

Before Richard could answer, Jack leaned out the window.

'G'day, Dave. Didn't think you'd be on this shift'.

The guard's face softened a notch.

'Jack? What are you doing here? You know we're closed'.

Jack nodded towards the passenger seat.

'Was asked to play taxi and bring this gentleman down from Busselton. He's come a long way to meet with the O'Connells'.

The guard frowned, torn between duty and recognition, then shook his head.

'I don't know, mate—orders are, nobody gets in when we're closed'.

A tense silence lingered for a moment. Richard was weighing his next words when the door to a nearby office opened.

And she stepped out.

The same figure from the label. The same features as 1944. The same Maggie.

It was impossible, utterly absurdly impossible, and yet there she was in the flesh, sunlight catching in her hair.

For a heartbeat, he could almost believe time itself had folded, until his reason caught up. No, not Maggie, but someone who carried her face, her bearing, her eyes lit with the same dark fire.

Without thinking, he called out.

'Maggie!'

The woman stopped dead, her hand still on the doorframe. Her head turned slowly towards him, eyes narrowing in confusion… or recognition.

For a heartbeat, the world seemed to be still around them.

The woman hesitated only a moment before stepping away from the doorway and striding towards them, her expression curious rather than guarded. The security man melted back a pace, clearly deferring to her.

'We're closed today', she said, her voice carrying the easy warmth of the Australian bush. 'But I have to ask… how do you know my name? Have we met before?'

Richard straightened, summoning the courtesy drilled into him over a lifetime.

'Miss… I must apologise for what must seem a terribly rude outburst. I've travelled a very long way, and when I saw you just now… you are the image of someone I knew a long time ago. I came here because of this'.

From the inside pocket of his jacket, he took out a monogrammed envelope with the Aldridge crest on it. Inside, carefully pressed flat, was the label the sommelier had removed from the O'Connell Estate wine bottle back at his club and, alongside it, the small photograph of Maggie from 1944. He handed them both to Miss O'Connell.

'Your face, Miss O'Connell, is on this label. And that face belongs to a woman I once... knew very well indeed'.

Her brows knit as she took in his words. Then, slowly, her expression shifted, curiosity melting into delight, the kind of joy that starts in the eyes before it reaches the mouth.

'Well', she said at last, 'you'd better come up to the homestead and meet Gran'.

Chapter 4: The Homestead

The short drive from the cellar door to the homestead wound through more vineyards, the late-afternoon sun casting long shadows across the neat rows. The air was warm and rich with the scent of the vineyard and eucalyptus, and Richard found himself gripping the armrest as though to anchor himself in reality.

Jack handled the wheel with an easy familiarity, nodding now and then at the familiar landmarks. 'Haven't been up this way in a while', he remarked, glancing towards the young woman beside Richard. 'Good to see you again, Miss O'Connell. Is your grandmother keeping well?'

She smiled warmly. 'As sharp as ever. She'll be wanting to meet our guest straightaway'.

Jack gave a small grin, then fell quiet again, wisely letting the silence hold as they rounded the last bend. Beside Richard in the back seat, Miss O'Connell watched him with a mix of curiosity and quiet excitement.

The homestead came into view: a sprawling, single-storey house of pale stone and timber verandas, its corrugated iron roof gleaming in the sun. Beyond it, gum trees swayed gently in the breeze. It was grand without being ostentatious, the kind of place built for generations, not just for show.

They pulled up in the shade of a wide pepper tree. Richard stepped out, his knees a little less steady than usual, and followed the young woman up the veranda steps.

Inside, the air was cool and faintly scented with lemon polish.

And then, from the doorway at the far end of the hall, she appeared.

Maggie.

Not as she had been in 1944; the years had left their marks, but unmistakably her. The same eyes, the same smile, the same presence that had carried him through the worst of the war. She stood very still for a moment; her gaze fixed on him as if afraid he might vanish if she blinked.

'Richard...'

He took a step forward, then another, his throat tight. 'Maggie'.

For a heartbeat, neither moved. And then she was in his arms, holding him fiercely, as though to make up for all the decades stolen from them.

They moved into the sitting room, its pale walls lined with shelves and low tables crowded with framed photographs, a private gallery meant for family eyes only.

On the mantelpiece, the first picture stopped him cold: a faded black-and-white print of their wedding day, taken in the vineyard all those decades ago. Beside it sat a small photograph of a baby boy, perhaps only months old, his mother's eyes and—Richard's heart lurched—his own jawline.

The boy appeared again in later pictures, taller now, his smile easy, his stance confident. One faded colour photograph showed him in jungle greens, helmet tilted back, an M16 slung at his side, the red earth and dense scrub behind him unmistakably Vietnam. Beside the frame, mounted under glass, lay his campaign medal, the striped ribbon of yellow, red, and blue bright against the bronze disc. A quiet honour, placed here not for show but for remembrance.

Then came the image of him on his own wedding day, standing beside a striking Aboriginal bride. Richard's gaze caught on the young woman's hand, resting lightly on her groom's arm. There, unmistakable even through the gloss of the photograph, was the ring: heavy gold, with a single deep-blue sapphire. His ring. The one he had taken from the little leather case in France and slid onto Maggie's finger over half a century ago. For a heartbeat, he felt the air go from his lungs. Maggie had kept it, and somehow, through all the years and silences, it had come to rest on the hand of the young woman who had married Maggie's son.

And then nothing. No photographs of the couple together after that.

The next images were different. Two children, a boy and a girl, clearly twins, appeared as infants in Maggie's arms, then as sun-browned youngsters playing among the vines, then as older children at a farmhouse table with books and maps spread before them. Always with Maggie. Always here, on the estate, never anywhere public.

It was a childhood shaped by the vineyard, the bush, and the quiet company of their grandmother. Richard noticed there were no school uniforms, no crowds, no seaside postcards with other children. Just the three of them, Maggie and her twins, in the still, safe corners of this land. And then proudly in one corner stood another frame: a young officer, clearly one of the twins, in parade dress, cap under one arm, medals gleaming at his passing-out parade. The story the wall told was clear enough for anyone who knew how to read between the lines, but Richard kept his thoughts to himself.

Lord Richard had lost all track of time, lost in this new world of Maggie and the photographs of a life that might have been. Day had turned to night without his noticing.

He was brought back to the present by a burst of laughter drifting in from the veranda, Maggie junior's voice ringing out, followed by Jack's amused correction in French.

A moment later, the door opened, and the two stepped inside, still smiling.

'Jack's been giving me a French lesson', Maggie junior explained, her eyes sparkling.

'She's a quick learner', Jack added with a grin, 'though she just asked me for a donkey instead of a coffee. Nearly had me spitting my drink'.

Maggie junior swatted his arm, blushing with laughter. 'It's not my fault! You make it sound too easy'.

The warm evening air followed them in, carrying with it the playful echo of family and friendship.

Richard rose, making his apologies.

'Jack will run me into town; he's dropping me at the hotel in Margaret River before heading home. I should take my leave before I overstay my welcome'.

Maggie would have none of it.

'Don't be ridiculous, Richard. You are my husband, and I've missed you all my life. You are staying with me; I'll not lose another moment'.

Before he could protest, she reached up to her neck and unclasped a fine, understated chain. Hanging from it were two worn gold bands: her simple wedding ring alongside a slender engagement ring, the stones dulled slightly with age but still catching the light. She set them gently in his palm.

'Put them on my finger'.

His breath caught as he slid the rings into place, his hand trembling slightly. Then his eyes fell to his own left hand, to the matching band he had never removed since it was first placed there in 1944. Some had noticed over the years, fewer still had asked, and those who did learned quickly that Lord Aldridge's private life was not a matter for discussion.

The room was silent for a moment, the only sound the soft sigh of the wind through the veranda shutters. Outside, Jack made his polite goodbyes and left alone, his vehicle carrying away the only clue that Richard had planned otherwise: the leather holdall in the back seat, now bound to spend the night elsewhere.

For a long moment, they simply stood there, his hand covering hers, both staring at the two matching bands that had outlasted war, grief, and decades of silence. Then Maggie reached up and touched his cheek with a tenderness that undid him.

She led him down the hallway she had walked for most of her lifetime, into the bedroom that still carried her quiet orderliness. From the top drawer of the dresser, she drew out a leather-bound photo album, its edges worn soft with use. Maggie settled beside him on the neatly made bed and laid the book across their knees.

Slowly, she turned the pages. Children with gap-toothed grins and sunlit harvests, she named each face in turn: their son Richard, his wife Sarah, and their grandchildren Richard and Maggie, weaving their stories in a low, steady voice.

Richard listened, the weight of the years pressing upon him, yet softened by the warmth in her tone. The children from the vineyard lived on in every smile, every glance caught by the camera.

At last, she closed the album and laid her hand over his.

'For all the years they told me you were gone', she said softly, 'you were never absent. Not really'.

And for the first time since France, 1944, neither of them dreamed of absence. Richard was exactly where he belonged.

Dawn came early in Margaret River. Lord Richard woke in Maggie's bedroom, the scent of her still lingering on the pillow beside him, her steady breathing a quiet reassurance in the half-light. For a moment, he simply lay there, watching the first pale threads of light seep through the curtains, wondering at the strange fortune that had brought him here.

The air was still cool, edged with the dry, resinous scent of the bush after the night. Careful not to wake her, he reached for his cane and pulled on the clothes he had worn the day before, the only ones at hand, his bag still stowed in Jack's Land Cruiser. The shirt was creased, the jacket smelled faintly of travel, but it would serve well enough.

Stepping out onto the veranda, he drew a breath of the cool air. The silence of the early hour pressed close; only the rolling laughter of kookaburras and the whisper of wind through the pepper trees broke it.

He walked without a plan, leaning on the cane as his feet carried him along the veranda and down the path that skirted the vines. The homestead revealed itself slowly in the grey light: cottages huddled against the trees, a scatter of tools leaned where someone had left them, the faint glow of an early riser's light in a window.

At the far edge of the grounds, beneath a great jacaranda whose spreading branches glowed with the last of the spring blossom even in the dawn, he found two weathered wooden crosses. Beside them stood a carved wooden post, its surface patterned with spirals and curves softened by time and weather. The meaning lingered nonetheless: a marker placed by hands that knew the old ways, declaring this ground to be sacred.

For a moment, he thought he saw something shift at the corner of his vision, shapes that dissolved when he looked straight at them. Not threatening, not even solid, more like shadows of belonging. He felt no fear. Instead, a stillness settled over him, as if unseen eyes were measuring and weighing, deciding whether to accept him.

He stood before the graves, head bowed. Whoever lay here, they had been loved. And as he stood in the quiet, a thought came unbidden: when his own time came and he believed it was not far off now, despite feeling more alive than he had in years, he would rather lie in such a place as this, close to Maggie, close to the land, than in the cold marble vault in West Farleigh Manor.

When he looked up again, a tall figure in fatigues was approaching across the paddock, his stride steady, his eyes already fixed on Richard.

Richard froze. The resemblance was unmistakable: the stance, the bearing. This, surely, was the mysterious person Maggie had spoken of the night before. Her grandson. His namesake.

The younger man halted a pace away, extended his hand. 'Captain Richard O'Connell', he said simply.

Lord Richard took the hand, gripping it firmly despite the tremor in his own. His voice was low, almost reverent. 'I thought so. My grandson'.

The captain's eyes flicked to the crosses beneath the jacaranda. 'So, you've met my parents', he said quietly. 'Richard and my mother, Sarah. She had another name, too, in the old tongue, but Sarah was the one everyone here knew. I always come here after an assignment, just to let them know I'm back safe'.

He touched one of the crosses lightly, a gesture at once respectful and intimate. Then, after a pause, he added, 'I was given another name as well when I was born. My maternal grandfather spoke it over me in the old tongue. Out here, some still use it, but in uniform, I'm Captain Richard O'Connell, or just O'Connell to my CO'.

He looked back at the older man. 'They'd have liked to have known you'.

'And me to them', Lord Richard responded.

Maggie's voice broke the moment from the veranda. 'Breakfast! And after that, the Cook's Tour. There are several people I want you to meet'.

The kitchen was alive with warmth and the smell of fresh bread. A great iron kettle hissed gently on the stove, and platters of bacon and eggs were set out with a simplicity that spoke of long habit.

They ate together at the scrubbed pine table with Maggie at the head, the two Richards opposite one another, and young Maggie darting in and out with plates. The conversation was easy, broken with laughter, and for the first time in his life, Richard felt part of a family rather than apart from one.

Afterward, true to her word, Maggie led him on the Cook's Tour. They walked the verandas, the gardens, and then down the track to a cluster of cottages. Children played between them, darting through the dust, their laughter mingling with the sound of wind in the vines. The adults paused in their work to nod or wave.

'These are the families whose parents and grandparents helped me set up the vineyard', Maggie explained. 'They stood by me when no one else would. I promised them that if this place endured, so would they. That promise is kept here. Many of their children and grandchildren have gone on to become teachers, doctors, solicitors, and even captains of industry. And the legacy continues. The estate funds scholarships to see them through university, to give them the education their grandparents could only dream of'.

At the largest of the cottages, Maggie introduced an old man seated in a cane chair, Elder Miran, the twins' maternal grandfather and a respected elder of the Noongar people. His gaze was steady and sharp despite his years, one hand resting on a carved walking stick whose patterns seemed to hold stories of their own.

For a while, Elder Miran regarded Lord Richard in silence, then said one word: 'Warrior'.

Richard returned the nod with equal gravity. 'If I am, then so are you, sir'.

Elder Miran's lined face creased into a slow smile. He tapped the stick lightly against the ground, as though sealing the thought. 'Kindred spirit', he murmured. 'Maggie was right to bring you'.

Maggie stepped closer. 'When your grandson came of age, Elder Miran took him out on a walkabout. Days in the bush, no maps, no help, only the old ways to guide you. Your grandson learned to track, to read the land, to listen when the earth speaks. Those lessons have stood him in good stead in the Regiment. More than once, he's told me it was the bush that taught him how to endure, how to survive'.

The elder gave a soft grunt of agreement. His sharp eyes moved back to Richard. 'Not just survive', he said. 'To be a man of spirit, not all learn that'.

For a long moment, the two old men regarded one another across the years and the bloodlines that bound them. Richard saw it more clearly now, the echo of his own Anglo features in the set of his grandson's jaw, tempered by the darker eyes and copper tone that spoke of Miran's people. The boy was marked by both heritages and carried himself with a bearing that was unmistakably his.

Richard felt a quiet jolt: though he had never known his grandson, some part of himself, the iron will, the unyielding presence had clearly passed down. The bush had honed the boy into a survivor, but it was his own blood that had given him that edge, that air of command.

For the first time in many years, Lord Richard felt a flicker of peace. His legacy would not only endure, it would thrive.

Chapter 5: No Accident

They had barely returned to the veranda when the crunch of tyres on gravel broke the morning calm. A white police Land Cruiser rolled to a stop. Senior Constable Dave Harris climbed out: solid build, sun-faded uniform, Akubra hat. His easy 'G'day' carried weight beneath it.

He greeted Maggie, the Captain, and young Maggie, but his eyes fixed on Lord Richard.

'Sir, I'm afraid I need a word with you'.

The air shifted. Conversations died.

'There's been an accident out on Caves Road early this morning', Harris said. 'Single vehicle. The driver didn't make it. Found by a couple of local fellas out hunting kangaroos'. He hesitated. 'We recovered some belongings from the wreckage, a notebook with the words O'Connell Vineyard written inside, along with a bag we believe was yours. From the direction of travel, it looks like the driver was heading back towards the estate, maybe to return it to you'.

Harris's expression hardened a fraction. 'We think we know who the driver was, but we'll need you to make a formal identification'.

No one spoke.

Maggie's hand went to her mouth. 'If you'd gone back to the hotel last night…' She didn't finish.

'I'll come with you', Captain Richard said firmly. 'Might need a translator in more ways than one'.

Lord Richard asked for half an hour to wash and shave. Harris, though clearly impatient, agreed. But then Lord Richard realised that he didn't have his washbag, it had been taken away with his clothes in Jack's Land Cruiser. His grandson came to the rescue with a spare wash kit, battered but serviceable, and pressed it into his grandfather's hands. 'Not Savile Row standard, but it'll do the job'.

When Lord Richard returned, cleaner but still in yesterday's clothes, he found a sight that would stir any motoring enthusiast: a fully restored two-door Mark 1 Range Rover, parked beside the police Land Cruiser.

He moved towards the Range Rover, but Harris gestured to his own vehicle. 'Better if you ride with me'.

A strange request, but Richard said nothing.

As they drove out, dust curling behind them, Harris kept his eyes on the road. 'Hard to roll a Land Cruiser', he remarked. 'Unless someone's really pushing it'.

'Or helping it along', Lord Richard said evenly.

Harris didn't answer, but his jaw tightened.

Richard turned his gaze to the passing landscape, gum trees, sunlit paddocks, flashes of the sea, yet his thoughts were elsewhere. His instincts prickled, the same way they had at the refuelling stop on the flight from the UK. This time, though, he didn't dismiss them as an old man's paranoia.

In London, there were people who would profit from his death. Jonathan is foremost among them. His nephew's hunger for the Aldridge title and the bank was no secret. A 'tragic accident' in Australia would serve him well.

And Jonathan was not a man who left things to chance.

By the time they rolled into the Margaret River police station, the sun was high and the cicadas shrilled from the gum trees. The building was low, whitewashed, and shaded by a wide veranda.

Leaning against the rail, phone in hand, was a Police Auxiliary Officer. He wore his uniform with the easy looseness of someone on a smoko, the sort of cigarette-and-coffee break every country copper took when the day grew long, one boot hooked over the bottom rung. To anyone passing, he was just another officer killing a few minutes. Yet his eyes were sharper than they needed to be, following every movement as the two vehicles pulled in, the police Land Cruiser driven by Senior Constable Harris, and, close behind, the Range Rover with Captain Richard O'Connell at the wheel.

A casual thumb tapped his screen, as though finishing a text to a mate. In reality, the message was already on its way: Aldridge present. Accompanied.

Lord Richard climbed down from the passenger seat of the Land Cruiser while his grandson got out of the Range Rover. They exchanged a quiet word, then Harris gestured towards the station doors.

'This way, my Lord'.

Richard raised an eyebrow. Harris gave a faint shrug. 'Your passport was in the wreckage. Title's right there on the particulars, hard to miss'.

Captain Richard peeled off towards a bench beneath the shade of a pepper tree, where two Aboriginal men sat with paper coffee cups in their hands. Their boots and khakis carried the dust of the bush, and their eyes, though calm, missed nothing.

'Uncles', the younger Richard greeted them warmly. His voice slipped into their language with the ease of long practice, and the conversation turned quiet, the words too soft for anyone else to catch.

Inside, the air was cooler but held the faint tang of disinfectant. Harris led Lord Richard through a short corridor to a plain room where a sheet-draped shape waited.

The constable drew back the cloth just enough for the face to show.

Jack.

Or what was left of him.

'I'm sorry', Harris said quietly. 'Found by those two fellas outside. Looks like he fell asleep at the wheel. Rolled it clean over. These bush roads'll do that to you'. He was already shaking his head, tone final. 'Case closed. No further action required'.

Lord Richard said nothing. His face remained composed, but in his gut the verdict rang hollow. Even on that first drive from Busselton, his old field instincts had noticed the small things—the way Jack checked his mirrors, judged each corner, eased off the throttle on gravel. Too careful a driver to simply drift off.

Back outside, Captain Richard was finishing his conversation with the two men. As he walked back towards his grandfather, he gave the barest flick of two fingers a subtle signal to say nothing.

Lord Richard followed his gaze back to the Aboriginal men. They sat now in silence, but something in their stillness spoke volumes. Without a word exchanged, he understood: they had seen what happened. Hidden deep in the scrub, in places only they could reach, they had watched Jack's Land Cruiser forced off the road and into the gully.

The knowledge settled like a stone in his chest.

As Lord Richard reached for the door of the Range Rover, the Auxiliary reappeared from the station's side door, Lord Richard's overnight bag dangling loosely from one hand.

'Nearly forgot this, sir', he said with the faintest grin, as though sharing a small kindness. The cheap paper tag tied to the handle had been replaced with a sturdier plastic one, the kind police often clipped on for evidence tracking.

Richard took it without hesitation, nodding his thanks. The weight was the same, the leather cool and familiar beneath his fingers. If the tag felt newer, crisper, he paid it no mind. After all, the bag had been through the wreck and the station's custody.

'Much obliged'.

The drive back towards the homestead was made in quiet contemplation. Lord Richard sat with the bag on his knees, his gaze fixed on the passing trees, while his grandson remained steady at his side. Captain Richard O'Connell knew the news they carried would reopen wounds his grandmother had spent a lifetime trying to forget.

When at last the Range Rover pulled into the homestead drive, Captain Richard was out almost before the engine stopped. He went straight to his grandmother, meeting her on the veranda, and put his arm gently around her shoulders. She looked up at him, saw the resolve in his eyes, and let herself lean into his strength.

From the car, Lord Richard watched them. For the briefest moment, pride stirred in his chest. His grandson was stepping into his duty as naturally as breathing. Yet beneath that pride lay a hollow dread. He knew the past he had carried in silence was about to surface, and that Margaret's heart was about to be broken all over again.

Chapter 6: Fremantle 1944

The smell of salt and diesel hung over Fremantle Harbour as the troopships nosed into their berths. It was the end of the war, and the docks were alive with colour and noise, flags snapping in the sea breeze, bands striking up, families waving frantically from the quay.

Maggie stepped off the gangplank, heavily pregnant, her kitbag slung over one shoulder. She had imagined this moment a hundred times during the long voyage from Europe: the smiling faces, the welcoming arms, the quiet pride of a nation greeting its returning daughters.

Instead, there was silence. Not total silence; the cheering still rang for others, but around her, a pocket of cold disapproval seemed to form. Women turned away; men averted their eyes. In the narrow lens of Perth society, she was not the war widow of a hero but an unmarried woman carrying a bastard child.

Her hand rose briefly to her collar, feeling for the thin string hidden beneath her uniform. The twin rings pressed warm against her skin: the heavy gold with its deep blue sapphire, and the plain band Richard had placed on her finger when they spoke their vows. Their rings were the only proof she had of what they shared. But here, unseen, they could not shield her. To the watching crowd, she looked bare, unclaimed. And they judged her for it.

Her parents were there: her father, a respected barrister, stiff in his summer suit; her mother immaculate in hat and gloves. Yet neither moved towards her. His gaze slid past her as if she were a stranger. Her mother's mouth pinched into a thin line, her gloved hands tightening on the parasol she carried. They turned their backs before she reached them, joining the crowd in applauding someone else's daughter. In that single gesture, Maggie understood that to them, she was dead.

She could almost hear their verdict in the clipped tones of the matrons along the wharf. Shameful. Disgraceful.

When the time came, Maggie did not face it alone. A handful of her nursing colleagues from the war, women who had seen her courage in field hospitals from Normandy to Caen, came quietly to her side. They knew the whispers, the raised eyebrows, the judgment that awaited her, but none of that mattered in the moment. In a modest room above a friend's surgery, with the smell of carbolic and eucalyptus mingling in the air, they helped her bring her son into the world.

They laughed when she cursed like a digger, soothed her when the pain grew sharp, and wept with her when at last she held the boy in her arms. 'Richard', she whispered, naming him for the man she believed lost forever.

Life in Perth soon became unbearable. The sidelong glances, the whispered gossip, the polite refusals whenever she looked for work all spoke the same language. Maggie knew she had to get out.

It was a notice in The West Australian that caught her eye: parcels of land in the south-west being offered to returned veterans under a government settlement scheme. A way to start over. A chance to breathe.

Her application sent shockwaves through the local establishment. A sheila expecting a land grant? They scoffed. The official in charge seemed almost affronted when she turned up in person to press her case. But Maggie was not one to be turned aside by frowns and formalities. She just kept coming back, week after week, until at last the grant was hers.

The plot was in Margaret River, wild country then, the roads rough, the soil untamed. But when she stood there for the first time, the gentle undulation of the land and the soft Mediterranean climate stirred a memory deep inside her: the vineyards of France, where she and Richard had walked between the rows, hands brushing, voices low, dreaming of a life they might have.

'Why not?' she murmured to herself. 'Let's give it a go'.

There was one problem: she had no money, no hired help, and a newborn to care for. Most would have given up before they began. But Maggie simply rolled up her sleeves. She reached out to the people others ignored: unmarried mothers like herself, maimed war veterans, and the marginalised Aboriginal families pushed to the edges of town. She couldn't offer wages, not at first; what she could promise was a roof in the old cottages and food drawn from the land itself: vegetables in the garden, fish from the river, bush game, and knowledge shared from the Aboriginal people. It was rough living, but it was enough to keep them going. And she offered something more: if the vineyard flourished, they would share in its prosperity. In truth, what Maggie was building was less an estate and more a settlement of kindred, a community bound by work, trust, and the promise of tomorrow.

Years passed. The vines took root. The child she carried grew into a fine man.

That son, Richard O'Connell, fell in love with the daughter of an Aboriginal elder. When they married, polite society clucked its disapproval, but Maggie's family were blind to skin colour; they only judged a person by the worth of their heart and the strength of their word.

A year later, Richard's wife was pregnant with twins. When the time came, the babies were delivered quietly at home with the help of a local midwife. It wasn't unusual in those parts, and no one thought twice about it. Afterwards, Maggie urged the young couple to take a few days in town. 'Go', she said, smiling, 'have a rest. I'll spoil them rotten until you're back'.

That evening, there was a knock at the door.

The policeman on the step looked as though he'd rather be anywhere else. His hat was in his hands. His voice was gentle, but the words hit like a hammer.

There had been an accident on Caves Road. Richard and his wife were gone.

Maggie stood in the doorway for a long time after he left, the twins crying in the next room. Her own grief could wait; for their sake, she would have to be strong. She always had been.

In the days that followed, she buried her son and her daughter-in-law together beneath the great jacaranda tree at the edge of the vineyard, the place she could see from the veranda each morning. There, their spirits would remain forever at the heart of the land they had loved, the blossoms falling like a blessing each spring.

Elder Miran, her son's father-in-law and the twins' maternal grandfather, came to stand with her, the chaplain reading the Anglican prayers while Miran marked the ground in the old way. He painted ochre symbols on the fresh earth, then set a carved post beside the crosses, spirals, flowing lines, and animal tracks cut deep into the wood.

'So, the ancestors will know this place', he said, 'and so the land will hold them'.

As Maggie tried to steady herself for the sake of the twins, Miran came quietly to her. His voice was low, but the warning was clear: There are shadows here, Maggie. You must keep the twins hidden, he said. And so, she did.

The children grew up on the vineyard, educated not only from books but by the eclectic mix of people Maggie had gathered around her. They learned languages, bush skills, and the hard-earned wisdom of those who had lived on the margins. From their grandfather, they learned to walk as one with the outback, to read the land and the wind, to understand the ways of their ancestors — lessons that would shape them for the rest of their lives.

Chapter 7: Present Shadows

The late afternoon sun slanted low across the paddocks, gilding the tall grass in bronze. Lord Richard sat very still on the veranda, Maggie's words circling in his mind like hawks riding a thermal. The vineyard lay quiet around them, the air heavy with its scent and the gum trees, a peace he had never thought to find again, and one he loathed to leave.

Maggie rose at last, brushing his hand as she passed. 'I'll put the kettle on'. With that, she disappeared inside, leaving the two men alone at the table.

Grandfather and grandson locked eyes. The thought that passed between them was like static, sharp, immediate, and undeniable. Neither wanted to step away from the stillness they had found here, but both knew they must. The fight would not wait. London would not wait.

Lord Richard broke the silence first. His voice was low but steady.

'London is where it began, Richard. Not just the city of my youth, it's where the Syndicate first coiled itself around our family. The Aldridge name, the Bank, even my seat in the Lords... all of it has been used as camouflage for other men's ambitions'. He shook his head, the lines in his face deepening. 'I've seen too much already. Falsified records. Shadow accounts. Silences that point to rot at the very core. I told myself I could look away, bury myself in duty, but the war taught me that evil ignored only grows stronger'.

He leaned forward, gaze hardening.

'If we want Maggie, this vineyard, you, all of it, to have peace, then we can't wait for it to come to us. We'll have to root out the poison back there'.

Captain Richard listened without moving, then gave a slow nod.

'Afghanistan taught me the same thing. And I don't think what's happened here has been chance. Too many shadows in the wrong places, too many eyes watching. My father's death...' He paused, the words tight in his throat. 'They called it an accident. Maybe it was. But I don't believe in coincidences anymore'. He sat back, jaw set. 'If that trail leads back to London, then that's where we go. Better to face them head-on than wait for them to strike again'.

The old man's eyes softened for a heartbeat, pride flickering beneath the gravity. As soldiers, they needed no further words. The pact was made.

Before his grandfather could speak again, Captain Richard was already at the study telephone, dialling a number he knew by heart, the direct line to his CO at Campbell Barracks, Swanbourne. The call was answered almost immediately.

Using the clipped shorthand only combat veterans understood, Richard brought his CO up to speed in under a minute. No explanations, no wasted breath—just the facts.

When he finished, his CO's reply was four simple words:

'What do you need?'

Richard's answer came just as quickly, five favours:

1. A leave of absence.
2. Two tickets to London on the next flight out of Perth. (The ASAS, Australian Special Air Services, had a standing arrangement with Qantas: any destination, next available flight, no questions asked.)
3. A couple of men down in Margaret River to watch over the family.
4. Backup in London from the 'friends' in Hereford, if needed.
5. New sunglasses.

The CO didn't even pause. He agreed and went one better. Rather than two minders, he was sending a full protection squad, written up as a training exercise. They were prepping to lift off from Perth within the hour. Once the handover was done, Richard and his grandfather could use that same chopper to get back to Perth in time for their flight.

Richard hesitated for half a beat, then added with a dry smile:

'Oh, and can I keep the company phone?'

The CO chuckled, the sound more like gravel than humour.

'No. But you can have an upgrade. It'll be waiting at the usual place, together with those sunglasses you wanted'.

Then came a cryptic add-on, half a joke, half a nod to the truth: 'I suppose you'll be wanting a full *ASIO-style Gerald* to go with them…

Richard didn't miss a beat.

'Why not throw in a company car while you're at it?'

There was a pause, then the CO's voice returned, half exasperated, half amused.

'I'll see what the Friends can dig up. Don't complain if it's not exactly a regulation issue. Delivery to Lord Aldridge's London address'.

It was nearly dark when the low thump of rotor blades finally reached them, distant at first, then building, rolling across the valley like thunder.

Maggie's brow furrowed. She didn't need to rise from her chair to know.

'That's no farm chopper', she said.

Captain Richard was already moving. His eyes locked on the treeline, then up at the approaching lights.

'No, Gran. That's ours'.

Within minutes, a dark-green AS350 swept over the treeline, banking hard and settling in the open paddock beyond the fence. The downwash sent a ripple through the grass, rattled the veranda railings, and whipped Maggie's hair across her face.

Five men spilled out, dressed like country hands in ballcaps, work boots, and dust-stained jeans. To a casual eye, they might have been shearers or vineyard workers, but the way they moved—smooth, economical, each scanning a different angle marked them as something else entirely. One gave Richard a sharp nod.

'Perimeter's clear. We'll keep an eye on the property until you're back'.

There was no time for long goodbyes. Richard slung his pack over one shoulder; his grandfather mirrored the movement, slower, but with the same soldier's economy.

On the veranda, Maggie stepped forward. She pulled Captain Richard into a fierce hug, whispering something only he could hear, then turned to his grandfather. For a heartbeat, she simply held his face in her hands, eyes shining, before kissing him gently on the cheek. 'Both of you come back to me', she said.

Neither man trusted himself to answer. They only nodded, then turned towards the waiting chopper.

They climbed into the rear cabin; the door sliding shut with a heavy clunk. The pilot gave a thumb-up, then pulled the collective. The skids lifted clear of the earth, and the homestead shrank below Maggie standing on the veranda, apron whipping in the wind, the ASAS men already in position.

She raised her face to the sky, eyes closed for a moment, lips moving in a prayer older than words. *Bring them back to me. Keep them safe on their road.*

From the shadows at the edge of the veranda, Elder Miran stepped forward, his presence as quiet as the dusk itself. He had been watching without intruding, letting Maggie's strength stand on its own.

'They will', he said simply.

Maggie opened her eyes, surprised, then nodded once, as if she had known all along.

They landed at the barracks and a car whisked them quickly to the Burswood Hotel on the Great Eastern Highway, where they would stay overnight before heading to the airport.

The next morning, before departing the hotel for their flight, Lord Richard and his grandson sat with coffee. A waiter approached Captain Richard with a folded slip of paper. Richard read it, excused himself, and promised to be back in half an hour.

Thirty minutes passed. He hadn't returned.

Lord Richard was about to rise, unease beginning to prick at him. He caught himself glancing at the empty chair opposite — the image of his grandson still fresh: chinos, an open-necked Oxford shirt, and his tweed jacket slung neatly across the back of the chair. Every inch the officer off duty, understated, steady, and watchful.

Then an apparition swept into the café, pastel jacket, silk scarf, enormous sunglasses, and an exaggerated runway strut and came up to the table where Lord Richard was sitting.

'Dickie, darling St. Clare. Gerald St. Clare', he announced loudly, extending a languid hand. 'I believe you're looking for a friend to accompany you on that beastly long flight to London'.

Before Lord Richard could speak, the sunglasses came off, revealing the hard eyes of a battle-seasoned ASAS operator.

Lord Richard blinked.

'You look more suited to a Paris catwalk than a warzone'.

'That's the point, darling', Gerald replied with a wicked grin. 'The watchers won't see a soldier. They'll see... well, me'.

As 'Gerald' flamboyantly led the way out of the airport and the battleground that awaited in London, Lord Richard rose more slowly. He reached over, lifted the tweed jacket from the chair, and slung it over his arm. Whatever game his grandson was playing, he wasn't about to leave a perfectly good coat behind to mark their passage.

Whilst Lord Richard and Gerald were on their way to London, in the hushed, high-ceilinged office at the top of Aldridge Bank, Jonathan's plain black handset buzzed. Fewer than a dozen people in the world had that number.

He answered with a single word.

'Speak'.

The voice was flat, unadorned.

'We missed in Perth. Lord Richard is still alive. Worse, there may be a legitimate living heir. The tracker on his bag just pinged from a hotel near Perth Airport. And… there's a photo from outside the Margaret River police station of him with another man. I think they're on their way to London'.

A pause. Then the secure line clicked once more, and a compressed image file came through. Jonathan opened it, the pixels resolving into a grainy shot of his uncle standing shoulder to shoulder with a younger man. The resemblance was impossible to miss. Jonathan's stomach turned cold. This was no coincidence. This was blood.

The words hit Jonathan like a thunderclap. He stared at the far wall, not seeing it. This wasn't just a setback; it was a direct threat to everything he had built.

Without a word, he ended the call and crossed to the drinks cabinet. The heavy stopper of the decanter came free with a dull pop. He poured a brandy big enough to coat the glass in amber.

The Syndicate would not be pleased. Piece by piece, they had been burrowing into Aldridge Bank, intent on turning its respectable name into their shield, a future gateway for laundering the money that fuelled organised crime, terrorism, and human trafficking. And their policy on failure was crystal clear.

Failure was terminal.

Jonathan swallowed half the brandy in one go, forcing the burn down with it. Then, acting on instinct rather than protocol, he picked up the secure handset again and keyed into the WebEx bridge, bypassing Alpha.

The ritual was familiar: a sterile whiteboard flickering to life, initials populating the screen in place of names. The voices that followed were distorted, clipped, drained of humanity.

Jonathan spoke quickly.

'Lord Richard Aldridge has resurfaced. Perth. Evidence suggests he may have found an heir. He is believed to be en route to London'.

The pause that followed was heavy, broken only by a single question, flattened by a scrambler:

'Risk?'

Jonathan hesitated. This was Alpha's role, not his. But he pressed on.

'If confirmed, catastrophic. He must be stopped'.

The whiteboard refreshed. One line appeared in stark black text:

TRACK HIM. IMPERATIVE. CONFIRM IF THIS IS AN HEIR AND REPORT BACK THROUGH THE PROPER CHANNELS.

The bridge clicked dead. No farewells. No indulgence.

Jonathan set the handset down with more force than he intended. His heart thudded in his chest. He had gone over Alpha's head, and they all knew it.

He drew a breath, then reached for a second line: the local net. A few clipped instructions, nothing written down. Spotters at Heathrow were to be alert for an elderly peer travelling in discreet company. The uncle must not slip past them.

Across Westminster, in a discreet office overlooking the Thames, the UK Alpha sat in silence as his own secure line went dead. Jonathan had jumped the chain. Reckless. Dangerous. The Partners might tolerate it once, but not twice.

Alpha smoothed the quarterly objectives sheet on his desk: three lines, two ticked, one still blank:

- Strengthen European clearing capacity.
- Consolidate feeder trusts in the Channel Islands.
- Secure Aldridge Bank acquisition.

His gaze drifted to the Thames below, where the water shimmered dully under a pale midday sky. Parliament rose stark, its familiar outline softened by the haze. Almost to himself, he murmured:

'Deliver, Jonathan. Or it's both our P45s'.

In Whitehall, a P45 meant redundancy. In the Syndicate, it meant something far simpler: a bullet in the back of the head.

As the plane from Perth landed and Lord Richard cleared customs and immigration, outside, a spotter leaned casually against a pillar near the tourist brochure rack, coffee cup in hand. He looked like any chauffeur waiting for his client, but his eyes never left the sliding doors from customs.

And then, there they were.

Lord Richard was walking with his deliberate, measured stride. Beside him, the flamboyant apparition in pastel, scarf fluttering, sunglasses the size of windshields.

The spotter blinked, then murmured into his phone:

'He's back. And the old *queen's* brought himself a toy boy'.

Jonathan's voice was cool.

'Stay with them. I want to know where they go and who they see. Don't be seen'.

The spotter never realised the 'toy boy' had already fixed him with a glance that lingered just a fraction too long. Behind those ridiculous sunglasses was a concealed pinhole camera, quietly logging faces one by one. Later, the images would be passed through secure systems in Hereford and GCHQ, but Gerald didn't need a computer to tell him what his gut already knew.

The way the man shifted his weight, the watchfulness in his eyes, the false ease of his stance, all of it shouted hostile. Gerald's instincts had marked him long before the tech ever would.

'Oh, Richard, darling, those dreadful beige chairs just outside baggage claim — honestly, who chooses that shade?' Gerald said loudly, fluttering a hand for show.

Lord Richard allowed himself the faintest smile. The enemy was watching and already underestimating them.

And that was their first mistake.

Chapter 8: The Tail and the Trap

The Bentley was waiting at the kerb, polished to a mirror finish. At its side stood Mason, Lord Richard's driver of decades, immaculate in a dark suit and gloves.

'Welcome home, my lord', he said, and for a heartbeat his composure slipped. The sight of Gerald, pastel scarf and sunglasses in place, provoked the faintest flicker of astonishment before professionalism reasserted itself.

Lord Richard gave the smallest nod. 'You got the message, then'.

'Of course, my lord'. Mason opened the rear door as though nothing at all were out of the ordinary.

Gerald noticed. Pausing at the open door, he gave Mason a languid, perfectly executed blown kiss. The driver's eyebrows twitched upward a fraction before he caught himself and closed the door with the same quiet precision he always had.

'Straight to my London home', Richard instructed.

The Bentley eased into the Westway traffic, and almost at once, a black London cab merged in three cars behind. Inside, the passenger was little more than a shadow, face half-hidden.

As they rolled towards the city, Lord Richard leaned forward and pressed a button. The glass partition rose with a soft hum. In his years of service, Mason had never known his lordship to use it, which meant whatever followed was important.

'We have a tail', Lord Richard murmured to his grandson, who was still in Gerald mode. 'Black cab, three cars back. Clever choice cabs are everywhere in London, but they've slipped. No London cabbie worth his salt would sit in slow-moving traffic with a bus lane wide open'.

Gerald kept up the performance, brushing his grandfather's cheek with theatrical flair for all to see.

When the Bentley arrived at the townhouse, there were not one but two vehicles parked discreetly in the mews behind the house. Both carried trade plates, clearly demonstrators sent over by the Friends in Hereford.

One had been left in plain view of the street: a Suzuki soft-top SUV in a garish shade of teal, the sort of thing you might expect to see outside a Knightsbridge salon. The other, a dark green Defender 90 hard top, squared-off, purposeful, had been tucked safely into the rear garage, well out of sight of any watchers.

Richard's heart lifted at the sight of the Defender. It was the kind of machine he could trust, a soldier's car all utility, no frills. But he was still in Gerald mode, and Gerald swooned over the Suzuki.

'Oh, darling', Gerald exclaimed, hands clasped with theatrical delight, 'just look at this adorable little runabout! Perfect for nipping down to Harrods or popping off to a cocktail party. I absolutely must take this one'.

Behind them, Lord Richard's long-suffering chauffeur muttered just loudly enough to be heard, 'Knew which one he'd pick. Why they even bothered sending two over for him to look at…'

The soldier smothered a smile. Outwardly, Gerald simpered over the Suzuki; inwardly, Richard was already claiming the Defender as his own. The Friends knew him too well. Better still, the right set of eyes would never even know it was there.

His gaze drifted to the Bentley waiting in the mews. For a moment, he caught himself wondering what the Friends might do with it, if asked a few discreet modifications, perhaps. Nothing so theatrical as smoke screens or ejector seats, of course, but the thought lingered, a private joke, before he pushed it aside.

The black cab parked across the street from Lord Richard's townhouse. Inside, the watchers relayed to Jonathan.

'They're in for the night'.

'Good', came the reply. 'Just sit and watch'.

Inside the house, both men moved quickly.

Lord Richard placed a quiet call to an old club acquaintance, Buster, a senior member long since retired but still commanding an unusually large 'family' scattered across the city.

'I need a couple of watchers on my back', Richard said.

'No problem. At least I can do for a lord of the realm. When?'

'Now. There's a black cab across the way with a couple of unsavoury types. Discreetly track them, tell me where they go, and get some pictures if possible'.

'Consider it done'. The line went dead.

Meanwhile, Richard, still in Gerald mode, was placing his own 'takeaway' order. To anyone listening, it sounded like a flamboyant request for late-night champagne and oysters; in truth, it was a coded call to pull in a very different delivery. Within hours, a discreet courier drop would provide him with the specialist kit he might need: full tactical gear, surveillance packs, encrypted comms, even a compact weapons loadout sealed in innocuous packaging. The kind of equipment no Aldridge heir should ever have reason to need unless war was already on the horizon.

Back in Jonathan's office, the watchers reported again.

'The old queen and his toy boy are in for the night. Even ordered a takeaway which has just been delivered'.

Jonathan allowed himself a thin smile. 'Good. Pack it in. Head back to the warehouse. I'll meet you there. We'll discuss the next steps'.

It was a mistake.

By pulling them off, Jonathan had just led Lord Richard's allies straight to one of the Syndicate's most sensitive sites. And fate, with its usual sense of irony, had chosen that night for the Syndicate's Alpha to visit.

Jonathan arrived minutes later, his Mercedes rolling into the warehouse yard with headlights low. Inside, the air smelled of oil, steel, and stale cigarette smoke. A few of the Syndicate men were already gathered, murmuring in low voices around a crate that served as a table.

And then Alpha entered.

He did not knock, did not announce himself. A dark overcoat, a trilby brim pulled low, the kind of attire that seemed too plain to notice yet impossible to overlook. A scarf covered the lower half of his face, not theatre, not disguise, just enough to deny anyone a clear look. He passed through the warehouse floor like a ripple across still water. Men who would have stared down police raids or rival gangs shifted aside without being told. Even in silence, he rearranged the air around him.

Jonathan stiffened as Alpha approached. He had met Syndicate lieutenants before, men who mistook arrogance for authority. But Alpha was different — the Syndicate's man in the UK, and every inch the power he represented. He wasted nothing: no word, no movement, no glance.

The voice came low, flat, each syllable deliberate.

'You broke the chain. You thought you could leapfrog me, wave your uncle in front of the Partners, and come out untouchable'.

The silence was worse than shouting.

'You embarrassed me. You embarrassed this office. And worse, you made them notice you. That is not ambition. That is suicide'.

Jonathan opened his mouth, but Alpha cut him dead, calm as a knife sliding under ribs.

'Do not mistake patience for forgiveness. The Syndicate has endured centuries because it excises weakness without hesitation. One more stunt like that, and you won't even need me. You'll sign your own death warrant the moment you open your mouth'.

The scarf hid Alpha's expression, but his eyes, sharp, pitiless, pinned Jonathan where he stood. The final words landed soft as silk, hard as a verdict:

'Bring me Aldridge Bank, whole and unchallenged. Fail, and you won't even leave a shadow behind'.

He turned and left without another glance. The echo of his footsteps faded into the cavernous dark, each one a hammer-blow reminder of Jonathan's place.

Jonathan stood alone, gripping the edge of the crate until his knuckles whitened. For the first time in years, the air tasted of fear.

At Lord Richard's townhouse, his phone buzzed once. A series of grainy images arrived as snapshots from Buster's watchers, texted through in haste. He handed the phone across.

'Here, you know how to make sense of this', he said.

His grandson forwarded them onto the secure laptop, keyed in the code, and enlarged them on the screen: *Alpha entering the warehouse. No clear face.*

The secure laptop's screen dimmed, leaving only the crackle of the fire and the low hum of the city beyond Eaton Square. Captain Richard stretched, the Gerald affectation slipping from him like a discarded coat.

He poured two whiskies, one for his grandfather and one for himself, and for the first time since landing in London, allowed his shoulders to ease.

Lord Richard was still studying the grainy shots of a figure at the warehouse in a dark overcoat and trilby, the so-called Alpha. No clear face, but something about the posture tugged at memory.

Before he could voice it, the doorbell rang.

Gwen, Lord Richard's long-suffering housekeeper and fixture of the household for decades, appeared a moment later, ushering in a tall woman with dark hair pinned neatly back. She carried herself with brisk assurance, though her eyes softened as soon as they found Lord Richard.

'Fiona', he greeted, his smile weary but genuine. 'You've heard I'm back'.

Captain Richard's antennae twitched at once. Heard? Their arrival had been carefully obscured. He studied her as she crossed the threshold, no hesitation, no nerves. If she were a leak, she was a convincing one.

'I hear everything', she replied with a glint of mischief. And when her eyes flicked briefly to the younger man, there was the faintest trace of amusement, as though she'd felt his scrutiny and chose not to take offence.

Lord Richard turned to gesture. 'Allow me to introduce my…'

'Richard', the younger man cut in smoothly, extending his hand before the word grandson could land. His gaze stayed steady on hers. 'Captain Richard O'Connell'.

For a heartbeat, Fiona faltered. The resemblance was striking: the same eyes as the elder Richard, though sharpened by youth and hard service; the soldier's bearing rather than the lord's measured poise. She took his hand, her grip firm.

'Doctor Fiona Markham', she said evenly. 'Lord Richard and I are old friends'. Her eyebrow lifted ever so slightly.

Lord Richard watched the exchange over the rim of his glass, the ghost of a smile playing there.

Conversation lingered for a while, the whisky glasses slowly draining. Then Fiona's gaze drifted towards the sideboard, where an unopened bottle of wine caught the firelight. She reached out, turning the label towards her.

'Did you ever resolve your problem?' she asked gently.

Lord Richard's expression shifted, just for a moment. He glanced at the bottle as if remembering the O'Connell estate label, then back to her, the silence heavy with shared history.

'You might say the matter has… progressed', he said at last, his voice quiet.

Fiona's eyes warmed, but her professionalism soon returned. 'Good. Then perhaps we should open this. One glass won't harm the check-up I intend to give you, and from the looks of you, that trip seems to have done you the world of good. Better colour in your face than I've seen in years'.

'My dear girl, travel broadens the mind', Lord Richard quipped, easing the cork from the bottle. 'And, occasionally, restores the body'.

'I'll still be the judge of that', she said with a smile, settling her bag on a chair as the glasses were poured.

'I'll not keep you longer', she said briskly. 'But don't think that glass of wine has spared you from a proper examination. I'll be back soon enough'.

Lord Richard smiled wearily. 'You've always been persistent, my dear'.

'I prefer thorough', she corrected, with the faintest tilt of her head.

The fire had burned low by the time Fiona rose, gathering her things.

'I'll see you out', Captain Richard said, rising with quiet ease.

In the hallway, away from the firelight, his voice dropped a shade lower. 'Doctor Markham, perhaps it would be best if we arranged a fuller consultation at your surgery. For my grandfather's long-term care'.

The words were out before he could pull them back. Grandfather. Until now, he had sidestepped the truth, keeping the bond between them unspoken.

Her eyes searched his, sharp enough to catch the slip. For a moment, it seemed she might press him, then her gaze softened. 'Professional diligence', she said softly, granting him the courtesy of leaving it there.

He inclined his head, a flicker of a smile at his lips. Whether it was admission or a test, he let her decide.

She held his gaze a heartbeat longer, then inclined her head. 'Very well. Gwen has my details. She'll know how to reach me'.

As he opened the door, the night air spilled in from Eaton Square. She stepped past him with the same brisk assurance she had entered, but the faintest curve lingered at the corner of her lips.

Richard watched her go, filing away every detail, professional, yes, but also personal. On various levels, the check was only just beginning.

Captain Richard closed the door behind Fiona and let out a slow breath, the soldier settling back into his frame. For a heartbeat, the house was quiet, the fire whispering in the grate.

Then Gerald swept back in, all flamboyance and timing.

'I think it's about time I got myself a proper job. Always fancied myself as a banker'.

Lord Richard's lips twitched, glass raised.

'I know just the merchant to call', he replied, dry amusement glinting in his eyes, and immediately phoned his nephew.

Across the city, Jonathan sat back in his chair, staring at the phone as if it had personally mocked him. He loathed the thought of wasting time on his uncle's painted boy, but the opportunity was too convenient to ignore. A preening distraction, nothing more, the kind of weakness his uncle always pretended he didn't have.

If he could manoeuvre the fop into a honey trap, just a few compromising photographs, it would be enough to start. A smear in the right circles, whispers seeded in the right ears, and soon enough, the Aldridge reputation would begin to fray.

Still, it grated on him that he would have to pay for the privilege, footing the bill to humiliate some jumped-up plaything. Jonathan's jaw tightened, mind narrowing towards the darkened warehouse in Limehouse. His uncle might have returned, but Jonathan would see to it he never stood tall again.

Chapter 9: The Mask and the Motor

The Suzuki, courtesy of the Friends in Hereford, handled the tight spiral of the West India Quay car park with the assurance of a mountain goat. On the surface, it was a frivolous little runabout, the sort of thing you expected to see outside a Knightsbridge salon. But as Richard eased it up the ramp, the steering precise, the engine note sharper than expected, he realised it had bite.

He had half expected body roll and wheezing protests; instead, the thing clung to the tarmac like a cat to curtains. A hairdresser's toy on the outside, but there was muscle under the gloss. Enough to make him raise an eyebrow.

Almost, he thought, as satisfying as the Range Rover he had rebuilt bolt by bolt in his youth. Almost.

Still, something was missing. The final ten per cent. The grunt that only a proper engine delivered. He suspected the Friends might have hidden it somewhere, and one day he meant to find out.

He parked in a far corner of the top deck, killed the engine, and sat for a long moment. Here, above the bustle of Canary Wharf, he allowed himself to be Richard: soldier, heir, grandson. Then he opened the door.

He gave the Suzuki's polished flank a fond pat, leaning in as if admiring his reflection.

'So many mirrors, darling', he murmured, just loud enough for his own amusement. 'You'll probably use them to spot some beastly tail, but I shall use them for something far more important: looking at me'.

Moments later, the man who stepped out onto Hertsmere Road was not Richard at all. Pastel jacket. Silk scarf. Oversized sunglasses. The exaggerated strut of a man who had never walked a straight line in his life. Gerald. Richard stayed behind, locked away in the Suzuki.

It was a short mince across the cobbles to the Bank. Aldridge & Co's headquarters occupied the restored warehouses of West India Quay, technically part of Canary Wharf, though with its brick and iron girders polished into something venerable yet secure, it felt a world away from the glass towers next door. A statement of continuity in a city that preferred shine to solidity.

Aldridge & Co had once kept its headquarters deep in the Square Mile, like every other ancient City institution. But the IRA truck bombs of the early nineties had shattered more than glass and stone. Overnight, the old City streets felt too cramped, too vulnerable. While the American giants took their places in the glittering new towers of Canary Wharf, Aldridge & Co chose a different course.

In 1994, it shifted its headquarters to West India Quay, into a row of restored brick warehouses where the Bank could claim both modern security and old-world gravitas. From there, it was a short run down the A2 to Kent, and barely ten minutes by car to London City Airport, a convenience the directors valued almost as much as the reinforced concrete cores and discreet security cordons.

Gerald admired his reflection in the glass doors before swanning inside.

The induction was every bit as tedious as Jonathan intended it to be. HR forms, compliance declarations, right-to-work checks: the paperwork labyrinth every new hire was supposed to dread. Gerald, however, breezed through it as though signing autographs at a stage door.

The passport was genuine, again courtesy of the Friends, like the Suzuki. The CV was impeccable, the references glowing, the background checks so spotless they could have doubled as a mirror.

The compliance officer reached the final page. 'Any accommodations you'll require while working here?'

Gerald tapped the small beige device in his ear with mock solemnity. 'My hearing aid. State of the art, or so they promised me in Harley Street. Without it, I'd never survive these ghastly open-plan offices'.

She made a note, satisfied. Nobody questioned it further.

From a mezzanine above, two men watched the exchange through the glass. They weren't bankers. Not really. Suits and ties covered the Syndicate just well enough to blend in, but their eyes were trained elsewhere, not on balance sheets but on threats.

One leaned closer. 'He's in. Box him in the Archives, keep him out of the way. We'll let the boss know'.

The other smirked faintly. 'Still don't see what all the fuss is about. Looks like no threat to me'.

'Maybe. But the boss doesn't like surprises. We'll keep the leash tight'.

Behind the tinted lenses, Richard's gaze drifted upward and spotted the 'gentlemen' instantly, whilst the sunglasses recorded their images for later analysis.

Richard let Gerald pout into a gilt-framed mirror and flutter his scarf, but in the corner of his vision, he had already filed their faces.

Let them watch. He was watching too.

Jonathan walked up to him. 'Welcome to the Bank', he said. 'I have the perfect spot for you to start. Somewhere you can really... make a difference'.

Gerald clapped his hands with exaggerated delight. 'Oh, Jonathan, how *thoughtful*! I do so adore a challenge'.

Jonathan's eyes glinted. 'Excellent. Follow me'.

They descended into the lower levels of the building, the air growing cooler and drier. Jonathan stopped before a heavy steel door, which he pushed open.

'The Archives', he said, as though unveiling a priceless gift. 'Everything the Bank has ever held: records, history, correspondence. You'll be surrounded by the very soul of Aldridge & Co'.

To Gerald, it was all 'marvellous, darling', delivered with a flourish.

To Richard, the man behind the act, it was exactly what he had hoped for. A gift-wrapped reconnaissance opportunity.

Jonathan led him inside, sweeping a hand towards rows of dusty shelves. 'I'll leave you to… familiarise yourself. I'll be back later to take you out to celebrate your first day. Meet the team'.

Gerald gave a theatrical little wave. 'I'll be ready for cocktails!'

The door shut behind him.

The Archives smelled of paper and time. Floor-to-ceiling shelving groaned under the weight of boxes, some labelled neatly, others scrawled in faded ink, almost worn away.

His sunglasses were already busy, silently recording everything for later analysis in case he missed a detail. Even on this initial sweep, it was clear: the Syndicate's infiltration of the Bank went back decades, perhaps generations, and was deeper and more entrenched than his grandfather had ever imagined.

At the far end, partially hidden by a collapsed stack of folders, sat a battered carton with a black-stencilled title:

OPERATION SIBLING

Contents: Perth, W.A.

Richard froze. To an intelligence officer, the message was unmistakable: open me.

Inside were photographs: his grandparents' wedding in France; his grandmother stepping off a troopship in Fremantle, visibly pregnant; and then, the one that made his stomach knot, grainy black-and-whites of a wrecked car on Caves Road. His parents, unmistakably dead in the driver and passenger seats.

There were birth certificates and a marriage certificate for his parents… but no record whatsoever of himself or his sister. In these files, they simply did not exist.

Then, buried under a ledger, he found the most damning item: a bundle of wartime cables in German.

He read them fluently. They detailed the betrayal of his grandfather to the Nazis in 1944 and the source of that betrayal. The cables pointed unerringly to his grandfather's own sister.

From the depths of Gerald's flamboyant man bag, Richard slid free what looked like an oversized leather-bound diary. Inside was the Friends' handiwork: a wafer-thin scanner sheet linked by concealed cable to a compact digital recorder.

He laid each document onto the page, one after the other, and depressed the discreet stud under his thumb. The scanner whispered as it captured, committing every line of ink and every grain of photographic silver to its CompactFlash store. He swapped cards twice, tucking the full ones into a hidden fold at the back of the bag.

By the time the door creaked open, he had restored everything to its precise order.

'Time for cocktails and to meet the team', Jonathan called.

Richard's first instinct was to snap the man's neck then and there; he was more than capable. But in an instant, Gerald took over.

'Interaction? Darling, I'm always up for that, especially with this team'. He gave a languid sigh. 'But alas, I have the most beastly migraine, and all I crave is a darkened room. Alone!' he trilled, mincing past Jonathan with a flutter of fingers and sweeping up the stairs as though the whole affair bored him.

Jonathan was beside himself. The honey trap he had spent the day so carefully arranging had slipped through his fingers in seconds. No matter; the bait was set, and tomorrow would bring another chance.

Meanwhile, Gerald minced out of the Bank and into the car park where the little Suzuki was waiting. The performance never dropped, but behind the act, his eyes were steel. Every polished surface, car doors, shop windows, and the dark glass of the Quay building became a mirror for his surveillance sweep. Flamboyant, yes. Careless? Never.

By the time he slid behind the wheel, the act dropped away. Gerald vanished; Richard returned. He guided the Suzuki out of Canary Wharf and towards Lord Richard's townhouse.

The drive passed in silence, headlights glancing off glass and steel. By the time he reached Eaton Square, the mask was gone entirely. A debrief was overdue, and the evidence could not wait.

On the laptop screen, file after file stacked into place. The truth was damning: the betrayal by Lord Richard's sister; the duplicity of Edward; Jonathan stepping seamlessly into his father's place; and finally, the killing of the son Lord Richard had never known he had. The old man's fist tightened on the table edge as the air in the room grew heavier with each revelation.

The stakes had risen a notch or three. Watching and waiting was no longer enough. It was time to go on the offensive.

The embryo of a plan formed. Under the guise of ISO accreditation, they would comb through the Bank's archives with a fine-tooth comb. Lord Richard knew just the person: Mary Jenner, former head of compliance. She had left to set up her own consultancy, but she knew the Bank like the back of her hand. More importantly, Lord Richard trusted her enough to bring her into the full picture.

That evening, he picked up the phone himself.

'Mary? It's Richard. I wouldn't ask if it weren't important, but I find myself in need of your help… if you can come to London, I'd be most grateful. I'll see to every expense'.

Her reply came without hesitation. 'Don't insult me with expenses. If you need me, I'll be there first thing tomorrow. No questions asked'.

A pause, then her voice softened. 'And Richard, if you need help in any way, you'll have it. You don't even need to ask'.

As she spoke, Lord Richard covered the handset with his palm and glanced across the room. His grandson leaned forward, still in Gerald's tailored disguise but eyes sharp with a soldier's instinct.

In a voice too low for the line to catch, the younger man murmured, 'Grandfather, your office might not be the best place for a first meeting. Assume it's bugged. Better to set neutral ground'.

Lord Richard gave a slight nod, then uncovered the receiver. 'You're right', he said — to both of them, in a sense. Into the phone, his tone returned to business. 'I'll book you a room at the Marriott. Safer there, and we can talk freely. I'll meet you first thing in the morning, at breakfast, before the Bank stirs. You'll need to be brought up to speed from the start'.

'I'll travel overnight', Mary replied immediately. 'Expect me at breakfast'.

The line went dead. Lord Richard set the receiver down slowly. The board was tilting, the pieces moving. By dawn, the circle would widen, and the Aldridge counter-offensive would begin.

A little after eight, Mary Jenner stepped into the hotel's breakfast room. Lord Richard was already seated at a table by the window, where the pale January sun caught his profile, softening the lines of age. For a man of his years and for one supposedly in decline, he looked remarkably well, a touch of colour high in his cheeks. Across from him sat a younger man, wearing glasses, in a well-cut suit, posture alert, his expression calm but unreadable.

Mary smiled warmly as she approached. 'Richard. You look remarkably awake for someone who called me at ten o'clock last night'.

'Old soldiers never sleep deeply', Lord Richard replied with a twinkle. 'Mary, thank you for coming on such short notice. Allow me to introduce your new assistant'.

Mary raised an eyebrow, humour in her voice. 'Assistant? Richard, with respect, I have my own people. Competent ones. I don't need handpicked minders foisted on me'.

The young man inclined his head politely, saying nothing.

Lord Richard gave a patient smile. 'Indulge me, just for this assignment. Trust me, he's precisely who you'll want by your side'.

Mary's lips pursed. She was about to object more firmly when the young man reached up and removed his glasses. Not the ostentatious sunglasses Gerald was known for, but a subtle set of frames chosen to mask the line of his jaw and shadow his eyes just enough.

The effect was instant. Mary's breath caught; she blinked, then leaned back in her chair as recognition settled in. The Aldridge family resemblance was undeniable, not in caricature, but in the shape of the mouth, the tilt of the head, the eyes that mirrored Richard's own.

Her first instinct was disbelief. She had known the old man for decades, had heard whispers of family tragedy and secrets, but had never imagined he kept someone this close. Then came a flicker of admiration, almost reluctant. For all her years in compliance, she had never seen a secret kept this well. Finally, a surge of resolve hardened in her chest. If Lord Richard trusted her enough to reveal this, then the game had changed completely. This was no longer a consultancy gig. This was a covenant.

'My God', she whispered. 'He's yours'.

Lord Richard nodded once. 'My grandson. For now, he must remain under the radar. That means someone else in public, Richard here in private, and for this assignment, your assistant'.

Mary recovered quickly, her professional calm returning, though the steel in her eyes had sharpened. She looked from one to the other, understanding now the depth of what she was being pulled into.

'Well then', she said softly. 'If we're playing for stakes this high, I suppose I'd be a fool to refuse such an assistant. But know this: if I take him, he's mine to manage. Agreed?'

The younger Richard gave a faint smile, a soldier's courtesy. 'Agreed'.

Lord Richard leaned back, his expression composed. 'Then it's settled. Mary, I'd like you to take the lead on the archive audit, framed as ISO compliance. My grandson will make sure you have all the support you need. Between you, I'm confident the answers will come, and soon enough'.

Mary reached for her coffee, her hand steady, though her mind was already racing. She thought of ledgers and anomalies, yes, but also of shadows and predators. This wasn't just a job; it was stepping onto a battlefield she hadn't known existed, one where her skills still mattered. She straightened her shoulders.

'You'll have them', she said. 'But Richard, this is no longer an audit. This is war, dressed up in paperwork'.

The old man gave a slow, grim nod. 'At last, Mary, you see it exactly as we do'.

Chapter 10: The Old Queen Returns

Morning prayers at the Bank had always been more theatre than governance. A ritual of nods, murmurs, and reports delivered in tones designed not to offend. Numbers flickered on the screens, directors droned their forecasts, and the real business, the quiet understandings and off-ledger arrangements, was carried elsewhere.

The session was winding down when the air shifted. A ripple passed down the table as Lord Richard entered. He hadn't been expected; his sudden presence was enough to still voices mid-sentence.

The old chairman looked different. Not merely rested, but purposeful: the set of his shoulders, the clarity in his eyes, carried an authority most had forgotten he possessed. For a moment, even Jonathan's mask faltered.

Lord Richard let the silence stretch, commanding the room without raising his voice. Then he spoke.

'Ladies and gentlemen. We face a century that will not forgive shadows. Transparency and rigour are no longer optional. To that end, I have authorised a full review: ISO certification. It will be demanding. It will touch every part of this institution. And it will be done'.

The word 'review' landed like a dropped stone. A ripple of discomfort moved along the polished table.

Jonathan leaned back in his chair, voice silk over steel. 'ISO certification? Uncle, forgive me, but this Bank has thrived for centuries without box-ticking exercises. Our reputation is certification enough'.

Lord Richard's eyes fixed on him. 'Reputation is bought and destroyed overnight in the twenty-first century. We will have proof. We will have standards no one can question. That is how we will endure'.

Several directors exchanged nervous glances. The implications of proof and standards brushed too close to ledgers better left unexamined.

It was Lydia McCarthy, the youngest director, who broke the tension. Her voice was clear, cutting through the murmurs. 'It's exactly what we need. The world has changed. If we demonstrate compliance at the highest level, we lead, not follow'.

Lord Richard gave her a measured nod. 'Precisely'. He gestured towards the door. 'Most of you will remember Mary Jenner'.

Mary entered with composed assurance, her eyes sharp, the picture of quiet authority. At her side was her assistant, Connor Richards, reserved, silent, watchful.

Mary placed a slim folder on the table. 'Our approach will be thorough, but discreet. We begin with the Archives. Then, policy, practice, and executive oversight. My role is to test the Bank as if I were the regulator and ensure that when real scrutiny comes, we excel'.

Jonathan's jaw tightened, his smile a shade too thin. 'Delightful. I look forward to watching you… work'.

'Indeed you will', Lord Richard said, voice even but edged with iron. 'Mary reports directly to me. You will provide whatever access she requires. That is all'.

He paused, then added lightly, almost as an afterthought:

'Oh, and one other thing. This place is starting to look rather dowdy. We haven't touched a thing since we moved in back in '94. About time it was redecorated. Work will begin tonight. I've already engaged contractors. Please make sure your desks and your teams are clear before you leave. They'll do their best to manage it overnight so you're not disturbed too much'.

The directors shifted uneasily, some exchanging glances. Only Jonathan's eyes narrowed, though he said nothing.

The meeting dissolved into whispers. Some directors offered Mary polite greetings. Lydia shook her hand warmly. Jonathan remained silent.

Lord Richard had arranged for a quiet conference room on the top floor, neutral enough to avoid attention, but secure enough for Mary to work without interruption. By mid-morning, she was set up, papers stacked in neat piles, her assistant beside her with a laptop open and phone on silent.

Mary's skill was in making the extraordinary look routine. She moved through rosters, payroll histories, and compliance reports with a practised eye, highlighting anomalies almost as soon as she saw them. To anyone passing in the corridor, it was just another consultant fussing with files.

But within hours, she had marked three names. Four, if she counted the one whose file was too clean. Not senior figures, Jonathan wasn't reckless enough to place them that high, but mid-level officers. Treasury. Compliance. Risk. All positioned where oversight could be nudged, where paper trails could be blurred.

She slid the sheet across to her assistant. 'See these? Jonathan's fingerprints are all over them. These aren't just ordinary hires. They're Syndicate plants. And a couple… I'd wager they've been involved in more than just moving numbers. Some of this blood money is literal'.

The young man nodded once, eyes hard, committing the names to memory.

Mary leaned back, exhaling through her nose. 'Richard was right. This isn't just an audit. It's a purge waiting to happen'.

Back in his office, Jonathan swirled a measure of brandy, the faint clink of crystal masking his irritation. Finally, he stalked down the hall and pushed into his uncle's office without knocking.

'Where is that bloody boy of yours, Gerald, when one might actually need him?' His voice was sharp, half-sneer, half-frustration. 'He's usually underfoot at every turn. Now? Vanished'.

Lord Richard looked up from the papers on his desk, his expression mild, almost amused. He let the silence drag, then replied evenly: 'Gerald has a way of appearing precisely when he's needed. I wouldn't trouble yourself over him'.

Jonathan's jaw tightened. He gave a curt nod and turned away, but Richard watched him go, the faintest trace of satisfaction in his eyes. Jonathan was rattled. The Syndicate could feel the noose tightening, even if they didn't yet know who was holding the rope.

Back at the Marriott Executive Apartments at West India Quay, the city had gone quiet. Mary was sorting her notes when there came a discreet knock on the connecting door to her suite. She had accomplished in hours what would have taken others days, even weeks, to achieve.

When she opened the door, her assistant was there, standing just behind Lord Richard, both men composed but watchful.

'Time for a debrief', Richard said simply.

Mary stepped back to let them in. On the table, she had laid out her findings: names, annotations, and thin trails of evidence that together formed a damning picture. Three, perhaps four individuals, all embedded in the Bank under Jonathan's patronage. Not high-level, but dangerous nonetheless. Their hands were not clean.

Richard studied the papers, his face unreadable. Then he looked at his grandson. 'These are the lowlifes you told me about'.

The younger man gave a single, sharp nod.

Richard's tone hardened. 'Then we deal with them. Tomorrow morning, my office. One by one. They'll be given a choice: resign quietly, or be dismissed for gross misconduct. Those close enough to retirement may go with their pension intact. The Bank was built on honour, and I won't strip that away. But the younger ones…' He set the papers down with finality. '…if they refuse to resign, their details go to the FCA. They'll never work in banking again'.

Mary met his gaze across the table, her own expression steady. 'It's a clean cut', she said. 'Swift and unmistakable. Jonathan will know you've struck back'.

Richard leaned back in his chair, eyes narrowing. 'Good. Let him know. This is just the beginning'.

The room fell into silence, the only sound the faint hum of the Docklands night outside. Three minds, now aligned, are already moving the pieces for the morning to come.

Chapter 11: The Old Queen Has Teeth

Morning prayers began without their chairman. The directors gathered in the boardroom, as they did each day, murmuring through reports and forecasts with the solemnity of liturgy. But today, the chair at the head of the table again sat empty.

Jonathan smirked faintly, leaning back in his seat. 'So much for the great return. Short-lived, wasn't it?'

A couple of the older directors chuckled nervously, though none too loudly.

Lydia McCarthy, clear-eyed and sharp, spoke up before the mutters spread further. 'Or perhaps he's simply working. Some of us still believe in leading by action, not appearances'.

That ended the whispers. Papers shuffled, chairs creaked. Without the chairman, morning prayers quickly wound down. One by one, the directors dispersed into the day's business.

Lord Richard was not absent. He was already at work.

His office bore the marks of overnight disruption: faint chalk notations on the plaster, pencilled crosses at seemingly random points along the skirting, and, most telling of all, small squares of tape placed with surgical precision. To an untrained eye, it looked like decorators preparing for a long-overdue freshening. In reality, each piece of tape sat squarely over a pinhole camera, each chalk mark aligned to a hidden microphone or transmitter, all carefully identified by the Friends' sweep team. None had been removed. To pull them out would raise suspicion. Instead, the sweepers had left them in place, blind and muffled, silent witnesses to a fiction of ordinary redecoration.

Helen Briggs from HR sat primly in the corner, lips pressed thin, notebook open. She was here not as an ally, but as the silent witness the Bank's procedures demanded.

The first to be summoned was Pritchard. Grey-haired, heavyset, with the weary look of a man who had spent thirty years at the

Bank's middle ranks. Nominally an operations manager, but in truth one of the Syndicate's facilitators, tucked neatly into the Bank's veins.

Lord Richard didn't waste time on ceremony.

'You've served this institution for thirty years', he began, voice level, eyes fixed. 'You can leave today with your pension intact. Or you can stay and have me place these documents before the Financial Conduct Authority'.

He slid a single page across the desk. A neat dossier summary, stripped of embellishment, its contents damning enough to drain the colour from Pritchard's face.

'There's no appeal', Richard continued evenly. 'Decide now'.

Silence stretched. The only sound was the faint rattle of a DLR train gliding past and the soft hum of the building's air systems, muted by thick glass. Pritchard's hand shook as he took up the pen. Thirty seconds later, his name was inked across the page. Thirty years of service ended in silence.

Lord Richard didn't look up as Pritchard left. He was already reaching for the next file.

Later that morning, Gerald, the chairman's friend, swept into the Bank, silk scarf knotted just so, hair immaculate, and the faintest whiff of cologne trailing in his wake. Staff turned to stare, as they always did; Gerald thrived on it.

Lord Richard's PA intercepted him on his way through the Bank. 'The chairman would like to see you at once'.

Gerald clicked his tongue and rolled his eyes. 'Of course he would. Probably wants to scold me for something I haven't done again'.

Inside the office, Lord Richard didn't waste time. His voice was sharp, pitched just enough to carry to the hidden microphones.

'I've looked after you. Got you this job, kept you in comfort, and this is how you repay me? Where have you been these past two days? Don't tell me you've been languishing with one of your beastly migraines after half an hour in the archives'.

Gerald affected a wounded look, sliding effortlessly into the role. 'Darling, you wound me. Do you think I'd risk my complexion among dust and mildew? Perish the thought'.

Richard huffed theatrically. 'Well, the good news is you're spared the basement today. Instead, you'll be helping Mary Jenner. She's here on compliance work. I'll have my PA fetch her'.

A few moments later, Mary was shown in. She took a seat, cautious but curious.

'Mary', Lord Richard said formally, aware of the ears beyond the walls, 'this is Gerald. An... old friend of the family'.

Gerald inclined his head with a dazzling smile. 'Charmed, I'm sure'.

Then Richard grimaced, waving towards the corner. 'And while you're here, Gerald, do something useful for once. Switch on that blasted machine. The one meant to keep the air clean. No idea why it never works'.

Gerald gave the faintest flicker of a knowing smile. He crossed to the boxy unit in the corner and pressed a hidden sequence of buttons. The purifier's fan whirred to life, and at the same time, Richard pulled open the desk drawer. Nestled inside was the real safeguard the Friends had left behind during their sweep the previous night: a cigarette-pack-sized jamming device. The soft electronic pulse filling the room told him both machines were now doing exactly what they were meant to.

In the side room down the corridor, Jonathan's receiver howled with static. The feed dissolved into dead air.

Back in the office, Lord Richard's voice softened at once. 'Mary, allow me to speak plainly. Gerald is no friend. He is my grandson in disguise'.

Mary's eyes widened, her professional mask cracking for the briefest instant. She looked from the flamboyant Gerald to the hard-eyed man beneath, suddenly seeing through the powder and polish.

'My God', she whispered. 'The resemblance... it's uncanny'.

Gerald let the performance slip just enough, his posture sharpening, his voice dropping half an octave. 'Now you see why the Syndicate hasn't caught on. They expect Gerald, and Gerald is exactly what they get'.

Mary sat back, breath steadying, comprehension dawning. The depth of the deception floored her, but it also explained why Richard was winning battles no one else even knew were being fought.

Meanwhile, across the building, Jonathan slammed his fist on the receiver. The line was dead. For the first time, the Bank's bugs had gone silent. And that, more than anything, terrified him.

While Jonathan fumed, Mary and her assistant had returned to the same conference room where they'd worked the day before. Mary sat down, opened her files, and within moments was back in her element: columns of numbers, policy gaps, names cross-checked against duty rosters. Gerald perched dramatically at her shoulder, sighing about the 'oppressive lighting' and brushing an invisible speck of lint from his lapel. For all his preening, though, his eyes never stopped moving.

When Mary finally leaned back, stretching the stiffness from her shoulders, Gerald set down his leather satchel with a conspiratorial grin.

'Darling, I think it's time you had some toys'.

He opened the bag and slid a few objects onto the table: a leather-bound diary, a lighter that gave a faint hum when flicked open, a pair of glasses far plainer than the flamboyant ones he usually wore.

Mary's brows arched. 'Good Lord. What on earth—?'

The Gerald mask slipped, just for a moment. His posture straightened, his voice steadied, and though the silk scarf and tailored suit remained, it was Captain Richard O'Connell who handled each item, explaining with a soldier's precision what they could do. The oversized leather-bound diary that was, in truth, a scanner. A pocket signal jammer disguised as a lighter — not the heavier unit the Friends had left in Lord Richard's office, but a personal safeguard he could carry anywhere. Glasses that tagged and traced.

He showed her how each worked, his movements efficient, his tone stripped of Gerald's affectations. The air was quiet except for the faint hum of the lighter-jammer, a subtle reassurance that this room was clean, private, and theirs alone.

Mary listened, rapt. For all her years in boardrooms and compliance committees, she had never seen power distilled quite like this. When the demonstration ended, she gave a slow, almost wicked smile.

'Can I keep these when we're finished? I know several CEOs who would collapse into abject terror if they thought I had them in my handbag'.

Gerald slipped effortlessly back into character, one eyebrow arched, a feline smile curving his lips.

'Well, my dear, I do have friends in very low places. Let me speak to them. Perhaps they can arrange a little something for your... corporate toolkit'.

Mary laughed, shaking her head, though she couldn't quite hide the spark in her eyes. For the first time since she'd stepped into the storm, she felt the odd thrill of being armed not just with rules and audits, but with secrets.

The moment was broken by a knock at the door. Jonathan leaned in, his smile tight, his eyes glittering.

'Gerald. Come along. You owe me cocktails, remember? Your first day here, I promised you'd see how the city really plays after dark'.

Gerald rose at once, as if the invitation were salvation. 'At last! Something civilised. Lead on, Jonathan, before I wither entirely under the fluorescent glare of governance'.

He swept out with his usual flourish, leaving Mary to gather her papers in silence. She watched him go, unease prickling at her edges. For all the frivolity, she sensed the currents beneath. Jonathan was taking Gerald, and whatever game was about to begin, it wouldn't end with cocktails.

Chapter 12: The Honey Trap

The West India Quay Footbridge arched over the water; its steel frame lit in soft amber. Gerald crossed it at an unhurried pace, pastel scarf fluttering in the breeze, Syndicate shadows pacing him a dozen steps behind. Ahead, Canary Wharf rose in glass and steel towers glittering against the night.

At the foot of one tower, a club front gleamed in the floodlights, its entrance roped off with thick velvet cord. The line was long: the wealthy, the ambitious, and the desperate, all waiting their turn for entry.

Jonathan didn't even glance at them. The moment he and his party approached, a bouncer unclipped the rope with practised deference. They were waved straight to the door.

But a larger bouncer, standing slightly apart, stepped forward. His hand came down on Gerald's shoulder with just enough pressure to bruise.

'Bag', he said flatly, nodding to the pastel satchel Gerald carried.

Gerald clutched the bag closer with a gasp of mock horror. 'Darling, really? Do I look like the sort of man who carries anything more dangerous than moisturiser?'

The bouncer didn't move. His hand came out, palm up, waiting. For a heartbeat, Richard weighed his options: a distraction, a takedown, something fast and messy.

Then Jonathan's voice cut in, smooth as ice.

'That won't be necessary'.

The bouncer hesitated, his eyes flicking to Jonathan.

'You work for me', Jonathan said softly, just loud enough for Gerald to hear. 'And I don't waste my time having my guests pawed over like criminals. Do you understand?'

A beat. The bouncer stepped back, his jaw tight. 'Yes, sir'.

Gerald fluttered his scarf as though the whole exchange had been an inconvenience beneath him. 'Well. That was frightfully awkward. Shall we?'

Jonathan didn't even dignify him with a reply. He simply turned and strode inside, Gerald mincing theatrically after him.

Inside, the club split into two worlds.

The first, a main lounge of dark wood, soft lighting, and expensive cocktails, was what the public saw. Music pulsed low from the DJ booth, a sleek, beat-driven undercurrent more felt than heard, calculated less to entertain than to oil the wheels of conversation. Cut-glass chandeliers caught the light, scattering it across marble floors polished to a mirror sheen. Waiters in crisp black waistcoats moved silently between the tables, balancing trays of champagne flutes and hors d'oeuvres no one really tasted. It was exclusivity on display, a veneer thinner than it looked.

The second, reached through a discreet side corridor guarded by another door, was where the real business happened. Here, the lighting dropped, the air heavier with cigar smoke and expensive perfume. Booths of tufted leather lined the walls, curtains half-drawn to promise privacy. The hum of conversation was low, punctuated by bursts of laughter that never quite reached the eyes. This was the Syndicate's hunting ground. Privacy reigned, rules bent until they snapped, and every indulgence was discreetly captured by the club's hidden cameras and directional mics. Perfect material for blackmail.

Jonathan's party was led there without hesitation.

Jonathan had chosen the bait well. A young man lingered at the edge of the table, a sharp suit, sharper smile, carrying himself with the ease of someone who knew exactly why he was there. His name, murmured in introduction, was Tristan.

Tristan wasted no time. He slid in beside Gerald, his hand resting on Gerald's thigh with practised ease, the scent of expensive cologne mingling with the faint tang of champagne. Gerald responded with just enough warmth to feed the cameras, every gesture calculated.

He let the laughter come easily, allowed the occasional lingering touch, even leaned in close enough for Jonathan to believe the bait was taking. But every move was controlled. Gerald never compromised himself, not once.

The champagne glass he'd been handed early in the evening remained mostly untouched, the bubbles long since gone.

After an hour, Gerald gave a theatrical yawn.

'Darling, I'm simply exhausted', he drawled, placing the barely drunk glass on the table.

Tristan's smile faltered, his frustration barely masked. Jonathan, however, was positively content. He had the photographs he wanted: intimate angles, suggestive frames, enough to spin a convincing story.

What he didn't have and what he didn't realise was a single shred of actual leverage.

Gerald let the heavy club doors swing shut behind him, pastel scarf trailing like a banner. The night air off the Thames, a few lingering smokers out front barely glanced at him, just another eccentric banker heading home.

He minced across the plaza until he reached the West India Quay car park. A casual glance in a window's reflection, another in the polished side of a parked taxi, no shadows where they shouldn't be. Almost.

The bouncer from the club peeled out of the darkness, shoulders rolling like a bull entering a ring.

Gerald stopped, turned and fluttered his hand. 'Well, hello, big boy. But not tonight, darling; you are simply not my type'.

The man's lip curled as he advanced, shoving him hard in the chest.

'Please don't make me angry', Gerald lilted, voice sweet as sugar. 'You wouldn't like me when I'm angry'.

The second shove drove him back a pace. The bouncer sneered. 'Why? You gonna turn into the Hulk?'

The smile vanished. The pastel mask fell away. Richard stood in his place.

'No. Much worse'.

Before the man could blink, Richard's hand shot out, seizing his wrist and rolling it inward with brutal precision. The shoulder gave with a sickening pop, and the bouncer crumpled to his knees, gasping in agony.

Richard leaned close. And then Gerald returned, smile sweet as poison, voice dropping to a conspiratorial murmur, silk over steel.

'Darling, I did warn you… you really wouldn't like me when I'm angry'.

He let the man collapse against the wall and walked on without another glance.

At the far corner of the car park, under a sodium lamp, waited the Suzuki, totally garish, and utterly out of place among the polished German saloons. Gerald slid behind the wheel, the pastel jacket creasing awkwardly against the Suzuki's seat. For a moment, the performance lingered. Then he sighed, peeled off the sunglasses, and started the engine.

Not Gerald. Richard.

Richard flipped the switch under the dashboard, and the Suzuki's personality instantly changed, as the friend's modification tweaked the engine. The Suzuki surged out of Canary Wharf and into the Limehouse Link. Concrete walls closed in, amplifying the engine note until the whole tunnel became a throbbing drum. Gerald slouched theatrically behind the wheel; one hand raised in a languid wave to late-night pedestrians at the exits. But in the dark reflections of the glass, Richard's eyes stared back.

From there, the road opened westward, the Suzuki shouldering through the city traffic with blunt authority. By the time it nosed up to the kerb outside Lord Richard's London townhouse, the masquerade was fraying. He killed the engine and sat for a moment, breathing. One last time, he pulled the pastel scarf tighter, a final layer of armour. Then Gerald got out of the Suzuki...

But it was Richard who walked in through the front door, casting off the pastel jacket, the silk scarf, and Gerald himself.

The butler, waiting discreetly in the hall, accepted the discarded garments without comment. His expression remained unreadable, his silence that of a man long accustomed to serving more than one face of the same master.

'I need a shower', Richard called over his shoulder. 'Get the slime of that place off me'.

The butler moved discreetly to take his coat, then withdrew without a word. Richard lingered a moment, turning back to his grandson. Their eyes met.

'You can rely on him', Richard said quietly. 'He's seen more than most'.

Ten minutes later, his grandson emerged into the sitting room, not in his usual chinos and open-necked Oxford shirt, the understated look of an officer off duty, but as Captain Richard O'Connell, ASAS. Black tactical gear, gloves, boots. Every line of his said one thing: the man was ready for war.

'We need eyes in the warehouse', he said flatly. 'Tonight's as good a night as any. Simple in-and-out, plant the surveillance kit and get clear'.

His grandfather gave him a long look. 'Where have I heard that before?' he said with dry trepidation.

Captain Richard's mouth twitched into the ghost of a smile. 'I won't be alone this time. I carry the skills Elder Miran gave me, and the spirits of my ancestors walk with me'.

Lord Richard's eyes narrowed. 'Spirits won't stop a bullet'. To which his grandson responded, 'You'd be surprised'.

Richard left the townhouse, his grandfather's last words weighing heavily as he crossed the private courtyard to the garages. The Defender waited in the shadows, while the Suzuki was left conspicuously parked out front for all to see. Tonight, he was in full Captain Richard mode, and as much as the little Suzuki had grown on him, only the Defender would serve for what he was about to do.

He slid into the driver's seat and pressed the hidden switch beneath the dash. A faint relay clicked. The low idle of the tuned diesel shifted into a steady, almost feline murmur. The extra work that had been done, turbo and exhaust mods courtesy of the Friends in Hereford, gave it a quiet confidence the standard TDI had always lacked.

'Stealth mode', Richard muttered, more out of habit than expectation. The Defender wasn't clever enough to answer back, but the discreet wiring loom and toggle panel gave him everything he needed: cut-down exhaust notes, scrambled comms, and a short-burst radio uplink if the situation went bad.

He allowed himself the faintest smile.

'After all, we don't want to wake the neighbours'.

The Defender rolled away from the kerb, tyres humming softly, its bulk moving with more grace than its boxy frame suggested. The modified diesel had grunt enough to surprise anyone still underestimating it.

But that was exactly how it went: in, out, quiet, unseen, the way Richard preferred it.

Across the city, in a discreet Mayfair office, Jonathan poured himself a measure of whisky and scrolled through a fresh batch of images delivered straight from the club. Frame after frame showed Gerald draped in suggestive poses, Tristan leaning close, laughter caught mid-motion.

Jonathan's smile widened with every click. 'Checkmate, Uncle', he murmured. 'Your little protégé won't survive this'.

He raised the glass in a solitary toast, convinced he had regained control.

But the images, so carefully staged, were nothing more than shadows on a screen. Gerald had given the Syndicate exactly what they wanted to see, and not a fraction more.

The trap was set.

By the time the first light of dawn touched the London skyline, Richard was back, the kit in place, the Syndicate none the wiser.

Within minutes, the first stills from the surveillance kit hidden in the warehouse began to come through, grainy, compressed, but clear enough. The images were damning: crates stacked high with drugs, guns, and cash. Worst of all was the corner where young boys and girls sat huddled, the human currency of the Syndicate. No sign of Alpha, but this was more than enough.

But the question remained: what were the Syndicate going to do with their photos?

Chapter 13: The Raid

The next morning, as he sat with Mary in full Gerald mode, his phone vibrated softly in his pocket. He excused himself, stepped to the window, and pressed it to his ear. A voice from Hereford followed, calm, clipped, the kind that never wasted a syllable.

'Your intel lit up the boards. We're going tonight. Rendezvous 23:00, Limehouse Basin. H-hour 00:30. Minimum noise. You're welcome on the team if you want to come, but we'll need your grandfather covered. They tried before in Margaret River, and if they even suspect he's alone in the house, they may try again'.

Gerald's smile froze. The camp lilt was gone in an instant, shoulders straightening, eyes hard. Mary saw the mask drop like a stage curtain, Gerald dissolving, Richard O'Connell revealed beneath.

'I want in on the raid', Richard said, measured.

'That's possible', the voice replied.

The line went dead.

That evening, in the study, the choice hung unspoken between the two men.

'Should I go', Richard asked at last, 'or leave it to the Friends? I don't like the thought of you here alone if they decide to come directly'.

Lord Richard raised a hand, silencing him. Without a word, he crossed to the writing desk, drew a key, and opened a drawer not touched in years. From within, he lifted a small wooden case and laid it on the blotter.

The case opened with a quiet click. Inside lay his old Webley service revolver, steel still blued, still oiled as though waiting for this very night.

'I've kept it clean', Lord Richard said evenly. 'Insurance. If the Syndicate thinks I'll go quietly, they're in for a disappointment'.

Richard's eyes flicked from the weapon to his grandfather. The revolver was clearly from the war, yet in remarkable condition. He wondered if it had last been drawn in France in 1944, carried home with his grandfather like a relic of another life. Whatever its history, there was no bravado in the way Lord Richard held it now, only the calm resolve of a man ready for war once more.

'Be careful', his grandfather said quietly.

'I will. And you, Grandfather'.

'I'll be back before you know it'.

'That's what I said to your grandmother in '44', Lord Richard murmured. 'And we both know how that ended'.

The Defender slipped off the A13 and into the dark underbelly of Limehouse Basin, engine hushed to a discreet murmur. Two unmarked Land Rovers waited in the shadows beneath the railway arches, lights off, silhouettes cut by the sodium haze on the water. Figures moved with unhurried precision, men who'd done this before.

Richard killed the engine and stepped out. The squad leader, a compact major with Hereford in his voice, looked him over once, then flicked two fingers in greeting.

'Captain O'Connell'.

'Major', Richard said, crisp, deferential. No swagger; another professional reporting to the man holding the chalk.

On the bonnet of the nearest Land Rover, a ruggedised Toughbook glowed, its chunky trackpad smudged with dust. A schematic of Tobacco Dock sprawled across the display, overlaid with blunt icons marking Richard's micro-cams, planted nights earlier. In the corner, Athena's uplink ticked steadily: time stamps in green, packet counts climbing line by line, signal strength bars winking as each feed held or dropped. Functional, inelegant, but it worked.

The major tapped the map with a gloved knuckle. 'Inside picture's good. Your cams are pushing stills every thirty seconds: mezzanine, east walkway, cold store row C. External's patchy, one CCTV blind on Wapping Lane we'll exploit'.

He swept a finger to a boxed office on the mezzanine. A feed showed a man pacing, backlit by a desk lamp, two heavies posted at the door. 'Target Alpha. Office Two, mezzanine north. Paces, smokes, points a lot. Classic'.

Another window: rows of cage doors and a chain. Faces behind mesh, still, watchful. 'Human currency in cold store C, bays 3–7. Minimal guards in the aisle. We treat this like a hostage rescue'.

He looked up. 'Priorities: one, grab Alpha alive. Two, extract every last person from C-row. Three, data sweep if time allows phones, ledgers, anything not nailed down. We go in hard but careful: no collateral, no cowboy noise'.

'Understood', Richard said. 'Your op, Major. Slot me where you need me'.

A beat, the sort of mutual sizing-up that lasts less than a second. The major's mouth tugged, faint approval. 'That'll do'.

Richard nodded towards the Defender. 'One condition. She comes with us. If anything kicks off at the London house, I need to be able to move fast'.

'Every man rides his own warhorse', the major said, amused. 'Defender sits at the back of the stack with White. Engines stay warm'.

He pointed to the plan again. 'Red goes mezzanine for Alpha. Blue hits the cold store, unlocks and lifts. White holds vehicles and forms the exfil corridor along Wapping Wall. Suppressed only. No shots unless you have to. Cameras are looped for…' he checked the Athena overlay, '…a six-minute window before the next sweep. Thames patrol passes at +07; we're gone before they wonder why the lights flickered'.

'You're with Red', he added to Richard. 'Secondary on breach, primary on hands-on if Alpha runs. Blue lifts the currency and pushes to vehicles, White covers and receives. If it unravels, we fall back to the arches and disappear west on the A13. Clear?'

'Clear', Richard said.

A discreet buzz from the comms unit at his collar told him the net was live. Comms green. Uplinks stable. He gave the Toughbook a final scan: Alpha still pacing; guards bored; cold store quiet. A good minute to start bad work.

The major closed the laptop with a firm click and slid the folded map into the oilskin. 'Mount up'.

Doors thudded softly. Engines turned over: two Land Rovers, one Keswick Green Defender idling low beneath the tracks.

The convoy rolled out in a staggered line, dark and deliberate, peeling east along Narrow Street towards Wapping: three vehicles, one plan, and no room for mistakes. Behind them, a second element staged out of sight, ready to move in with ambulances and vans once the hostages were free.

The approach to the warehouse was silent, tyres crunching on gravel only as much as they had to. The perimeter guards didn't stand a chance, dropped cleanly, radios pinned before they could press transmit.

Inside, the team moved like clockwork, clearing each section with ruthless precision. But when Red hit the mezzanine office, Alpha was gone. On the cam playback, you could see it: a brief phone call, a glance at the door, then a slip through a service stair during a twelve-second blind spot when a lens was wiped by a bored guard's sleeve. One minute pacing; the next, air.

Consolation came fast and heavy: crates of weapons; shrink-wrapped bricks of heroin; bundles of cash in plastic; ledgers; phones, usable intel by the boxload.

And in the far corner, the most damning evidence of all: frightened, thin children huddled behind mesh, the living currency of the Syndicate. Richard's jaw clenched so tight it ached. Every instinct screamed to tear the place apart, to meet justice here and now. But training was held. He forced the fury down, channelled it into precision, covering Blue's team as they cut chains and led the captives out.

Within minutes, the extraction vans took them, heaters on, medics waiting. A total success, apart from the one thing they had come for.

Alpha was gone. One minute pacing the mezzanine office, the next vanished through a blind stairwell, leaving nothing but smoke and silence.

Captain Richard returned to the London townhouse to find his grandfather waiting with two whiskies already poured. He accepted the offered glass, the weight of it solid and familiar, and raised it in quiet thanks to his grandfather, to the house that sheltered them, and to the unseen spirits who had carried him safe through another assignment.

In a quiet office overlooking the grey spires of Westminster, Alpha sat alone at a polished table. A single lamp cast a pool of light across the leather blotter, leaving the rest of the room in shadow. To anyone who might walk in, it looked like a senior official catching up on late paperwork.

He keyed into the encrypted bridge. One by one, the Partners came online: no faces, only distorted voices and shifting initials across the black screen.

Alpha's report was delivered in the clipped cadence of a quarterly review.

'London region compromised. Tobacco Dock raided. Product seized. Distribution chain fractured. Ledgers and electronic devices captured. Estimated loss to forward revenue: thirty-eight million pounds. Ancillary exposure: significant. Hostages were recovered, children. Public relations risk elevated'.

The distorted chorus cut back immediately.

'You assured us the Bank would shield operations'.

'You gave us no warning'.

'This quarter will bleed red'.

Alpha did not flinch. His reply was calm, deliberate, the voice of a man who knew panic was weakness.

'The responsibility is mine. The breach will be corrected. Aldridge Bank will deliver as planned'.

There was silence, heavy, dangerous, before one final voice answered, cold and absolute.

'See that it does. Or your region will be restructured'.

The line clicked dead, leaving only the soft hum of the scrambler.

Alpha closed the laptop and leaned back in his chair. One hand brushed his temple as if to ease a headache. His voice, when he finally spoke aloud into the silence, was little more than a whisper.

'Restructured... or buried'.

The next day, the Deputy Leader of the Government rose at the despatch box, the green benches murmuring into silence. He adjusted his papers with a practised hand, gaze sweeping the chamber before fixing squarely on the Speaker.

'Mr Speaker, I can report to the House that, as of this morning, a coordinated operation involving the Metropolitan Police, the National Crime Squad, and Customs & Excise has resulted in a significant disruption of organised criminal activity in the East End. A number of individuals are now in custody, evidence has been seized, and further inquiries are underway'.

He allowed the words to settle, then leaned in, voice tightening with manufactured conviction.

'This Government promised the British people that we would take the fight to the criminals who threaten our communities. Today, we have delivered on that promise. This is proof of what can be achieved when our agencies work together with resolve and determination'.

The benches behind him erupted in the ritual thump of approval. Cameras caught his measured smile, the carefully rehearsed expression of a minister presenting competence to the nation.

Chapter 14: Night of Two Fires

The raid had torn a hole in the Syndicate's armour. For all their money, their reach, their confidence, the humiliation cut deep. Product lost, ledgers seized, lives freed. In boardrooms and safe houses alike, whispers spread: the UK region was slipping, and Alpha's grip was weakening.

Inside the Syndicate's hidden chamber, the atmosphere was not merely tense; it was ritualistic. Shadows moved across polished walls, voices distorted by machines, but the weight in the air was older than technology. It felt like a conclave, an unholy liturgy, every word heavy with consequence.

'The wolves circle us. Who are they?' one voice growled.

'The balance has been broken', another murmured.

'Mercy is weakness', a third intoned, its Scottish burr cold as stone.

The doves, those who once argued for patience, subtlety, and infiltration, were silent now. Their time had passed. The hawks had won the floor.

Alpha spoke little. His report on the raid was factual, clinical, and delivered without tremor. But even through the distortion, those who listened heard the echo of failure. They smelt it — like blood in the water.

It was not just the numbers, though the numbers mattered: thirty-eight million lost, distribution chains cut, partners unsettled. It was the symbolism. A fortress breached. A trade exposed. The veil of untouchability torn away.

The hawks seized the moment.

'Fear must be restored'.

'The streets must burn'.

'Blood is the only language they will heed', a voice with a hard Russian lilt said flatly.

No dissent rose. No voices counselled restraint. The verdict was unanimous, carried on the chill wind of inevitability. The Syndicate would move from silence to spectacle. The hand of power would no longer hide in the glove.

The order was given:

ERADICATE THE ALDRIDGES. SIMULTANEOUS STRIKES. NO BLOWBACK. NO TRACE.

A pause, then new lines appeared, stark as death warrants:

LONDON: MAKE LIKE A LOVER'S QUARREL. MARGARET RIVER: A FARMING ACCIDENT.

One by one, the Partners dropped off, leaving only two initials glowing: London and Melbourne.

On one side, London Alpha, his office window black against the Thames. On the other hand, Melbourne Alpha, blinds drawn over Collins Street, the faint clatter of trams drifting through.

The Partners' directives lingered on the whiteboard, together with a hidden threat written between the lines: fail, and you will be replaced.

London Alpha exhaled through his nose. 'Timing's impossible. Night in both hemispheres doesn't line up'.

Melbourne Alpha tapped his pen, restless. 'Then Margaret River first. London later. A few hours' gap won't matter, so long as the result's clean'.

The whiteboard cleared. Nothing remained but a blinking cursor. The Partners had spoken.

In Margaret River, the sergeant in charge of the protection squad walked the perimeter as he did every night, torch in one hand, the other brushing the stock of the carbine slung across his chest. Hard-nosed, methodical, not much given to superstition.

One moment, the rows of vines lay silent under the moon. Next, there was a man standing at the edge of the track, tall, weathered, eyes dark as the soil.

The sergeant stiffened. No one had approached without his men spotting them. No one.

'Name yourself', he barked.

The old man inclined his head, voice low and even. 'Evil comes. Dark spirits are descending on this vineyard'.

The sergeant narrowed his eyes, unsettled in spite of himself. 'We'll be ready', he said, tight-voiced.

The elder smiled faintly. 'You won't be alone'.

And as if the land itself exhaled, figures emerged from the trees and shadows, half a dozen Aboriginal men, silent as stone, watching with calm intensity. It was as though they had been there all along, part of the night itself.

Sergeant Davies let out a long breath he hadn't realised he'd been holding. Suddenly, the whispered rumours he'd once heard around barracks made perfect sense—stories of Captain Richard O'Connell, a man who walked in two worlds and always came back alive. Perhaps it wasn't a myth after all.

When the mercenaries came, they met an army they hadn't expected. The assault broke on the vineyard like waves on rock. Gunfire cracked once, twice, then the darkness swallowed the attackers whole. Not a single building touched. Not a single life lost.

As night moved across the globe, back in London, Lord Richard sat in his leather chair, a book open on his lap, brandy glass within reach.

Across the house, Captain Richard moved room to room, restless. Then it came; that tickle at the back of the neck, sharp and undeniable. The same sixth sense that had kept him alive in the killing fields.

He froze. 'Grandfather...'

Lord Richard raised a brow, half dismissive. But when he saw the look in the younger man's eyes, something in him stirred, a memory of his own narrow escapes, long ago.

He reached for his old service Webley and tucked it under his book.

The entry was silent, practised. A lock turned with a whisper, not a splinter. The door eased inward as though it had never been touched. Four men in black slipped through one by one, suppressed pistols raised. They moved like shadows, not raiders, no shouting, no crash of boots, only the soft intent of men preparing a scene they would not stay to watch.

From their view, the kill was simple. Lord Richard, in his chair, head bowed, an old man waiting for the end. All it would take was one placed shot, a gun in his hand, and the papers would write the rest.

They spread to finish it, and the shadows moved.

Captain Richard stepped from the dark like a ghost, his Glock barking twice. Two men fell before they even registered the threat. The others swung round too late. Lord Richard raised the Webley from beneath his book and fired. The revolver roared, a thunderclap in the confines of the room. One slug punched the third man off his feet.

The last fled, panic overtaking training. He made it two steps into the hall before Captain Richard met him there, silent, efficient.

Then stillness returned. Acrid smoke hung heavy. The tickle eased.

Grandfather and grandson exchanged a look across the wreckage, pride, yes, but also a grim acknowledgement. The war had followed them home.

Captain Richard pulled a phone from his pocket and dialled a secure code. 'Package neutralised. Four bodies. Sweep and sanitise'.

The voice on the other end was calm. 'Understood. Thirty minutes'.

By dawn, the townhouse was immaculate again. No signs of a fight. No hint that four men had ever existed.

In Melbourne, Alpha stared at a blank feed. Margaret River had gone dark. No reports, no bodies. Nothing.

In London, Alpha waited for confirmation that never came. His own secure line buzzed once, then silence.

The whiteboard flickered alive, three words stark against the blank screen:

DELIVER. OR BE REPLACED.

Both Alphas sat in silence, the weight of failure pressing down. Across two continents, strike teams had vanished into thin air.

And the Aldridges still lived.

Chapter 15: Face in the Shadows

Later that morning, the lamps in Lord Richard's study glowed against the morning gloom, their amber glow softening the ranks of leather bindings and the brass of the old desk set. Beyond the tall sash windows, London pressed close: tyres hissing on wet tarmac, a siren far off, rain ticking on slate. A rare shower in what had been an unseasonably bright, dry January. The house held its breath around them; the stillness pressed close until even their breathing seemed loud.

On the desk, the encrypted link to Hereford was already live. Hard-eyed men in plain civvies filled the split screen; soldiers by posture if not by uniform. Their voices, when they spoke, were low and economical, the professional calm that comes after violence.

'The raid was a success', the lead operator reported. 'Primary stairwell was barricaded; we went through with thermal and bang. Resistance brief but nasty: shotguns, knives, improvised shields. We've secured weapons, drugs, and cash. And the children…' his jaw flexed '…are safe'.

He glanced off-screen, then back. 'But Alpha… slipped the net. He left four minutes before the breach via the loading bay. Driver knew the drill, CCTV caught him switching plates under the canopy before they killed the lights and ran dark to the river road'.

A wiry tech with a skewed headset leaned into the frame. 'We might still have something. One of your micro-cams caught a partial as he exited, brim down, bad angle, sodium lights'. His fingers tripped over the keyboard. 'Running an enhancement and angle match now. It'll take a few minutes. Stand by'.

On the split screen, the blurred image swam and steadied, broke apart and re-formed. Lord Richard sat motionless, watching the grain come under discipline. A jawline sharpened. A mouth tight with habit. The particular tilt of a head he'd seen before, somewhere between command and contempt, the chin lifted half a degree above everyone else in the room.

The tech stacked filters. 'Counter-rotate the brim… correct the perspective… bring in ear geometry… cross-reference press pool stills'. A progress bar crawled. The darkness retreated.

The study went silent. Even the Hereford operators seemed to hold their breath.

Lord Richard felt the knowledge move towards him like a tide. His mind tried to push it back: not him, not that boy who had kicked a football on the lawns at West Farleigh Manor, not the son of the officer who bled next to me at Tilly. But the machine didn't care for pleading. The last artefacts fell away.

The software pinged green. A name populated the margin.

The Right Honourable Alistair Greville, Deputy Leader of the Government of the United Kingdom.

Lord Richard's hand closed around the edge of the desk, knuckles whitening. A personal friend for forty years. The boy who had raced the spaniels in his gardens; the young backbencher he had once counselled over claret by the very fire now burning low at his back. A man who had stood in this room and spoken of service, duty, and the cost of both while binding himself to rot.

No wonder the earlier image had nagged at him. He had known the face most of his life.

'And yesterday', Lord Richard said, voice flat as a parade square, 'he stood in the House and took the bow. He praised the 'heroic success' of a raid he would have tried to abort, had he known', he said softly.

On the link, the Hereford commander cleared his throat. 'We'll need to tread carefully. He's one heartbeat from Number Ten'.

'And the head of a criminal syndicate', Lord Richard answered, each word landing like a gavel. 'Drugs. Guns'. He swallowed, the last word rough in his mouth. 'Children'.

'Which makes him', Captain Richard said, 'a wounded predator. That's when they're most dangerous'.

The Hereford lead nodded once, businesslike again. 'We'll keep processing. That brim, he favours it. We'll trawl every pool photo from the last two years and build a confidence map. If he thinks he's unseen, he'll be sloppy'.

'Good', Lord Richard said. He closed the laptop with deliberate care, palms resting a moment on the cover as if to contain the fury beneath. When he spoke again, his voice was calm, edged with steel. 'He will come for us'.

He looked to his grandson. 'I'm not certain he knows that we know. They are desperate now. They've already tried the hit, both here and at the vineyard. Next, they'll try to discredit me and force a resignation. Jonathan's waiting in the wings, and they think that lever will hold. They suspect me, but they don't know for sure. That ignorance is our only shield'.

Captain Richard inclined his head. 'Then we let him think his mask is intact'.

Later that afternoon, the Palace of Westminster hummed like a hive. The division bell had stopped ringing, but its echo seemed to hang in the coloured tiles of the Central Lobby. Messengers darted, whips conferred, journalists loitered with studied nonchalance. Beyond a set of swing doors, the green benches of the Commons exhaled the last of a long debate.

Greville came out, borne on a wake of cameras and congratulations. He had that particular Westminster glow about him: the varnish that comes from applause in the chamber and a headline already half-written. He dispensed nods, shook hands, and accepted praise with a statesman's modesty and a performer's timing.

Lord Richard stood to one side beneath a stone arch, his cane resting lightly in his hand. When Greville's eyes found him, the

Deputy Leader of the Government's smile broadened with genuine warmth, or a flawless copy of it.

'Richard!' Greville took the older man's hand in both of his. The flashguns loved the tableau: veteran peer and triumphant minister. 'Quite a morning, eh? A clean strike at organised crime. Just what the country needed'.

'Just what it needed', Lord Richard agreed, matching the smile. Up close, he could smell the winter rain in Greville's coat and the faint ghost of the Commons' floor polish. 'Remarkable how swiftly justice can come when it's least expected'.

Greville chuckled. 'Oh, justice takes a prod now and then'. His eyes searched Richard's face for a beat, reading him as men in politics learn to read a room. Whatever he saw seemed to please him. 'I must say, splendid to have your steady hand these past weeks. Calming, when others lost their heads'.

'One does one's best', Richard said. He let the smallest pause bloom between them. 'One hopes the net closes as tightly on those who give orders as on those who take them'.

Greville's eyes didn't so much as flicker. 'Quite', he said, with perfect blandness. 'Quite'.

A whip muttered in his ear; a private secretary hovered with a red box. Greville squeezed Richard's arm, affable, familiar. 'We must catch up properly. My office will find a slot'.

'I look forward to it', Lord Richard said.

He watched the Deputy Leader of the Government move away towards the cameras, the smile back in place, the aides reforming like a school of fish around a shark. Greville didn't look back.

He believed himself unseen.

Across the river, a sudden shower thickened, drawing a grey veil over the lights of Whitehall. In his Westminster office, the Deputy Leader of the Government poured a finger of whisky and stood for a time with his back to the room, watching droplets chase each other down the glass. The raid had been too close; four minutes, his driver said, but close only counts in horseshoes and hand grenades. He allowed himself a small, private smile.

The old Marquis had been in the lobby. Steady as ever, courteous as ever. Not a flicker. Whatever rumours Alpha's partners had heard, the old man had seen nothing. He wouldn't dare, even if he had.

Greville turned from the window, set the glass down, and picked up the secure phone. His voice, when he spoke, was clipped and efficient.

'Jonathan. Release the photos to the press. And this time, get it right. This is your last chance'.

He ended the call, picked up his glass again, and let the whisky sit on his tongue until the burn chased away the last taste of fear.

He did not see, in the reflection on the window, the faintest crease in his own smile, the hairline crack that comes when a mask is worn too long.

Chapter 16: Syndicate Strikes Back

The next morning, Jonathan played his hand perfectly, or so he believed.

The photographs hit the press with surgical timing. The tame Syndicate hounds bayed on cue, headlines blaring scandal and betrayal. Alongside them ran whispers of 'irregularities' at the top: nothing concrete, nothing regulators could seize on, but enough to smear. Overnight, the Aldridge name was tarnished.

Jonathan made his move, standing before the cameras with an air of reluctant duty. He spoke of his uncle's failing health, hinted at Lord Richard taking a back seat at the bank, and solemnly assured the city that he, Jonathan, would be 'looking after things' until a replacement was found.

It was a performance of calculated loyalty, a balancing act between sympathy and ambition. The Syndicate had everything it wanted: the Chairman's credibility in tatters, his heir apparent sliding into place, the institution still theirs to exploit.

Jonathan deluded himself that his performance had been masterful, where others had failed. In his mind, he had not only saved the day but also earned himself consideration for Alpha's seat at the Syndicate's table. The thought tasted sweet.

Meanwhile, back at Lord Richard's London home, appearances told a different story. To all intents and purposes, the old man was holed up, besieged by press camped at the gates, flashbulbs popping, headlines braying for blood.

In fact, the truth was very different. While the cameras kept vigil on an empty façade, Lord Richard and his grandson had already slipped away under the cover of Hermes' discretion, spirited quietly to West Farleigh Manor before dawn. From the study there, far from prying lenses, they were already planning their coup de grâce. The Syndicate had manoeuvred itself into exactly the trap they had laid.

The first step was simple: bring the two Maggies over from Margaret River, as discreetly as possible.

Lord Richard reached for the handset in his study. The call went out across the world, and after a few tones, a familiar French voice answered.

'Luc speaking'.

'It's Richard'.

'Ah, mon ami'. Luc's tone warmed immediately. 'I received your hamper, very elegant. Fauchon, no less. My wife has already hidden the macarons from me'.

Richard allowed himself the faintest smile. 'A small token of thanks, Luc. You got me out of England when few others could. Now I need your help once more'.

'Then it will be done. Tell me what you require'.

'My family, two women, mother and granddaughter, must be brought from Margaret River back to England. Quietly, with no eyes on them. No detours this time; straight to Biggin Hill. They'll travel under business cover, nothing to draw attention'.

There was a pause, then the soft scratch of Luc's pen. 'Busselton to Biggin Hill. Gulfstream IV, my best crew. Their papers will say they are representatives for the Margaret River consortium, travelling to the trade show in London. A perfectly dull explanation'.

'Dull', Richard agreed, 'is exactly what we need'.

'You shall have it. And, Richard...' Luc's voice carried that subtle mixture of humour and respect, 'next time, send two hampers'.

The line clicked dead. The arrangements were in motion.

The terminal was its usual discreet efficiency, the kind of service Biggin Hill's VIPs demanded. Passport control and immigration had already been handled on board; by the time the aircraft door opened, a black Mercedes was waiting at the steps.

'Mrs O'Connell. Miss O'Connell', the driver said with a polite nod. 'I'm Ben. Hermes Taxis'.

The elder Maggie's expression softened. She remembered Lord Richard mentioning the firm, the same outfit that had spirited him quietly out of England only weeks before. Trusted. Discreet.

Ben held the rear door without fuss. Once they were settled, the Mercedes eased off the apron and out through the secure gate.

The road unfurled quickly, hedgerows giving way to open Kent countryside as they joined the M20, bound east for Maidstone.

Maggie looked out at the rolling winter fields, mist clinging low across the furrows. 'Not so different from Margaret River', she murmured.

Her granddaughter leaned closer, her voice quieter, edged with intent. 'Except this time, we're not here for the wine'.

Ben said nothing, eyes steady on the road. The Mercedes merged with the traffic, slipping towards Maidstone.

At Aylesford, Ben swung off the main road and into a discreet yard by the river. There, a gentleman's launch was waiting, polished mahogany gleaming despite the frost. Its boatman, cap pulled low, stood by with quiet readiness, one of Lord Richard's oldest retainers.

'Cases will draw attention if you take them on the water', Ben said. 'I'll run them back to the office. Hermes can have them delivered later by van before you arrive. No one will notice'.

The Maggies exchanged a glance, then nodded. Travel-light suited them. With only their small handbags, they stepped aboard the launch.

The boatman dipped his head respectfully. 'Welcome, madam. Miss. All ready'.

The engine purred to life, scarcely louder than the river itself, and the launch nosed out into the current.

They passed beneath the iron span of the railway bridge, where a train rattled overhead, then beneath the twin road bridges, the older with its weathered arches, the newer a single concrete span. On the right bank, the shell of the old gasometer still loomed beside a half-finished retail park, concrete and cladding pressing close to the water.

But just beyond, on the opposite bank, the grey stone of the Archbishop's Palace stood serene above the river, centuries of history enduring while the modern world crowded in. The elder Maggie shook her head at the contrast.

'France had its scars after the war, too', she murmured.

The town fell away soon enough, giving way to fields, bare woods, and the quiet sweep of the river valley. Mist gathered low across the water. At East Farleigh, they paused to pass through the lock, timbers creaking, water swirling dark around the hull. Above, the old stone bridge loomed—once fought over in the Civil War, now carrying only the hum of village traffic. Then onward again, past darkened meadows, until at last the lights of West Farleigh Manor winked above the bank.

The launch eased into the boathouse just as the last rays of the winter sun slipped behind the trees, the light fading beneath the willows at the edge of the estate. The boatman secured the lines and offered a hand as they stepped ashore.

The boathouse light cast a pale glow across the mist as the Maggies stepped ashore. Ahead, the path wound upward through frost-silvered lawns towards the looming silhouette of West Farleigh Manor.

At the top of the rise, the great oak doors swung open. Lord Richard stood framed in the light, overcoat drawn tight against the cold, a half-smile softening the steel in his eyes. His grandson hovered just behind, shoulders squared in that soldier's way of his.

Only weeks had passed since the boys lifted off from Margaret River, but it felt like an age. At the threshold, they hugged, that same quiet, stunned relief rising again — the feeling they'd first shared at the vineyard after the cruel decades the Syndicate had engineered, when each had been told the other was dead.

Maggie's granddaughter tipped her chin toward the house, eyes bright. 'So while I've been slumming it in Margaret River, keeping the vineyard afloat, you've been lording it here?' she said to her brother, sweeping a hand at the frost-rimmed stonework. 'And you told me your 'overseas assignments' with the ASAS were in draughty billets and dingy safe houses somewhere?'

Captain Richard gave a wry smile, leaning in just enough for only her to hear. 'Trust me, little sister, most of them were. This is one of the rare perks'.

Maggie shot back without missing a beat. 'Little sister? Only because you're five minutes older'.

He chuckled softly. 'Still counts'.

She laughed, the sound a relief against the Kentish mist, and for a moment the dangers fell away.

As they walked into the manor together, Maggie quietly thanked the spirits for keeping her boys safe.

They did not go straight upstairs. In the great hall, lamps glowed on polished oak, and a fire roared in the hearth. A table had been set with quiet care: roast beef, winter vegetables, and a bottle of claret breathing beside the silver. Nothing ostentatious, but a meal meant to welcome family home.

The four of them sat together at last: Lord Richard, his Maggie, and the two grandchildren she had raised half a world away. For a moment, it felt impossible; this circle restored after years of Syndicate lies. Yet here they were, alive, together, under one roof.

Conversation flickered easily at first: talk of the vineyard, the flight, Kentish weather compared with Margaret River. The younger Maggie teased her grandmother about managing the wine show in

London, while Captain Richard slipped into wry stories of army rations and the things soldiers call 'food'.

Laughter came, tentative at first, then freer, warming the room as surely as the fire. The elder Maggie sat watching them, her husband and the grandchildren she had raised, a glass of claret in her hand and tears she would not shed brightening her eyes.

Lord Richard caught her glance across the table. He did not speak, only raised his glass. She returned the gesture with a small nod, a silent acknowledgement of all that had been stolen and all that had been given back this night.

When the meal was finished and the plates cleared away, the candles on the table had burned low, their soft glow reflected in the polished glass. Richard rose, circled the table, and drew out her chair with a hand both courtly and gentle.

'Come', he said softly. 'There is something I want to share with you, before the night is done'.

She laid her hand in his without hesitation, and together they left the hall, the fire at their backs and the children's voices fading into the hush of the manor.

Later that night, the old house lay silent beneath the frost. In the master chamber, the fire still glowed low, throwing warm light across the carved beams. Maggie stood at the window, looking out across the lawns towards the river mist.

The door opened softly, and Richard stepped in, a bottle in hand. Not a Margaret River Cabernet this time, but a Kentish red from a vineyard further down the valley.

He set it down on the table with a faintly apologetic smile.

'Nothing like your Cabernet', he said, 'but at least it isn't vin ordinaire. One glass between us, for old times' sake'.

Her laugh was quiet, touched with memory. 'Better than what we used to drink in France'.

He poured into two thin-stemmed glasses, the ruby colour catching the firelight. They sat together on the edge of the bed, shoulders touching, sipping in silence. It was the same ritual they had shared as young lovers in wartime France, but richer now, aged like the wine, like themselves.

When his hand found hers, she let it rest there, firm and steady. The fire crackled low; the night closed around them. They were exactly where they belonged, in the same room, the same bed, the years between dissolving like smoke. The candle guttered. The house beyond remained watchful, but here, the world finally gave them back what the Syndicate had stolen.

Meanwhile, all around them, preparations were underway for the coup de grâce. Heated marquees were being erected in the grounds; invitations dispatched to a select list of honoured guests. Everyone assumed the gathering would mark Lord Richard's resignation from the bank after the scandal.

Those invitations included Jonathan.

And the Deputy Leader of the Government.

One thing haunted both Lord Richard and his grandson: the need to keep the Maggies' presence at the manor completely hidden. If word of their arrival leaked, the entire plan would unravel.

Part of the solution lay in the very nature of West Farleigh itself. The manor thrived on discretion; its staff were not merely employees but fiercely loyal retainers, bound to Lord Richard by decades of trust. Their silence was ironclad, as it was among the London staff, who had long since learned that service to the Aldridges meant guarding more than silver and ledgers.

The other part came courtesy of Buster. 'Groundskeepers' from his extended 'family' had been quietly installed, watchful men with soldiers' eyes ensuring that no unwanted visitor would step foot on the estate without being seen, or stopped.

Chapter 17: The Party in Kent

By dusk, the manor grounds glowed like a winter wonderland. Lanterns hung from bare oaks, torches flickered along the gravel paths, and braziers smoked beside the heated marquees. Inside the house, staff moved with quiet precision, setting silver on linen and guiding guests towards the great pavilion where the evening's announcement would be made.

From an upstairs window, Lord Richard watched the preparations for a moment with Maggie at his side. He touched the gold band on his finger, that quiet promise he had carried for a lifetime, and then turned to her with a faint smile.

'Time, my love'.

Outside, the guests began to arrive. Hermes drivers ferried ministers, judges, and financiers through the gates in unmarked saloons, slipping away before attention could linger. Ben himself stood watch at the manor steps, indistinguishable from the staff, his expression calm and unreadable as he directed the flow.

Luc, immaculate in an open-collared shirt beneath his tailored coat, mingled with a knot of bankers and civil servants, his glass raised in easy laughter, though his eyes never ceased sweeping the crowd. Mary Jenner moved easily among the city set, her cover as an external compliance consultant giving her reason to ask quiet, pointed questions that mapped the shifting alliances of the evening. One of Buster's family shadowed her discreetly, a woman with the tidy air of a secretary, but the watchfulness of a soldier. To most, she was a PA; to those who knew, a sentinel.

Jonathan moved through the throng like a man rehearsing for high office, shaking hands, exchanging compliments, and quietly preparing the speech he believed would cement his succession. Jonathan's gaze lingered on the Deputy Leader of the Government across the floor. A man of influence — useful now, dispensable later.

At last, the largest marquee hushed as Lord Richard stepped onto a small podium. Braziers glowed at either side, and the hush of expectation settled across the room.

'My friends', he began, his voice strong, 'thank you for joining me this evening. You all know I've had the honour of leading the Bank Aldridge & Co. and serving the House of Lords for longer than I care to count. Tonight, I intend to confirm my retirement… and name my successor'.

Jonathan's smile widened.

'But before I do', Richard continued, lifting his left hand, 'there is something I have kept from you, though I doubt many of you failed to notice it'. The firelight gleamed on the plain gold band. 'Some of you have asked, over the years, why I wear this ring and refuse to speak of it. The truth is simple. It was placed here in a vineyard in France, in 1944, by the extraordinary woman who stands with me tonight'.

He gestured, and Maggie mounted the dais, tall and proud despite her years. A ripple of astonishment coursed through the marquee.

'My wife, Margaret'.

Jonathan's smile faltered.

'And now', Richard's tone hardened, 'it is time you met the rightful heir to my name and to Aldridge Bank. My grandson, Captain Richard Aldridge: sixth Marquis of Hunton'.

The young officer in dress uniform joined them, every inch the soldier, every inch the heir. Applause stuttered, uncertain, as if the crowd demanded proof. Then they saw the ribbons glinting on his chest, his own hard-won medals on the left, his father's, Lord Richard's son, worn proudly on the right. The hesitation broke. The hall filled with sound.

A servant stepped forward, handing a heavy leather folder to Jonathan. On top of it, resting like an afterthought, lay a familiar pair of sunglasses. He opened it, colour draining with every page:

- A certified copy of Lord Richard's 1944 French marriage certificate.
- The birth certificate of their son.
- Birth certificates for Maggie and Richard, the grandchildren.
- And finally, a cream parchment bearing the seal of the College of Arms: confirmation that Captain Richard Aldridge (O'Connell) was indeed the sixth Marquis of Hunton, rightful heir to every title.

The sunglasses caught the light, the lenses reflecting only Jonathan's own stunned face. For an instant, Jonathan's eyes flicked up, defiance flaring. Then he saw the two tall men in dark suits at his shoulders. Not police. Not Special Branch. Syndicate men, there to deliver his reckoning.

His defiance ebbed to ash. They took him by the arms and led him out. The crowd parted in shocked silence as Jonathan was escorted into the night.

Applause began, hesitant at first, then swelling until the marquee shook with it. On stage, the family stood together at last.

Captain Richard stepped forward, his gaze steady. 'Many of you have read the headlines in London this week', he said, his voice carrying. 'You have seen my family's name dragged through the mud, stories seeded with malice, designed to wound. Let me be clear: those reports are false.

'Tonight, you have heard my grandfather's truth and seen the proof. In the days ahead, a press dossier will be delivered to every major outlet in the country. It will set out the facts, in full, and it will expose those who thought they could manipulate the narrative from the shadows.

'Some of you know, and others are only now beginning to grasp, that there are forces in this country who thrive in darkness, who believe themselves unaccountable. But they will not remain there. They will be dragged into the light, whether they wish it or not'.

A murmur rippled through the guests: shock, unease, grudging respect. Luc raised his glass; Ben's eyes narrowed at the door; Mary noted every pale face in the crowd.

'The Aldridge family has stood for honour and service for centuries', Richard concluded. 'That legacy will not be tainted by lies, nor stolen by those who think power is theirs by birthright or fear. That ends tonight'.

The applause roared again, but not all were cheering.

At the marquee's edge, the Deputy Leader of the Government lingered in the shadows, his aides close. For a heartbeat, his eyes locked with Richard's. He allowed himself the faintest flicker of relief, the look of a man convinced the young Marquis had not recognised him, that his secret remained intact.

He turned, lips tightening into a statesman's smile, as he slipped out into the night.

But Richard did know. He had seen that same cold calculation before, in another war, under another flag. Alpha believed himself unseen. In truth, he had already been drawn into the light.

The war was far from over.

Part II

The Hidden War

Beneath the glass towers of London, the Syndicate tightens its grip — but the heirs of truth are gathering their strength.

Chapter 18: Crossroads

Lord Richard and his grandson sat together in the study at West Farleigh Manor, the excitement of the day and the demise of Jonathan now ebbing away. Captain Richard had changed out of his formal dress uniform and now stood with his back to the fire, a fine single malt in his hand.

Lord Richard, the 5th Marquess of Hunton, sat back in his favourite wingback chair with a glass of his wife's excellent O'Connell red. Knowing how much he liked it, she had brought over a case with her. They had spoken little since the guests departed and the Maggies had retired for the night. Sometimes, silence said more than words.

At last, the younger man stirred. 'You must look at me and still see Gran's photographs'.

Lord Richard glanced up. 'Photographs?'

'The ones on the wall in Margaret River. Passing-out parade. Maggie and I are playing around the homestead. The vineyard at harvest'.

Lord Richard's mouth tightened. 'I studied those frames every night whilst I was there. They are the only memories I have of you, your sister, and your parents. Thanks to the Syndicate, those are all I have'.

'I know'. The younger man paused, then sat opposite, leaning forward with his elbows on his knees. His voice softened. 'But pictures don't tell the whole story. Maybe I should'.

So he did. He spoke of childhood mornings beneath the wide Australian sky, of chasing kangaroos through the scrub while Maggie laughed behind them. Of Elder Miran taking him and his sister on a walkabout, teaching them to read the land, to find water by the flight of birds, to listen until the silence itself spoke.

'Gran insisted we learn both', he said. 'Bushcraft and books. Shakespeare at breakfast, fire-making by dusk. She said we had to walk in two worlds if we wanted to survive in either'.

Lord Richard listened, hands folded, eyes fixed on his grandson. The photographs in his mind unshattered and came alive, not frozen faces but a boy with dust on his boots and firelight on his cheeks. For the first time, the still images had breath.

'And Maggie?' he asked quietly.

A smile tugged at Captain Richard's mouth. 'She kept us honest. Reminded us that bush skills didn't excuse us from fixing fences or keeping the books. If Elder Miran gave us the Dreaming, Gran gave us duty. Between them, we turned out all right'.

The silence that followed was companionable. But when Lord Richard spoke again, his voice carried a different weight. His gaze was fixed on the shadowed valley, where the river blurred into night.

'Don't be deceived by the quiet. The Syndicate is not finished. Jonathan was only their mask. Alpha is still out there, moving, planning. They'll want revenge for what we exposed, and they'll strike at what matters most: the bank, the land, the bloodline itself.

'It isn't new', he went on, his voice roughening. 'When I was a boy, I heard the quarrels whispered after dinner, how the Aldridge succession had almost broken the family apart. My father, the Fourth Marquess, carried the shame of his daughter Catherine's scandal. She bore a child by a man tied to the Syndicate, Edward.

'For a time, they thought they had succeeded, for there was no direct male heir to follow my father. Then I was born, and succession passed to me. All their scheming came to nothing.

'But the Syndicate learned what they needed to know: that division inside a great house is the crack where they can force the blade. They never forgot that lesson. They've circled us ever since, waiting for the next quarrel, the next weakness, the next Edward.

In this generation, it was Jonathan, Edward's son, who carried their banner'.

He drew a slow breath, his gaze never leaving the darkness. 'What we face now is only the latest shape of an old enemy'. His hand shifted on the rug, restless. 'If I must return to the Bank to keep the campaign alive, then so be—'

'No'.

The word cut clean across his sentence. The old man looked up sharply.

His grandson leaned forward, voice steady. 'You return to Margaret River, the vineyard with Gran and Maggie. That is your home now, your legacy. Reclaim the time the Syndicate stole from you in 1944, and let me take the fight to them. It's my turn'.

For a moment, even the night seemed to be still.

Lord Richard's lips parted, but no protest came. He had carried command long enough to recognise when it had passed to another.

The younger man went on, slower now, deliberate. 'Between you, Gran, and Elder Miran, I've been prepared for this moment all my life. My fight isn't in the desert or the jungle anymore. It's here, against the Syndicate, on their ground'.

He drew a breath. 'I'll resign my commission. Leave the Regiment behind. From tonight, my campaign begins'.

Lord Richard's hand closed over his grandson's wrist, grip unexpectedly strong. His eyes were fierce, yet softened with pride.

'Very well, but you won't be alone. I'll always be with you: your mentor, your counsel, your backup. Whatever comes, you'll never carry this war without me at your side'.

Captain Richard held his gaze, then nodded once. The pact was sealed.

They sat together, two Richards bound across generations — one at the dusk of his life, the other at its fiercest dawn.

Captain Richard glanced out through the study windows into the night, and in his mind, he could hear Elder Miran's words as clearly as if the old man were standing beside him rather than half a world away in Margaret River.

'The land will watch over your family while you face the demons. But remember, spirits guard only those who walk straight. Step aside, and they will turn their backs'.

Chapter 19: The Call

As dawn broke over West Farleigh, Richard made the call he had long dreaded, the one he could no longer delay, to his CO. The line clicked twice before it settled, the faint hiss in Richard's ear. Morning light filtered through the tall windows of West Farleigh Manor, pale across the lawns and oaks. On the far side of the world, it was already late afternoon in Swanbourne, the heat still shimmering on the parade ground.

'Colonel Jameson', came the familiar voice, dry as ever.

'Sir, it's O'Connell'.

A pause, then the faintest chuckle. 'Not for much longer then. London, Banking dynasty, you don't do things by halves'.

Richard smiled faintly into the receiver. 'Not exactly in the recruitment brochure, sir'.

'You realise', Jameson went on, 'if you'd stayed, and the paperwork caught up, I'd have had to address you as… what was it? Lord Captain Aldridge? No, no, couldn't have stomached that. You've always been O'Connell to me, and I'd like to keep my lunch down'.

Richard chuckled. 'I appreciate that, sir'.

The humour ebbed. 'It isn't just London', Richard said quietly. 'It's the vineyard. My grandparents, my sister… the Syndicate won't stop. They'll come again, and the vineyard's exposed. They'll be targets'.

Jameson's reply was calm, steady. 'After what the sergeant told me about the raid there, your grandfather Miran and his mob appearing out of the smoke, I doubt anyone's sneaking up on your family. Half the mess reckon the stories about you weren't myths after all'.

Richard blinked, then gave a short laugh.

'Truth is', Jameson went on, 'some of the lads reckon the vineyard would make a perfect training ground. Off the grid, rough country, skills we've neglected. Tracking, survival, bushcraft. The things you grew up with. Your mob might end up teaching us'.

That drew a genuine laugh. 'Gran will love that'.

'Oh, she's already won fans. The sergeant hasn't shut up about her cooking or your sister. Between you and me, I think the bloke's half in love with her. The point is, he'd guard that vineyard with his life. They all would. You're not leaving them unprotected'.

The knot in Richard's chest eased, just a little.

Jameson's voice softened. 'You've been a hell of an operator, O'Connell. Steady, dependable... occasionally reckless, but always for the right reasons'.

Richard's mind flicked back to a night in East Timor.

A valley choked with jungle, rain hammering down so hard it turned the clay track into a torrent. His patrol had been sent to extract a group of villagers marked for reprisal by the militias. The radios were useless, the map a bad joke, and every track seemed to vanish into the green.

He'd fallen back on what he knew: bushcraft, instincts drilled in by his grandfather. Reading the slope of the ground, the run of water, and the smell of smoke carried on the wet air. He'd trusted it, led them along goat paths no chart or briefing had foreseen, slipping them clear of ambushes they only glimpsed after they'd passed. Hours later, they staggered out onto a clearing where an INTERFET convoy was waiting. The villagers' relief and gratitude were something he would never forget.

Jameson had been there, boots in the mud, listening to the debrief. 'You got lucky', the Colonel had said then. Richard had only shrugged. 'Or we read the ground right'.

Now, across the line, Jameson's voice carried the same dry edge. 'That was Timor. And then there was your little 'holiday' in the Balkans. Don't think I missed the paperwork on that one. Temporary attachment, liaison this, exchange that... call it what you like, you ended up drinking with the Hereford lads. They still talk about the Australian who out-marched them on a recce patrol'.

Richard smiled faintly. 'They didn't like that much'.

'No', Jameson said dryly. 'But they respected it. Point is, O'Connell, you've got friends in Swanbourne, and you've got friends in Hereford. Don't forget that'.

Richard hesitated, then said, 'I won't forget'.

There was a rustle of papers down the line. Jameson's tone shifted back to business. 'Leave the paperwork to me. I'll put a word through the right channels. You won't have to fight your way through a heap of bureaucracy here or in London'.

'That simple?' Richard asked.

'Simple's the point. Let me and the Friends smooth things out. You'll have enough real battles outside your own front door'.

The line went quiet for a long moment. At last, Jameson said, 'The Regiment will march on. But your own campaign begins now'.

Richard closed his eyes, hearing the cadence of boots on tarmac in memory, the echo of voices on parade. For a heartbeat, he thought he saw them: a man in uniform, proud and steady; a woman with her hair caught by the sea breeze, her smile bright with love. His father. His mother.

The vision lingered, then faded. Richard drew a slow breath.

'Yes, sir. Beginning now'.

The line clicked dead.

Over the next few days, the question of departure could no longer be put off. The vineyard needed them; the homestead would not run itself forever. Messages were exchanged, flights quietly booked, and the Manor's staff took to their tasks with the brisk efficiency of people who understood the gravity of the moment.

Richard had insisted on discretion: no public farewells, no attention drawn.

Finally, the day came. On the stone steps of the Manor, silvered with dew, the household was gathered, luggage neatly stacked, a Hermes taxi idling in the gravel sweep — Ben at the wheel, as ever, patient and watchful. Today was the parting not just of family, but of paths.

Lord Richard stood straight, his hand resting lightly on Maggie's arm. Her eyes shone, though her voice was steady. Beside them, Richard's sister Maggie shifted her weight, torn between the pull of duty and the ache of leaving her brother behind.

Captain Richard came down the steps, boots ringing against the stone. He stopped at the bottom, looking at them one by one: grandfather, grandmother, sister — the heart of the vineyard he would now defend from afar.

His sister broke the silence first. 'Feels strange, me leaving before you'.

Lord Richard smiled faintly. 'It's only fitting. The vines won't wait on sentiment; they need you more than I do'.

Maggie Senior gave a brisk nod. 'Quite right. Someone's got to keep the books in order while we're off gallivanting. You're the steward now, girl; don't let the accountants talk circles round you'.

That drew a laugh, even though the tears threatened at the edges.

Her brother embraced her tightly. 'Look after Gran's wine', he whispered.

'And you look after our name', she shot back. 'Fair trade'.

Moments later, the taxi pulled away from the steps, carrying Maggie Junior toward Heathrow and the vineyard waiting half a world away. The others watched in silence until the car vanished beyond the trees.

Then came the second leave-taking. Mason brought the Bentley round, polished to a gleam, and held the door as Lord Richard and

Maggie Senior prepared for their journey south to Southampton. They would sail from there, choosing the long way home.

'It's indulgent', Lord Richard had admitted earlier. 'But after the years stolen from us, I'll not waste the chance of a slow voyage with the beautiful woman I have loved all my life'.

No one argued. Not Gran. Not Richard. Not even Maggie Junior, before she left.

On the steps now, Captain Richard clasped his grandfather's hand. 'The Syndicate won't touch you out there. Not again'.

Lord Richard's grip was iron. 'And you won't face them alone here. Remember that'.

From inside his jacket, Captain Richard produced a grey, boxy handset with a long retractable antenna, bulkier than any mobile phone, though discreet enough to pass as one to the untrained eye.

'It's a satellite phone', he said quietly. 'Works anywhere, even if you're in the middle of an ocean. If anything happens and you can't reach me, and I you, by phone in the usual way, this will still get through'.

Lord Richard turned it over in his hand, studying the device with a soldier's curiosity rather than an old man's bafflement. At last, he slipped it into his pocket.

'Very well', he said. 'At least it will let us keep in touch while I'm indulging in this cruise'.

'You'll need this more than I will', Captain Richard replied.

His grandfather gave a wry smile. 'Perhaps. But there's something you'll need more'.

From his own pocket, Lord Richard produced a small, battered notebook bound in dark leather. Its edges were worn, the cover softened by years of handling. He held it out without ceremony.

Richard hesitated, then took it. Inside, in his grandfather's unmistakable hand, were terse notes on each board member: initials, dates, curt assessments. *Reliable in a crisis. Wavers under pressure.*

Prone to self-interest. No explanations, no wasted words. One line stood out simply: *'AA?'* Enough to suggest his grandfather had been running his own quiet ORBAT: the soldier's 'order of battle', translated into the politics of the boardroom.

At the back of the book, in the same tight script, were numbers and names. A handful of trusted contacts: an old barrister in the Temple, a retired brigadier in Hereford, Buster's number written in block capitals. Not allies of convenience, but men who could be relied on when the usual doors were closed.

Richard looked up. His grandfather's gaze was steady.

'Always thinking ahead', Richard murmured, a faint smile tugging at his lips.

Mason closed the Bentley door with a dull thud. Richard stood back, watching as the car rolled down the drive, its red taillamps dwindling between the oaks. His grandfather and grandmother, a soldier and a nurse, reunited at last, reclaiming time the Syndicate had tried to deny them, were gone on their voyage.

Silence closed over the Manor steps. He was alone now.

Across the courtyard, a Keswick green Defender rolled to a halt. A man in a plain jacket stepped out, a discreet key fob in hand, and offered Richard a single, businesslike nod.

'The Suzuki and the other Defender have been returned to the dealership', he said, his tone clipped and neutral. 'They've sent this one over for you to trial in their place'.

Richard circled the vehicle once, the paint still carrying the faint scent of the factory. The interior gleamed, clean and purposeful, yet there was a quiet pulse from somewhere beneath the dash — the unmistakable hum of new electronics.

'It's not entirely standard, is it?' he asked.

The man's mouth twitched, almost a smile. 'No, sir. This one carries the usual Hereford extras — and a few prototypes the lab's been testing. Early integration suite. They're calling it *Project Athena'*.

Richard ran a thumb along the bonnet edge, approving. 'Greek goddess of wisdom', he said quietly. 'Let's hope she drives like it'.

Richard picked up his bag and squared his shoulders for his return to the London townhouse. The farewells were over. The campaign was about to begin, and London was waiting.

The Defender's heavy door shut with a solid clunk, sealing him into something that felt less like a car and more like armour. The smell of oil and leather wrapped around him like an old campaign tent.

The V8 fired with a deep, confident growl that cut through the drizzle, steady as a heartbeat. Beneath the bonnet, the Friends had tucked in a clutched supercharger. In normal driving, it freewheeled behind a bypass, the engine just a steady V8. Arm it, and an electromagnetic bite woke the rotors, boost arriving like a fist through silk.

On the dash, a discreet chime sounded as the systems came alive.

'System checks complete. Vehicle secure'.

Richard allowed himself the ghost of a smile. The tone was clipped, precise, yet there it was, the faintest curl of humour. Not all machines were without personality.

So you're Athena, he thought. *Let's see what you can do.*

He eased the Defender out along the manor drive, tyres whispering over the wet gravel, before swinging onto Lower Road. The route carried him through Maidstone and out to the M2, where the spires of Canary Wharf glimmered faintly on the horizon, drawing him towards London.

By the time he reached Belgravia, the city skyline had flared into chaos. Reporters still swarmed the front of the townhouse, cameras popping beneath rain-slick plastic covers, satellite vans wedged against the kerb. A fine, needling drizzle clung to coats and lenses alike, the sort of damp, grey February weather London did so well.

Even at this hour, questions were hurled into the gloom: fraud, succession battle, Aldridge in crisis. The Syndicate's fingerprints were all over it, feeding stories, poisoning the well, grinding at the name his family had carried for generations.

Richard's jaw tightened. The Defender's cabin was a cocoon of quiet, the engine's growl steady beneath him. Out there was chaos and deception. In here was the purpose. He swung the Defender into the rear garage, shutting out the din. Inside, the house was all quiet restraint: oak panels, polished floors, the faint smell of beeswax and old leather. The Fourth Marquis's portrait hung above the fireplace, stern-eyed in uniform, as though still passing judgement on the living.

Richard unbuttoned his coat and handed it to Gwen, the housekeeper. 'How many?' he asked.

'Dozens, sir. Some have been there since dawn'.

He crossed to the window and glanced out. Flashbulbs popped, voices rose. The mob wasn't going anywhere.

He made his decision quickly. 'Then let's give them something. But first, I need a shower and a change of clothes. Oh, and see if we can take some refreshments out to them. If they've been here since before dawn, they must be longing for a cup of tea'.

Gwen's mouth twitched, half in surprise, half in approval. 'Very good, sir'.

Thirty minutes later, Richard came down the staircase, tie knotted, shoes polished to a soldier's shine. From the hallway, he heard the front door open. The hubbub faltered as Gwen and two footmen stepped outside carrying trays: china cups clinking, silver pots steaming, plates of biscuits balanced with military precision.

For a moment, the crowd was stunned. Then, almost sheepishly, reporters accepted the cups, lowering their cameras to cradle the unexpected warmth.

'Bloody hell, proper china', someone muttered, half awed, half amused. Cameras dipped as cups were taken.

Another voice, sharper, carried over the drizzle. 'So the Aldridge hospitality is not a myth, then?' The line drew a ripple of laughter, easing the tension just enough to let hands wrap around the porcelain.

At the back, a grizzled correspondent raised his cup in salute. 'If only the politicians could take a lesson from this', he called dryly, earning chuckles even among his rivals.

The mood shifted, no less eager, but no longer hostile. That was when Richard appeared. He squared his shoulders, a parade-ground calm settling over him — different uniform, same mission. He stepped out onto the stone steps, pausing just long enough for the cameras to find their focus.

'Good morning, ladies and gentlemen', he said evenly. 'I'd love to have you all in for the interview, but the housekeeper would lynch me over your wet boots on the carpet. So just one of you. One camera, one reporter. My answers are for all of you, so make sure they're shared'.

There were mutters, a shuffle, but the grizzled correspondent stepped forward. He had earned his stripes in war zones and parliaments; if Aldridge was letting one of them in, it would be him.

'Very well, Lord Aldridge', he said. 'I'll keep the record straight'.

And so, it was the BBC anchor with her cameraman, and the veteran correspondent from The *Times*, who followed Richard into the townhouse while the rest of the pack waited in the rain.

Inside, the drawing room glowed with lamplight, portraits of Aldridges' past staring down from dark oak panels. Rain rattled the windows while the cameraman set up.

Richard gestured them to the low chairs before the fire.

'You've been out in the rain long enough. Sit — I'd rather not conduct this conversation with half-frozen guests'.

He crossed to the sideboard, uncorked a bottle of O'Connell Estate Margaret River, and poured three generous measures. The light outside had already softened into late afternoon.

'Tea is well enough outside', he said lightly. 'But for this, something stronger. My grandmother's vineyard. She'd be delighted to know Fleet Street and the BBC were finally giving it their attention'.

Glasses in hand, the interview began.

The BBC anchor leaned forward, eyes sharp.

'Captain Aldridge, the City is abuzz. You're stepping straight from a military career into the boardroom of Aldridge Merchant Bank. Some say it's a bold move. Others reckless. What do you say?'

Richard smiled, easy and unguarded.

'Reckless? Well, the worst that happens is the board throws me out on my ear. No incoming fire, no ration packs. I think I'll survive'.

The correspondent scribbled notes.

'But you have no banking experience. None at all'.

Richard spread his hands. 'Until last year, I could barely keep track of my own accounts. I imagine the board will find that... refreshing'.

The anchor pressed.

'What about the whispers in the Square Mile that you're now the most eligible bachelor in British high society?'

Richard gave a mock wince. 'You mean the tabloids weren't joking? Well, I suppose if people want to debate that over cocktails in Mayfair, who am I to argue? I've been called worse'.

The *Times* man cut in, adjusting his glasses, tapping the folder in his lap.

'Captain Aldridge, your grandfather promised the release of a dossier, evidence, he said, of manipulation from the shadows. Both of us have received it. Do you stand by its contents? And what of today's press release, circulated to every newsroom in London, stating the family's official position?'

Richard leaned back in the leather chair, one ankle loosely crossed over his knee, the picture of languid composure. He let the silence stretch just long enough for the camera to capture it, then smiled faintly.

'My grandfather has always been a stickler for accuracy. If he's put his name to those papers, then they're as solid as the ground under my grandmother's vines. The dossier speaks for itself. As for the press release', his smile thinned almost imperceptibly, 'well, it says everything that needs to be said. My part is simply to see that his wishes are carried forward and that the family legacy continues, uninterrupted'.

The BBC anchor tilted her head, lips curving as if to press him further, but Richard's easy delivery left little to grasp. He looked every inch the polished heir, the dutiful grandson, precisely the role he intended them to see.

'And your critics? Some say you're nothing but a figurehead, a soldier in a suit, a convenient face for an old family name'.

Richard considered the question and then said evenly, with the same self-deprecating ease,

'Well, if being a figurehead means doing what my grandfather asks of me, then I suppose I'm guilty as charged. I've always done what's asked of me, in uniform or now in a suit. I'll muddle through. And if the professionals need to take over later, all the better'.

The glasses were drained, the camera light winked off, and the interview was done. Richard escorted them to the door.

Outside, umbrellas jostled as the two journalists stepped onto the wet stone steps. Cameras flashed, voices clamoured. The veteran correspondent raised a hand for quiet, his voice carrying over the crowd.

'He offered us a glass of wine', he said dryly, 'and he even answered the dossier question honestly'.

The pack rippled with laughter, mutters, and fresh scribbling into notebooks. For once, the headlines wrote themselves.

Back inside, the heavy door thudded shut, muting the shouts and shuffle of the pack outside. The study seemed suddenly vast and silent, the fire's crackle the only sound.

Richard stood for a moment in the dim light, hands resting on the back of a chair. The smile he had worn so easily for the cameras slipped away, leaving only the hard line of his jaw. He adjusted his cufflinks with mechanical precision, a small ritual of order, of armour, before lifting his gaze to the Fourth Marquis's portrait. The stern eyes in uniform seemed to weigh him, as if measuring whether the heir was still playing the part or becoming part of it.

'First skirmish over', he murmured. 'Now for the main event'.

He reached for the half-finished glass on the sideboard, drained it in a single swallow, and set it down with quiet finality. Outside, the rain rattled harder against the panes, but in the study, there was only resolve.

Chapter 20: The Real Battle Begins

The Defender nosed into the multistorey tucked behind the old warehouses and the Marriott Hotel at West India Quay. Its engine note echoed against the concrete before falling silent. Richard killed the engine, slipped the keys into his pocket, and stepped out into the drizzle.

The air carried a mix of wet brick, diesel fumes, and the faint salt of the docks, a city smell, yet it stirred memories of other deployments. Jungle clay in Timor after a storm, the acrid haze of cordite clinging to kit, the heavy tang of stagnant canals in the Balkans. Different continents, same undertone: danger hidden just out of sight.

From the stairwell, he took in the long brick façades of the quay, Georgian warehouses scrubbed clean and refitted with steel-framed windows. The old dock cranes loomed like skeletal sentinels along the water's edge. Below, the West India Dock lay still and dark, houseboats riding gently against their moorings. One was lit with stained glass, a floating church among the moored barges.

He let his gaze travel across the quay. These walls had once held the empire's plunder: sugar, rum, tobacco, the wealth of half a world bled dry and shipped home in barrels and crates. Now they held their modern equivalent: balance sheets and ledgers, fortunes conjured in ink and digits, just as ruthless, just as corrupt.

Richard felt the thought settle like iron in his chest. He had worn a uniform to fight tyranny overseas. Here, the battlefield was quieter, the uniforms were tailored, but the fight was no less real. This time, it was financial plunder he was hell-bent on rooting out.

Among the restaurants and boutique offices sat the discreet frontage of Aldridge Merchant Bank, bronze letters over double doors that had once opened onto sugar and rum.

Richard crossed the slick cobbles, the weight of history under his boots. No Gerald swagger, no careful invisibility. For the first time since setting foot in London, he walked openly as himself.

The uniformed security man at the doors stepped forward. 'Sir, may I...' He froze mid-sentence, recognition dawning. It was the face from every morning paper, the name on every rolling news strapline.

'My apologies, Lord Aldridge', the guard said quickly, straightening. 'Welcome to the bank'.

Richard extended his hand. The man shook it, firm but a little uncertain.

'Nothing to apologise for', Richard said evenly. 'You've a duty to do. Never forget that'.

The guard nodded, almost grateful, and stepped aside. Richard pushed through into the lobby.

Upstairs, the boardroom windows looked out over the quiet dock. Inside, the directors were already gathered for their morning prayers, the day's newspapers spread across the polished table. Headlines ran bold above glossy photos:

'Aldridge Charm Offensive: Army Captain Wins Over Press with Wine and Wit'.

'Eligible at Last: The City's Most Wanted Bachelor'.

'Soldier-Turned-Banker: Reckless or Refreshing?'

Most were smiling, a few smirked with barely disguised envy. One or two looked guarded, already measuring him as a rival.

Richard paused at the threshold, his grandfather's warning still in his ears:

They'll circle you, boy. Test your hide. Don't flinch, don't fold. Let them show their teeth first.

He stepped inside. The main event had begun.

The murmurs began before he even crossed the threshold. '…straight from the army…', '…no banking experience…', '…just the old man's pet project…' The interview had done its work. They thought him a playboy, a puppet.

Every eye followed as he entered. The 'Chairman's seat' at the head of the table sat empty, waiting. But Richard's gaze went instead to the midpoint on the right-hand side, facing the door— the real power seat.

A middle-aged director lounged there, jacket unbuttoned, smirk already forming.

Richard stopped beside him. 'You're in my seat'.

The smirk faltered. After a heartbeat, the man shifted two chairs down without protest.

Richard slid into the vacated spot, unhurried, setting a leather folder before him. From this vantage, the head of the table was no longer symbolic — it was command, and he now held it, right where the action converged.

He let the murmurs build. Then he began marking the room as he would a patrol. The silver-haired Frenchman: hostile. The nervous younger director: weak link. And two places down, Lydia McCarthy. Calm, composed, eyes sharp. Neutral for now, but not indifferent. An ally in waiting.

At the right moment, Richard opened his folder and drew out a stack of black binders, stamped discreetly with the Aldridge crest.

'Miss Harrington', he said evenly. 'If you'd be so kind'.

Anna handed out the binders without fuss. Inside were the essentials:

- His Master's degree in International Finance from the University of Western Australia.

145

- Selected extracts from his military record—command citations, commendations, clear evidence of leadership under fire.

A few passages were blacked out, entire lines struck through. Certain operations remained classified, their details sealed, but the weight of the record was undeniable.

The Frenchman muttered in his own tongue:

'Un soldat déguisé en banquier… voyons combien de temps il tiendra'.

(*A soldier dressed as a banker… let's see how long he lasts.*)

Richard did not look up. His reply, delivered in fluent, unhurried French, landed like a blade:

'Autant que nécessaire, monsieur… et peut-être plus longtemps que vous'.

(*As long as necessary, sir… and perhaps longer than you.*)

The silence that followed was musical. Richard let it breathe, then, almost under his breath, added in a language no one in the room recognised:

'Ngany kaditj'.

(*I understand.*)

No one dared ask what it meant.

He closed his folder. 'Before today's formal business, I want something from each of you. By tomorrow morning, written reports, in your own hand, with your recommendations for stabilising the bank's public standing and containing the damage in the press. No committees. No joint submissions. Individual accountability'.

Chairs shifted. Pens stilled. Lydia gave the faintest nod.

'And with those reports', Richard continued, 'I want résumés and service records for all senior management and the board itself. Signed and dated'.

A low, derisive sound came from down the table, but Richard didn't bother to respond. He gathered his folder, rose, and turned toward the door.

'Meeting over'.

At the threshold, one of the quiet directors intercepted him. Early forties, sharp-suited, an air of reserve. He extended a hand.

'We haven't met. Adrien Aldridge'.

Richard took the hand, noting the grip. 'Aldridge?'

'A very distant cousin', Adrien said lightly. 'After university, I came in as an intern, kept the name quiet at first, but people notice these things. One posting led to another, doors opened, and somehow, I ended up here'. His tone was breezy, but the rise had clearly been rapid. Some men climbed ladders; others had theirs steadied for them.

'I only mention it so you're not blindsided later by some genealogist in *The Times*. We'll speak again'.

A precise smile. Then he melted back into the room.

As Richard reached the door, Lydia caught his eye. She gave the faintest inclination of her head—respect, or approval. He filed it away. Allies would be precious.

The first skirmish was over. The campaign had begun.

By the time Adrien stepped off the Thames Clipper at Westminster Pier, dusk was closing in and the night was getting colder under a cloudless sky.

Across the river, in an office curtained against the night, Alpha set down the phone. The green light on the secure line faded to black.

'Promising', he murmured.

The man sitting opposite gave a tight nod. Younger, sharper-suited than Jonathan had ever been, but with the same Aldridge cheekbones and the same hunger in his eyes. Adrien Aldridge.

'He handled the board as predicted', Alpha went on. 'More spine than some expected. That works to our advantage. A commander who thinks he sees the battlefield is easier to draw onto the ground we choose'.

Adrien's jaw tightened. 'He accepted me'.

Alpha's smile was thin, precise. 'You wear the right name. You sit at the right table. That makes you our bridge. Inside the tent, as they say'.

'And when the moment comes?'

Alpha's eyes hardened to stone. 'When the moment comes, Captain Richard will find his allies already compromised. Until then, let him enjoy his little victories'.

Outside, the river kept its silence, patient, watchful, waiting for the next move.

Chapter 21: The Squad

The chairman's office smelled faintly of leather and polish, though most of it was new. The redecoration had been carried out on Richard's advice, a cover for the bug sweep that had stripped the place bare only weeks earlier.

Fresh carpet, new drapes, refitted shelving, all chosen to reassure visitors that the bank's traditions endured, even if the fittings themselves were recent.

The sweep had found what Richard expected: microphones seeded in cornices and fittings, lenses hidden in gilt and brass. On his instruction, they had been left in place, the microphones still live, the lenses carefully painted over to preserve their view while showing nothing.

Whoever was watching or listening received the same comfortingly empty signals as before. When he needed to speak freely, a scrambler the size of a cigarette case would bathe the room in white hiss, turning every bug into static.

Behind the desk, only a handful of heirlooms had been returned: the antique blotter, the walnut pen box, and a gilt-framed photograph of Lord Richard in his younger years. Enough to project lineage, but not enough to give any wire or lens a second chance.

Richard placed his briefcase on the desk before he sat. To a banker, it would look like a chairman's accessory; to him, it was cover, a way to carry the tools of Gerald's trade without raising a single eyebrow. After all, he could not very well carry a man bag.

On one side, he drew a slim silver frame: his grandparents together at the vineyard, taken almost as soon as they found each other again — faces lined but eyes bright.

He set it carefully on the desk, angled so their smiles looked toward the door. To anyone else, it was just a photograph. To Richard, it was also a sentry. Buried in the frame's edge, barely wider than a pinprick, was a lens no bigger than a seed. It fed into a secure loop in his briefcase, logging every shadow that crossed the office when he was not there.

He allowed himself the smallest smile; his grandparents were watching the room, in more ways than one. Only then did he sit, the leather creaking beneath him. Uniform gone, suit and tie in its place. Soldier among bankers.

He set his folder down and began opening the desk drawers one by one. Most held neatly labelled files and the sort of stationery his grandfather would have insisted on: heavy cream paper, fountain pens in polished walnut boxes.

He moved to the whiteboard on the far wall and uncapped a marker. Slowly, deliberately, he began sketching names from memory, adding short code notes beside each. Not bankers, not colleagues, a squad under review.

- **Lydia McCarthy: Sharp.** Calm. Backed Grandfather when the wolves circled. Potential ally, but every ally has a price.
- **Jean-Paul, the Frenchman:** Vanity first. Loyalty for sale. Unreliable under fire. Enemy.
- **Adrien Aldridge:** Quiet. Too quiet. Called himself a 'distant cousin'. Polite, precise, unreadable. Unknown, watch carefully.
- **Young director, charcoal suit:** Nervous. Weak link. Fence-sitter. Could be swayed or snapped.
- **Silver-haired City veteran:** Dismissive. Condescending. Already probing for leverage. Enemy.

He stepped back, arms folded, scanning the board the way he once scanned a sand table before a patrol. Friend. Foe. Fence-sitter.

In the regiment, a squad was not about rank or medals; it was about trust. The man on your left and the man on your right had to be the ones you could count on in the dark, under fire, when the plan went sideways. Banking might not have bullets, but it had its own ambushes, and the stakes were no less deadly for those who depended on him.

Tomorrow's reports would tell him who had a clear head, who could think under pressure, and who needed to be cut loose. The résumés would show the training; his instincts would judge the spine.

He lingered for a moment longer, then reached into his inside pocket and drew out the rugged PDA the Friends had given him, matte black, its stubby stylus clipped neatly to one side, indistinguishable from the kind sold in airport electronics shops. Only this one carried an encrypted memory core and a covert lens tucked beneath its casing.

With practised precision, he snapped a series of images of the whiteboard from several angles, each stored silently into its hardened drive. Every name, every note, preserved.

Then, with the same methodical calm he would use wiping fingerprints from a weapon, he picked up the eraser and cleared the board until it gleamed under the lamplight. By the time he pocketed the phone, not a trace of ink remained.

He turned to go, hand on the light switch. The room went dark, and the PDA in his pocket gave a short, sharp vibration. He drew it out. The matte display glowed with a single line of text:

EXTERNAL ACCESS ATTEMPT DETECTED. SOURCE UNKNOWN.

Richard froze. The Friends had built safeguards into the device, a rudimentary tripwire meant to flag if anyone so much as rattled the lock of its encrypted core. Someone out there had just tried. Not a random probe, the timing was too clean, too deliberate.

For a moment, he stood in the doorway, the glow of the screen the only light in the room. The faint hum of the air conditioning now sounded like static, the creak of the old floorboards like a footstep too close.

And beneath it all, a colder thought: if the Syndicate realised this was no ordinary organiser but hardened kit, the mask of dutiful heir and convenient playboy would slip. They would know he was more than the tabloids painted.

The warning faded from the screen, but the unease remained. Perhaps the bait had not been swallowed whole after all.

He slipped the PDA away, closed the door behind him, and glanced once more at the photograph on his desk: His grandparents were watching the room, in more ways than one, smiling, sentries in silver.

Then he walked into the night.

The squad would come together. The house would be cleaned. But the enemy was already working its way inside, unseen but close at hand.

Chapter 22: Day Two at the Bank

Richard was in before the lights had fully warmed the corridors. His shoes clicked on marble, echoing in the hush of the early morning Bank. A cleaner with a buffing machine paused to let him pass, giving a curious glance; not many chairmen came in before dawn.

At the ground-floor desk, the same security guard from the previous day straightened as Richard approached, surprise flickering in his eyes. Most directors drifted in at mid-morning; a chairman at half-past six was another matter.

Richard stopped. 'Good morning. Remind me of your name?'

The man blinked, then answered quickly. 'Carter, sir. James Carter'.

Richard offered his hand, firm and deliberate. 'Thank you, Mr Carter, for yesterday, and for this morning. Keep doing your job; it matters more than most people in this building realise'.

The guard's grip was steady, though his expression carried the faint shock of a man not used to being acknowledged by anyone above his pay grade. Richard left him standing a little taller.

Upstairs, the chairman's office still carried the faint scent of polish and new carpet beneath the leather. Outside, the City was only just stirring, a grey dawn brushing the towers awake.

Inside, Richard set his briefcase on the desk and drew out the same ruggedised PDA he used the night before. A thin cable linked it to the silver photo frame of his grandparents, the pinhole lens disguised in its edge feeding straight into the device. With a few taps, the screen blinked awake and began scrolling through the overnight log: the night guard on his rounds, a pair of cleaners vacuuming at two a.m., one pausing to straighten a chair before moving on.

For half a second, one frame stuttered, a brief smear of static before the picture corrected itself. Richard's eyes narrowed. He noted the timestamp in his pad without fuss, the way he'd once logged an unexplained flicker on a night-vision scope.

Nothing to dwell on in the moment. Log it, move on, review later.

The rest of the feed rolled clean. No shadows where they shouldn't be, no hands where they didn't belong. Just polish and elbow grease.

He let the screen fade and exhaled slowly. No surprises. For now.

On his desk, precisely where he'd asked for them, lay the board's overnight submissions: neat stacks of paper clipped to résumés, names typed bold on ivory letterhead.

He took his coffee black and his reading straight. One by one, he worked through the reports, annotating with a fine pencil, building his internal map.

Some made his pulse steady.

- **Lydia McCarthy:** crisp recommendations, clean data, practical sequencing. She proposed trimming high-risk derivative exposure by a third, doubling down on mid-cap corporate lending businesses that actually employed people, and stabilising liquidity through a short-term sale of secondary assets. Her slides were clipped in the back, already formatted. A professional soldier's thinking in civilian form.

Others made his teeth itch.

- **Jean-Paul and Guillaume, the French quarter:** elegant prose, glossy charts, little substance. A Paris 'brand refresh', new office space, 'synergy with continental expansion'. All adjectives, no numbers. They would have been laughed out of a field briefing.

And one didn't sit in either pile.

- **Adrien:** his folder sat apart, deliberately, the way a weapon is laid where you can see it. Not naughty, not nice, just unknown. Richard's instincts were clear enough to write in the margin without looking up: keep a close eye on this one.

By the time he'd finished his first pass, the piles looked like a parody of Father Christmas: naughty and nice, and because accuracy mattered, he checked them twice. He allowed himself a wry smile at the thought, then sharpened his pencil and annotated each one with the same brisk shorthand he'd once used on sitreps: sound, weak, unreliable, spin. Humour had its place, but so did clarity.

He drafted a short email.

Subject: *Thank you & next step*

Thank you for your individual submissions. Please now combine your recommendations into a single consolidated proposal. I have a clear idea of the way forward, but I want to see whether we are on the same page.

11:00 sharp: *brief board session to discuss.*

He hit send.

The door clicked open a minute later. Miss Harrington arrived, perfectly punctual, coat over her arm, shorthand pad already in hand. She took in the lit office, the empty cup, the stacks already filed and marked.

Not surprised. It was exactly what she would have expected; only this version of Lord Richard was at least fifty years younger.

'Good morning, Miss Harrington', Richard said, rising. 'I'm going to get a coffee. May I bring you one? And by the way, I can't keep calling you 'Miss Harrington' forever'.

She blinked just once, the corner of her mouth almost twitching. 'It's Anna. White, no sugar'.

He gave a small nod. 'Anna, then. And mine's Richard, at least when we're not in front of the wolves'.

By the time he returned, two cups in hand, something had shifted. He placed hers on a coaster. Somewhere between the lift and the kettle, he'd moved up a notch in her private ledger. What Richard didn't know—couldn't yet know—was that he'd just acquired a guardian who would quietly fend off anything with teeth and make sure nothing sharp found its way into his back.

'I'm afraid I'll need to shut the door for an hour', he said. 'Something sensitive. I've sent an email out for a short board session at eleven; would you be able to make sure that everything is ready for it?'

'Of course'.

The door closed. The office fell into silence. Richard reached for his PDA again. Last night's captured images flickered onto the screen. Another keystroke sent them to the wall-mounted projector through the PDA's secure short-range link, where they bloomed across the whiteboard in sharp monochrome... The markers squeaked under his hand as he began to build out the squad over the ghostly outlines of his notes.

Chief of Staff: he wrote, underlining it. Lydia McCarthy.

Security: Mac, a Para to the bone, Regimental Sergeant Major before he finally hung up the maroon beret. Broad-shouldered, sharp-eyed, and with two decades of Balkans mud and Sierra Leone heat behind him. Retired, but only technically.

Comms: — left blank for now. The role was vital, but the right person hadn't yet stepped forward.

Admin/Logistics: a steady hand to keep the Bank's heartbeat regular without needing a spotlight.

Analysis (Archives): already covered Mary Jenner.

He frowned at the two vacancies. Logistics and comms. Who could fill these roles?

He glanced at his watch; Grandfather would be somewhere off the coast of Spain by now. But before he made the call, he opened the top drawer of his desk and activated the scrambler, bathing the room in static.

The satphone link connected on the third ring.

'Grandfather'.

'Grandson', Lord Richard said, his voice warm and steady across half an ocean. 'I was thinking of you'.

'How's the cruise?' Richard asked quickly, before the business came. 'And Gran—please give her a hug from me and let her know that I'm thinking of her?'

A low chuckle carried down the line, threaded with the hum of the ship's engines and the muted wash of the sea. 'I will. Your grandmother has already won three games of bridge and charmed half the dining room. As for me, I find the pace... agreeable. Slow, but in a way that feels earned. After all these years, we're finally regaining the time that was stolen from us'.

Richard let out a breath he hadn't realised he was holding. 'I'm glad. You both deserve that'.

For a moment, the static hummed like shared silence — a closeness bridging oceans. Then his tone shifted, steady and professional.

'I need recommendations. Five vacancies, five roles. I've got most covered, but I need someone to look after Administration and Comms'.

'Administration's easy', his grandfather replied. 'She's sitting outside your door, and she's been running that place since you were in short trousers. Don't underestimate her.

Comms, I'm afraid I can't help you there — but speak to Anna'.

Richard smiled despite himself. 'Duly noted. Thanks'.

There was another pause, lighter this time. Lord Richard's voice came back with a trace of mischief.

'Stay safe, boy — and remember: *Illegitimi non carborundum*'.

Richard's answering smile could be heard in his voice. 'And you, Grandfather'.

The line clicked dead. He ended the call, wrote Anna Harrington onto the board, and snapped another set of images back into the PDA for secure storage before cleaning the board.

At ten fifty-three, he straightened his tie and headed for the boardroom.

The power chair had been left vacant this time. Richard sat at eleven on the nose and opened the meeting. Several members drifted in over the next five minutes, late, flustered, avoiding his eye. He was not surprised to see they all lived on the naughty list.

'Thank you for your reports', he said, voice even. 'Some were excellent. Effort and time were evident'. He let his gaze settle, deliberately, here and there. 'Others were likely written at your clubs with one hand while the other reached for the glass'.

A few throats cleared. No one laughed.

'We have a storm outside', he continued. 'We will meet it head-on. Who will present a way out of our current predicament?'

Paper rustled. Eyes went to the shoes. Silence thickened.

Then a chair scraped. Lydia stood. She crossed to the screen, calm as if she were back in front of a university lecture hall. Clear slides, tight voice, recommendations laid out step by step. Her plan matched almost note for note the sketch Richard had drawn in his own hand that morning.

When she finished, Richard nodded once. 'Thank you'.

'We will also get ahead of the media', he said. 'Do we have a communications director?'

Blank looks. A few frowns. No hands. Down the table, the French quarter leaned together.

'**Pourquoi un directeur de la communication?** *Why a communications director?*' one murmured.

'**Nous ne sommes pas une agence de publicité. C'est une banque.** *We are not an advertising agency. This is a bank'*.

Richard didn't bother to hide his smile.

'**Et c'est précisément pourquoi vous avez besoin de quelqu'un qui sait quand se taire, quand parler, et à qui avant que les autres ne racontent votre histoire pour vous.**

And that is precisely why you need someone who knows when to stay silent, when to speak, and to whom before others tell your story for you'.

It landed. Clean.

'Miss Harrington', he said, glancing toward the door where she stood with her pad. 'Please begin the process for a senior communications appointment. We'll discuss names this afternoon'.

'Yes, Chairman'.

Richard rose. The meeting was over; everyone could feel it. At the door, he turned back.

'One more thing. I want a signed letter of resignation from each of you on my desk by the close of business. State your own reason; leave the date blank. I'll complete that part if and when it's necessary'.

The shock travelled the table like a quiet electric pulse. No shouting, no grandstanding, just silence, and a few pens already lifting.

'Thank you', he said, and stepped into the corridor. 'Ms McCarthy, walk with me, please'.

Back in the office, he asked Anna to join them. Once the door closed, he checked that the scrambler was still active before he faced the two women.

'First', he said to Lydia, 'your presentation was precisely what we need'.

'Thank you'.

'I'm building a small core team', he continued. 'Not another committee. A squad. I'd like you to serve as my Chief of Staff'.

Her eyes narrowed slightly, assessing. 'Scope?'

'Anything that doesn't need my signature, you handle. You'll have open access to me. What I need from you is steadiness, urgency, and the truth; even when it's hard to hear'.

Her mouth twitched, almost a smile. 'When do we start?'

'We already have'. He reached for the phone. 'You'll want to meet Security'.

The notebook lay open on the desk, old names in his grandfather's hand now joined by a few in his own. Mac's number was among them, a legacy contact, but one Richard had kept current.

He dialled. 'Mac? It's O'Connell. I need some help'.

The speaker crackled, and a bark of laughter filled the office.

'O'Connell, you slippery bastard. From the number you're calling on, I can see you're in London. What is it, back to that ASIO cloak-and-dagger work, or just here to wind up the boys in Hereford? They still won't stop whingeing about that Aussie officer who ran rings around them, made 'em look like crow recruits in the Balkans. Thought you'd buggered off to grow grapes'.

Richard pinched the bridge of his nose, half amused, half resigned. 'Will I ever live that down?'

He allowed himself a faint smile. 'Some things never change'.

'Too right they don't', Mac shot back. 'I can be with you in an hour, and don't think I'm polishing your boots this time'.

Anna's eyebrow twitched upward; Lydia's mouth quirked despite herself.

Richard leaned toward the microphone, tone dry. 'Careful, Mac, there are ladies present'.

'Ladies?' Mac snorted. 'Then you'd best tell 'em O'Connell's worse than a platoon of Paras on payday. If they can stand that, they'll manage me just fine'.

The line went dead, leaving the faintest echo of his laugh in the speaker.

Richard replaced the receiver, shaking his head. He turned toward Anna. 'Admin and logistics. From what Grandfather tells me, you've been running this place for years. Nobody else could do it half as well'.

Anna's eyes gave away nothing, but the faintest tightening of her jaw said she accepted.

'And the archives?' Lydia asked.

'Mary Jenner will continue her ISO audit', Richard said. 'There's a goldmine downstairs. We have already started unearthing skeletons'.

Lydia dipped her chin. 'I'll coordinate'.

Richard picked up a marker, activated the PDA, and turned the whiteboard toward them. Names. Arrows. The outline of something leaner and harder than a traditional bank chart.

'This isn't a board', he said softly. 'It's a patrol. We move light, we move fast, and we don't miss'.

Whilst Richard was updating the whiteboard, Lydia cut in.

'You talked earlier about a Communications Manager. Sensible in principle, but too slow in practice. Recruitment takes weeks. Right now, we need reach and credibility immediately. A PR firm gives us both: instant bandwidth, instant cover'.

Richard looked up, marker still in hand. A faint smile touched his mouth.

'Good. That's the thinking I need'.

He turned to Anna. 'Can you work with Lydia? Start sounding out discreet firms, especially ones that know how to move quietly as well as fast'.

Anna gave a small, silent nod. Lydia dipped her chin once, already half a step ahead.

Richard marked another line on the board. Inwardly, he thought: *Definitely the right choice for Chief of Staff.*

A soft knock interrupted. James Carter, the ground-floor guard, stepped in. His uniform was still damp from the drizzle, an envelope held carefully in one hand.

'I thought it best to bring this to you personally, sir', he said. 'It came direct by hand, a Downing Street courier. It didn't seem right to let it sit at reception'.

Richard rose and accepted the envelope with a nod. 'That was well judged. Thank you, Mr Carter, James'.

Carter inclined his head, but Richard didn't let him leave just yet.

'Don't you ever sleep, James? You keep longer hours than I do'.

A flicker of amusement touched the older man's face. 'Old habits, sir'.

Richard's eyes narrowed. The cadence was unmistakable. 'Army. What regiment?'

'Royal Military Police', Carter replied evenly. 'Invalided out after the Falklands. I lost the lower part of my right leg'.

He shifted slightly, and Richard caught the stiff angle, the faint gleam of the prosthesis beneath the light. For a beat, Richard said nothing, weighing him. A soldier's bearing, wasted here in a marble foyer, but as a doorman, Carter had eyes on every arrival, every exit, the sort of vantage point he could use.

'Well, James', Richard said at last, 'it seems you're better suited to this post than most realise. Keep your eyes sharp. I'll have my security consultant get in touch — I'd like him to meet you'.

Carter gave a short nod, pride flickering behind the professionalism, and withdrew as neatly as he had entered.

For a moment, Richard studied the closed door, weighing the thought. Good men in the right places were worth more than any security system. Carter had the instincts — and he'd make a point of introducing him to Mac soon.

He turned the envelope in his hands, the embossed crest of the Prime Minister catching the light. Unusual. Normally these things came couriered, logged, and official. *Hand-delivered* meant something else.

Across the desk, Anna's arms folded lightly. Her gaze narrowed just enough to show she'd noticed too.

Richard broke the seal, scanned the letter, and exhaled through his nose. 'Looks like the Prime Minister wants to see me. A car's already on the way'. He set the letter down and met Anna's eyes. 'Can you cover for me while I'm out?'

'Of course', she said, in the tone of someone who had never once failed.

She gave a short nod but didn't leave, standing like a small immovable shield beside his desk. Whatever the message in that envelope, Richard knew she would see him through it.

As he reached for his coat, he added almost as an afterthought:

'Oh, and Anna, would you mind getting onto the College of Arms. Let's see just how distant a cousin Adrien really is'.

Chapter 23: The
Prime Minister's Request

The car stopped at the black railings of Downing Street. A police constable checked the list, then waved him through with a polite nod. Inside the gates, the Number 10 door swung open as if it had been waiting for him.

Richard stepped into the entrance hall, the air warmer than the drizzle outside, and handed his coat to the waiting staffer. He had barely taken two steps toward the staircase when the inner door opened and a figure emerged. The Deputy Leader of the Government.

Alpha's expression broke through the public mask of geniality. 'Captain Aldridge'. His handshake was firm, his smile easy. 'Settling in, are we? Big chair for a young man'.

Richard summoned his most disarming grin, the one that had infuriated drill sergeants and charmed Perth debutantes. 'It is a big chair', he said lightly. 'Still working out if it's better for signing papers or mixing drinks'.

Alpha chuckled, exactly as Richard intended. To him, the spoiled heir act was confirmation of everything he already believed: Richard was a lightweight, a playboy in a suit, someone who would be eased out once the old man was gone.

'Well', Alpha said, patting his arm as if he were a favoured nephew, 'enjoy it while it lasts. These things have a way of… finding their proper level'.

'Quite', Richard murmured, still smiling. They exchanged pleasantries, and Alpha swept out toward his waiting car, entirely satisfied.

Richard watched him go, his face unreadable, before being led into the Prime Minister's office.

The Prime Minister stood as Richard entered, hand extended. 'Aldridge. Good of you to come on short notice'.

'Prime Minister'.

'Tea? Or something stronger?'

'Black coffee will do, sir'.

The PM gestured toward two chairs drawn up before the fireplace. 'Sit. We won't be disturbed. I've made that clear'. His private secretary slipped out, closing the door behind him.

Richard sat, waiting.

The PM wasted no time. 'You saw him on the way out?'

'Yes'.

'And?'

Richard gave a half-shrug. 'He thinks I'm a spoiled heir. A marionette'.

The Prime Minister's eyes narrowed in grim approval. 'Good. That suits us for now'. He leaned forward, elbows on his knees. 'I'll speak plainly. I know what you know, and your grandfather knows. I know what you passed on to Hereford. The man who just left this room is not simply the Deputy Leader of the Government. He is Alpha. The Syndicate's head in the UK. Drugs, weapons, trafficking, and worse'.

Richard said nothing. He didn't need to.

The PM's voice was low, edged with frustration.

'I can't touch him. If I sack him, I hand the Opposition a gift-wrapped scandal. Expose him, and I lack the admissible proof. Assassination?' His jaw tightened. 'We don't do that here. At least not yet. But for him…' He let the pause hang. '…I might make an exception'.

He sat back, the firelight hardening the lines of his face. Then, with the faintest smile, he added:

'You know, when I first came through that door as a junior minister, they all looked at me like I'd wandered in from the wrong street. Maybe I had. Council flat. My mother is a single mum working two jobs. I stacked shelves, pulled pints, and delivered papers before school. Got a scholarship to Manchester, scraped through on part-time wages and student grants. Joined the TA, spent time in uniform, living out of a tent while the real lads kept the peace. Nothing in my life came easy'.

The Prime Minister gave a small, wry smile. 'Some of my colleagues told me to pack it in when I first got to Westminster. 'No place for a Member of Parliament in uniform', they said. But I kept my slot in the Territorials. Said it kept me sane'.

He leaned back slightly, eyes narrowing with memory. 'Bosnia, '97. They called us up to support the engineers. Officially, I was already an MP, but I put my hand up anyway. A fortnight away in theatre, nothing glamorous, just bridging and roads. One night, our convoy hit a roadblock outside Pristina. Local militia, drunk, twitchy, every one of them with a finger on a trigger. We sat there under the headlights for an hour, waiting for it to turn into a massacre'.

He reached absently for his glass, voice steady but quieter. 'Didn't come to it, thank God. One of our corporals spoke enough Serbo-Croat to joke with their lieutenant, and we bought our way through with a fuel drum and a carton of rations. But the look on their faces and the sound of those safeties clicking on and off in the dark stays with you'.

The trace of a grin returned. That night did two things. It made me respect the regulars who lived like that for months, not days. Strange thing, politics — three years after that roadblock, I was Party Leader. All the speeches, the hustings, the late-night votes, and yet it was one jittery stand-off in Bosnia that catapulted me further and faster than any of them.

'Odd sort of CV, isn't it?'

He tapped the arm of his chair once, firm. 'That's why I see you clearly, Captain. You may have been born to a title, but you're not trading on it. You've fought for what you are. That's why I need you: someone who understands discipline, loyalty, but also how to walk into rooms full of privilege without blinking'.

The firelight flickered. The Prime Minister leaned forward again, voice lowering.

'Which leaves us one option. Someone outside the official machine. Someone who can manoeuvre, probe, and strike without my fingerprints on the knife'.

Richard leaned back, meeting his gaze. 'Then I'll speak plainly as well. I won't do this alone. A soldier without a squad is a target, not an asset. I'm building a team of trusted, discreet men and women who know how to fight in the shadows as well as the field. They'll meet me this weekend at West Farleigh Manor. That's where the planning begins'.

The Prime Minister's brows rose a fraction. 'West Farleigh Manor? You're opening the family seat to this?'

Richard's mouth twitched. 'It has the advantage of being mine. Secure grounds, private land, no curious civil servants. And the house has, according to my grandfather, seen its share of secrets before'.

A beat of silence passed before Richard added, 'You'd be welcome, Prime Minister. Hearing the plan from the source, not filtered by reports. It would give the squad confidence and make clear where the authority lies'.

The PM considered that, gaze drifting toward the fire. 'Tempting. But how do you suggest I travel? A Prime Minister's diary is public; his movements are tracked. If I vanish to Kent for a weekend, the press will howl'.

Richard nodded slowly, as if turning the idea over. 'Then don't vanish. Make it routine. An official weekend at Chequers, photographed with family, the usual handshakes'. He tapped a finger on the armrest, thinking aloud. 'But... Chequers is only a short distance from Farleigh by air. If we wanted to be discreet, we could lift you at first light on Saturday'.

He leaned forward, sketching an invisible line across the blotter on the Prime Minister's desk. 'Something low-key, civilian registry, a trusted pilot. By the time the press pack stir for breakfast, you'd already be on the ground at West Farleigh'.

The Prime Minister raised an eyebrow. 'And airspace? We're not about to blunder into Heathrow's landing path'.

Richard gave a half-shrug, the ghost of a smile tugging at his mouth. 'It can be done. Skirt the London Control Zone, ride the edge of Class G. File it cleanly, and the controllers won't give it a second glance. Fifteen minutes in the air, no more'.

'And security?' the PM pressed. 'My team won't like me slipping off the radar'.

Richard's grin was wolfish. 'Then bring them. Two of your close protection on board, the rest believing you're still tucked up at Chequers. No motorcade, no tails, no eyes on the lanes. To Alpha and his friends, you'll have spent a dull weekend hosting a trade union leader in the Chilterns. Nothing more'.

The Prime Minister's expression hardened, but a spark of amusement lit in his eyes.

'You've thought this through'.

Richard gave a quick shrug. 'On the spot, sir. Habit of the trade: sketch a plan before the boots are even laced'.

For the first time that day, the Prime Minister allowed himself a smile, not of ease, but of recognition. This was a man who could operate in ambiguity. He reached to the side table and handed Richard a slim red folder, the crest of the Prime Minister's Office stamped on the cover.

'This makes it official. Advisory clearance. No civil service chain, no committees. You report to me. No one else'.

Richard took the folder, weighing its significance. Officially, he was now a Special Adviser. Unofficially, he was being asked to fight a war in the shadows against a man the public believed to be the country's second-in-command.

The Prime Minister studied him. 'You've been a soldier all your adult life. This will require the same discipline, the same resolve, but a different kind of battlefield'.

Richard closed the folder. His voice was even. 'Then I'd better draw up the patrol plan'.

Inside his own car as it left Downing Street, the Deputy Leader of the Government loosened his tie and pulled a sleek phone from his pocket. The rain drummed on the roof as he pressed a number from memory.

'Adrien', he said smoothly. 'You saw him? Strutting into Number 10 like he belonged there'.

'What on earth did the Prime Minister want with him?' Adrien asked, irritation clear in his voice.

Alpha chuckled, low and mirthless. 'A photo opportunity, most likely. Or a word about the family bank. The boy hasn't a clue. A popinjay in a suit, thinking a smile and a handshake make him a statesman. His grandfather must be desperate'.

'They'll find him out soon enough'.

'Precisely. Let him enjoy the limelight. The higher he climbs, the harder the fall. And when he stumbles, Adrien, you and I will be ready to pick the pieces clean'.

A pause, then the voice softened, almost amused.

'And if he drags the Prime Minister down with him — well, some accidents tidy more than one problem at once'.

He ended the call, leaning back with a satisfied sigh as the car purred into Whitehall traffic. To the world, he was a senior statesman returning from Cabinet. To those who mattered, he was Alpha, still unchallenged, still untouchable.

A cluster of journalists loitered across the street, sheltering under umbrellas. The sight of Richard Aldridge emerging from the Prime Minister's residence drew a scatter of camera flashes, questions shouted over the noise of the weather.

'Captain Aldridge! Are you advising the government on defence?'

'Is this about Aldridge Bank? Can you comment on the rumours of impropriety?'

'Are you here as the country's most eligible bachelor or the Bank's newest playboy?'

Richard gave them the smile they expected: careless, aristocratic, the expression that said he was flattered but faintly amused. Instead of retreating straight to the waiting car, he strolled across the cobbles toward the pack. Cameras went into overdrive.

One face stood out: Michael Denning, the journalist who'd once remarked that Richard was the first man in Westminster to answer his questions honestly. Richard extended his hand.

'Mr Denning', he said with easy charm, shaking firmly. 'Don't worry — no great scandal today. Just excellent coffee and the Prime Minister's undying sympathy for my taste in tailors'.

The press chuckled, Denning most of all. Richard let the smile linger, then leaned in, lowering his voice so only Denning could hear as shutters snapped and pens scratched for the City's latest soundbite.

'Call by the townhouse this evening. Off the record first, then on. I'd like to set a few things straight'.

Denning's eyes sharpened; he nodded, the grin replaced by the professional focus of a man already filing his next angle.

Denning's brow arched, already calculating headlines. 'Sunday edition?'

The cameras saw a young heir in a tailored suit, a scion of old money drifting through politics like a debutante across a ballroom. A spoiled marionette, dancing on the strings of his grandfather. Exactly what they were meant to see.

What they could not see was the red folder tucked beneath his arm. Inside, a single sheet of paper bore the seal of the Prime Minister's Office, naming him Special Adviser. No civil service chain. No committee oversight. His orders came from one man only.

As Richard's car eased away from Downing Street, he let the smile fade, the mask falling away like a discarded coat. He pulled the folder closer, thumbing it open just long enough to confirm the Prime Minister's signature and seal. Then he slid his phone from his inside pocket and pressed a single number.

'Captain', came Anna's calm voice when the line clicked live. Efficient, unflustered as always.

'Anna', Richard replied, his tone gentle. 'It's Richard, not Captain. Not with you. Titles have their place, but this isn't it'.

A brief pause, then: 'Yes, Richard'.

'Thank you'. His tone eased. 'Could you set something up at West Farleigh Manor? Friday evening. Just a dinner to break the ice, nothing formal. Best if everyone's there by dusk, and perhaps suggest they bring an overnight bag'.

'Yes. And Saturday?'

'The real work. Closed circle planning session', he said, then leaned back slightly. 'Anna, could I ask one favour? Don't mention it to the others yet, but the Prime Minister will be joining us Saturday morning. I'd like that to be a surprise. I'll handle the introductions when he arrives'.

He hesitated, then with a faint smile added, 'And if you wouldn't mind, extend the invite to Mr Carter. He's earned his place with us. Make sure he can put in for the overtime, too'.

Anna's brow arched, but she only gave a brisk nod. 'Understood, I'll liaise with Mac. The Manor will be ready'.

'Perfect. Just… don't tell Mac about the PM. Better if he thinks it's a standard lockdown. I'd quite like to see his face when the PM shows up'.

Anna allowed herself the briefest smile. Richard matched it before his tone grew serious again. 'One last thing, could you remind them this isn't a reunion? It's a war council. Not guests, Anna. A squad'.

'Yes, Richard'.

'Oh, and Richard, I reached out to the College of Arms, as you asked. They were… surprised. Said this was the second enquiry they've had about Adrien Aldridge in as many days'.

Richard ended the call and slipped the phone away. His mind snagged on Anna's words. Someone else was digging into Adrien, someone outside his circle, moving on the same scent. Coincidence was a word he had long since stopped believing in. He made a mental note: Adrien's file stayed open.

Outside, the rain blurred the lamps of Whitehall into streaks of gold and grey. He sat back, already running through the weekend in his mind: the squad gathered at the manor, the Prime Minister slipping in under the radar, the first true step in a campaign fought not with battalions but with shadows and trust.

An enemy in the shadows, wearing the face of a statesman. A war that would demand everything he had.

He exhaled once, slow and steady. Then the smile returned, easy and careless, just in time as the car pulled into the wet London night.

The spoiled heir was back in place. The assassin was already drawing up the plan.

That evening, the rain had eased, but the streets still shone black with it. Michael Denning arrived at the Aldridge townhouse, his notebook already in hand.

Richard met him at the door himself, ushering him past the portraits and into the drawing room where lamplight softened the oak panels. A fire burned low, throwing shadows up the chimney breast.

'Off the record first', Richard said, pouring two glasses of Margaret River red and handing one across. 'You'll want context before you get your copy'.

Denning settled into the low chair, pen poised but still capped. 'And then on the record?'

Richard allowed a flicker of a smile. 'And then on. The public deserves their story, and some shadows deserve a warning'.

The reporter's eyes narrowed, curious. Richard lifted his glass, a silent toast, and leaned forward as the first questions began.

The next day, Richard cleared the morning with paperwork in the London office, then prepared for the drive down to Kent. By early afternoon, he was on the road, the red folder from the Prime Minister still tucked in his briefcase. West Farleigh Manor awaited the weekend, the squad, and the first test of what came next.

The manor house glowed against the cold Kent night. Discreet uplighters set into the gravel drive threw long shadows up the trunks of ancient oaks, their bare branches etched against the sky like black lace. The manor's stone façade was washed in a soft amber light, every mullion and gable picked out with quiet precision. Beyond the lawns, low garden lamps traced the edge of the yews and chestnuts, guiding the way without drawing attention.

Inside, the long dining room had been prepared with care: a fire in the hearth, silverware polished to a high shine, a bottle of O'Connell Estate Shiraz breathing at the head of the table. Portraits of Aldridge's past gazed down from the walls, their eyes catching the glow in ways that felt almost alive.

Richard had brought them all here for one reason: to turn names on a whiteboard into a squad.

Mac arrived first, shoulders squared, eyes sweeping the room as if he were still on parade. His old service blazer sat just so, shoes polished to a mirror shine, the sort of entrance that told you he'd driven himself down in something befitting a retired RSM, steady and dignified. He took in the exits, the angles, the line of sight through the mullioned windows before allowing himself the smallest of nods. One hand rested lightly on the ferrule of a stout ash walking stick that wasn't needed for support, but carried the way some men wore sidearms: a reminder that he had never really put soldiering aside.

The crunch of tyres on gravel announced the taxi's arrival from the station. The three women had shared the ride, each passing the journey in her own way: Lydia reviewing files with clipped efficiency, Mary scrolling data on her tablet, and Anna watching the route in silence, precise as ever.

Lydia McCarthy stepped out first, professional to the fingertips, files tucked beneath her arm, her heels clicking smartly on the oak floorboards. She glanced once at the paintings, weighing history against present duty, then slid into her chair with the precision of habit.

Mary Jenner followed, tablet still glowing faintly blue in her hands. The damp of her coat suggested the dash from the taxi, the last leg of her journey down from the city. She gave Richard a small, almost apologetic smile, as though embarrassed to arrive armed only with data.

And lastly Anna Harrington. Something in her composure seemed to straighten the room, as if order itself had just walked in.

At the doorway lingered one more figure: Carter, the bank's security guard. His suit was neat but plain, his posture betraying the old habits of a soldier more used to foyers and checkpoints than dining rooms.

Richard crossed to him at once. 'Mr Carter, James. Glad you came. And do claim the overtime'.

Carter gave a hesitant nod. 'Thank you, sir. It just didn't seem right to say no. I had to ring the wife, though, to explain I'd be staying over. First time in years, but she knows the job can mean shifts, but never nights away. Took a bit of persuading'.

Richard's expression softened. 'Then tell her from me, this one matters. And when it's done, you'll go home with my thanks, not just the bank's'.

Richard turned towards the head of the table. 'Mac, meet James Carter. Royal Military Police, Falklands. He lost a leg, but not his eyes'.

Mac's gaze swept him like an inspection. Then the ex-RSM extended a hand. 'RMP? You poor sod. Did all the dirty work and never got credit. You'll fit'.

Carter shook the hand firmly, a flicker of pride chasing away his unease. Richard saw the stiffness ease from his stance.

'Good', Richard said quietly. 'Then that's settled. Tonight, you're part of the patrol'.

Mac clapped him on the shoulder. 'Come on, lad. Time to earn that overtime'.

Laughter rippled around the table, easing the tension. For the first time that evening, Carter looked like he belonged.

Dinner began formally enough: soup, fish, wine poured with measured civility…

Conversation circled around neutral ground: the weather, the journey down, the quirks of old houses in winter. But the air was taut, each of them waiting for Richard to move past courtesy.

It was Anna who broke the façade. Halfway through the main course, she set her glass down with a sharp click.

'There's one thing I still don't understand', she said, her gaze level on Richard. 'That dreadful man Gerald, he was insufferable. Half the Bank thought he was why the Chairman was brought down. Whatever happened to him?'

A ripple of amusement ran around the table. Lydia raised a brow. Mac grunted. Even Mary looked up, lips twitching.

Richard cleared his throat. 'Gerald…' He let the name hang, then pushed his chair back. 'Excuse me a moment'.

He left the room. Five minutes later, the door burst open, and Gerald swept in, scarf trailing, vowels stretched to breaking point.

'Darlings! You cannot imagine the trauma of the drive down. Honestly, Kent is simply not what it used to be'.

The table dissolved. Mac roared, Lydia clapped a hand to her mouth, Anna stared in outraged disbelief, and Mary only smiled knowingly.

'You?!' Anna sputtered. 'All this time—'

Gerald dropped the act, voice steady now, sharp as glass. 'Yes. Gerald. A mask. A weapon. A very particular kind of camouflage. Effective enough to buy survival when it mattered'.

From his seat at the edge of the table, Carter gave a dry grunt. 'Knew it the moment I saw him stroll past the security desk. No banker walks in like that. Either a lunatic or a soldier in disguise'.

The laughter returned, lighter this time, tempered with respect. Gerald inclined his head in mock salute. 'And you, Mr Carter, are far too perceptive for a doorman'.

The laughter ebbed. The truth settled like stone.

Richard looked around the table. 'Gerald wasn't the downfall. Gerald was the bait. The man who walked into clubs and boardrooms loud enough to draw the eyes, while I watched who was doing the watching'.

He paused, letting that sink in.

'You've all chosen to be here', he went on, voice steady. 'But you should know why. There's a Syndicate: old money, old power, threaded deep through City and State. They've already turned Aldridge Bank into their nest. They'll happily burn my family name to cinders if it keeps their own accounts unsullied. What they don't want is scrutiny, not from regulators, not from Parliament, not from the press. That's why they discredit, why they distract. And that's why you've been called here'.

Around the table, expressions shifted: Mac frowning like a man scenting an enemy, Lydia's pen hovering mid-air, Mary's fingers tightening on her tablet, Anna cold-eyed with calculation, Carter impassive but listening hard.

Richard gave a thin smile.

'Choosing to come was the easy part. The hard part begins tonight'.

Trust, born in fire and humour, began to take root.

'Now, whilst I divest myself of Gerald, why don't we all retire to the sitting room for some parlour games? I'll be back shortly'.

They moved into the sitting room where pads and pencils were laid out. Richard joined them soon after, wholly back in Richard mode. He stood with his back to the fire, Mac at his side.

'You've all chosen to be here', Richard said evenly. 'That choice matters. But the Syndicate won't test us with kind words; they'll test us with pressure. Tonight is about starting to see how we think, how we work together, when the ground shifts beneath us'.

Mac dealt out the cards like a poker hand. Each bore a rough sketch of a situation. 'No wrong answers', he growled. 'But plenty of bad ones'.

Anna read hers first. A bank run begins at 09:00. You've got half an hour and incomplete data. First three calls you make?

'Clients, regulators, comms', she said without hesitation. 'Contain panic before it spreads'.

Lydia turned her card. An ally is late to a meeting. A stranger sits down in his place, claiming to be a substitute. What do you do?

'Ask a control question', she said quickly. 'Something only our ally would know. No confirmation, no deal'.

Mary, who had been quietly turning her card over, cleared her throat. A shipment of documents arrives, thousands of pages. Half are genuine. Half are forged. You've got an hour before they go to the board. What's your first move?

Her eyes flicked to the others, then back to Richard. 'Sample check. Pick five at random and drill deep. If I find anomalies, I widen the net. If they're clean, I triangulate against external records. An hour isn't long, so I'd aim to prove the forgery, not the truth. Lies leave fingerprints faster'.

Mac's eyebrows rose. Richard gave the smallest nod. 'Sound thinking'.

Then Mac slid a card across to Carter. 'Your turn, old man'.

Carter squinted at the handwriting, then read aloud. *A visitor arrives at reception, ID perfect, papers flawless. But something in his story doesn't fit. What do you do?*

The former RMP's reply came without pause. 'Delay. Offer him coffee, call for verification through a back channel he can't see. While he's sipping, run CCTV on his route in, check if anyone's shadowing him. And if the gut still says wrong, don't let him past the desk. Ever. Better to take flak for blocking the right man than regret letting in the wrong one'.

The table went quiet for a beat. Richard leaned back, eyes narrowed in approval. 'And that's why the front desk may be our strongest line of defence'.

He dealt with the last scenario himself. *Safe house. Midnight. There's a knock at the door. The man outside gives the right password, but something in his eyes tells you it's wrong. What's your move?*

Silence stretched. Anna shifted in her seat. Lydia said, 'Bolt the door. Passwords can be stolen. Instincts can't'.

Anna added quietly, 'And above all else, I'd call you. Because if it's wrong, I'd rather face it with you than open that door alone'.

Richard let the weight of that hang in the room before closing the folder.

'Good. Remember this. The Syndicate won't come at us with guns in the street. They'll come with confusion, pressure, and temptation. If you can keep your heads here, you stand a chance of keeping them when it counts'.

The fire popped, throwing sparks against the grate. For the first time, the room felt less like a board meeting and more like a patrol briefing.

The next morning, the dining room was transformed. Strong coffee, eggs, bacon, and toast. Papers lay beside plates. Richard stood at the head of the table, sketching out the framework of their campaign: financial probes, Syndicate watchers, Alpha's shadow across Westminster.

At the centre of the table sat a star-shaped conference phone, its LEDs blinking. Richard keyed in his grandfather's Iridium satphone number, waited for the static to settle, then raised a hand for quiet.

'Good morning, Grandfather. I have the team with me'.

A half-beat of silence, the faint lag of orbiting satellites, then Lord Richard's voice carried across the room, threaded with the hum of engines and the muted wash of the sea behind him. 'Good morning, ladies and gentlemen. I trust my grandson hasn't let you sleep too much'.

'Not a chance, sir', Mac muttered, to quiet laughter.

Lord Richard's tone warmed. 'And tell me, Anna, did Gerald put in an appearance last night? He was never one to miss out on a free glass of wine'.

Anna rolled her eyes, though there was humour in it now. 'Yes, my lord. As insufferable as ever'.

'Good', Lord Richard said, satisfied after a slight pause. 'Means the boy's learning'.

Carter shifted in his chair, eyes fixed on the speakerphone. The voice, the bearing, the quiet authority, it was the kind of presence he'd only ever seen in the very top tier of command. For a moment, he felt like he was back on parade, except this wasn't Sandhurst or Whitehall. This was something else entirely.

This, Carter thought, as the call rolled on, *is the premier division.*

The distant thump of rotor blades cut across the room. A few heads turned instinctively toward the window.

Mac frowned. 'A bit early for joy-riders'.

Richard didn't miss a beat. He flicked his marker against the whiteboard, sketching another box. 'The Staff tell me it's the air ambulance. Runs in and out of Maidstone hospital most weekends, much to their annoyance'.

Outside, the helicopter settled onto the west lawn. Two of the PM's close protection stepped out first, scanning the grounds. One of them slowed, eyeing a lone 'gamekeeper' standing at the tree line with a shotgun cradled loosely. To most, he was just part of the scenery.

'Bloody hell', the officer muttered to his partner. 'That's not a gamekeeper. That's ex-Para. What kind of estate is this place?'

His partner gave a dry grunt. 'The kind where the pheasants shoot back'.

Neither said another word, but their stance shifted: wary and impressed.

Moments later, the dining room doors opened. The Prime Minister entered, coat over his arm, drizzle still clinging to his shoulders. He paused, surveying the table with a half-smile.

'I was in the neighbourhood', he said lightly, 'and thought I'd drop in for a decent bacon sandwich. They just can't get it right at Downing Street'.

The room froze. Cups halted halfway to mouths; forks hung in mid-air. Lydia blinked, and Anna's pen slipped from her fingers.

Even the faint shipboard sounds in the background quieted, as if Lord Richard too had leaned toward the line.

Richard stepped in without hesitation. 'Prime Minister, allow me. Anna Harrington, Administration and Logistics. Lydia McCarthy, Chief of Staff. James Carter, our eyes and ears. Mac McAllister, Regimental Sergeant Major, retired. He's keeping us safe, and you can thank him for the 'gamekeepers'. And lastly, Mary, whose work in the archives has brought us this far in the campaign. And on the line, my grandfather, Lord Richard'.

The PM inclined his head to each in turn, the faintest flicker of recognition in his eyes.

Mac broke the silence, his voice low but carrying. 'Christ... it's the bloody Prime Minister'.

The PM's smile widened a fraction. 'I've been called worse, RSM'.

That earned a ripple of nervous laughter, just enough to break the spell. Lydia leaned back slowly, eyes narrowing as she studied the new arrival. 'Well', she said, voice cool, 'I suppose that settles it. This isn't just about the bank anymore'.

The Prime Minister gave her a nod of acknowledgment, neither confirming nor denying.

Richard uncapped a marker and turned to the whiteboard. With deliberate strokes, he sketched a pyramid. At its apex, he wrote a single name: Alpha. Beneath, he built descending layers of boxes: cash flow, shell companies, muscle, political cut-outs, the scaffolding that held the figurehead in place.

Next, he drew two more pyramids, one on either side, each crowned with a question mark. Then, above all three, he added a larger question mark that loomed over the whole diagram.

'This', Richard said, tapping the central structure, 'is the UK region, possibly even Europe. These', he indicated the flanking pyramids, 'are other regions. We don't yet know which. And this', he tapped the question mark above them, 'represents the ultimate controllers. Whoever sits above Alpha, and above everyone like him'.

He tapped the central pyramid again. 'For now, we go after what we know. The rest are tomorrow's battle'.

'The Syndicate looks solid, but it's a house of cards. These layers are the low-hanging fruit. We will target them first, expose them, isolate them, then flip them. Each time one falls, the rest scramble. Panic sets in, and it spreads. By the time Alpha looks down, there'll be nothing left holding him up'.

Lydia leaned forward. 'It's the oldest trick: set people against each other, then move in while everything wobbles'.

Mary cleared her throat. 'From the analysis that I've already done, there are some names that need closer examination. Some could be monitored, perhaps even flipped if they're weak. We don't want to burn all assets too quickly'.

She hesitated, glancing at her tablet. 'Two of the French directors in particular. On paper, they're clean, old Paris connections, but the numbers reek of Syndicate handling. They're valuable in Brussels, though. If they can be peeled away from Alpha's shadow, they might serve us better alive than gone'.

Lydia's eyebrow arched. 'Or they could undermine us completely while we sit around waiting for them to choose a side'.

Richard's smile was thin. 'I've already accounted for that. Their resignations are signed and waiting. All that's left is the date I write on them. Monday will show whether they're worth keeping on ice... or cut loose immediately'.

Mac folded his arms. 'And if they wobble?'

'Then they're liabilities', Richard said flatly. 'And we don't carry liabilities'.

He let that hang before adding, 'Kicks come first. Monday morning, they won't be given time to clear their desks. They will be escorted out, clean and final'. He looked across the table. 'Mac, get two of your most trustworthy lads for the escort. Quiet professionals. No mistakes'.

Mary cleared her throat softly. 'That's the visible fight. But there's another'. She angled her tablet so the faint glow lit the pages of her notes. 'I've been tracking trades on AIM — the small-cap end of the London market. Biotech, junior miners, start-ups. The kind of stocks that wobble when bad luck strikes'.

Richard frowned. 'Bad luck?'

She nodded. 'A lab fire here, a supply chain tangle there, a regulatory hiccup. Coincidence, maybe, but the timing is too clean. Every time, short positions are placed just before the blow lands. Someone knew the bad luck was coming and made money off it'.

Lydia's eyes narrowed. 'That's not trading. That's a protection racket in pinstripes'.

Mary's voice was quiet, but it carried. 'If the Syndicate can break companies like that at will, they don't need to own the whole market. They just need everyone to fear them'.

The table fell silent again, the scale of the thing settling in. Richard tapped the table once with his pencil, as if marking a target on a map.

'Then after the kickouts, that's our next priority. Mary, would you mind keeping an eye on the markets? As soon as you spot a short, let Mac know. Mac, make sure they don't have any 'accidents'. It might not be a killer blow to the Syndicate, but it'll sure as hell interrupt their cash flow'.

Mac gave a single nod. 'Consider it done'.

The Prime Minister leaned forward, eyes sharp. 'That's how you do it in the field. Disrupt the chain, scatter the unit before they know what's hit them. Logistics first, then disruption. Choke the supply and the fight ends itself'.

Richard gave a short nod of acknowledgement.

The PM glanced around the table, then back to him.

'And for the record, Richard, you're in command here, not me. My role is to keep the roof from collapsing while you dismantle the foundations. I'll hold off the press and Parliament as long as I can. If you stumble into the law, the Attorney General will see you don't stay there. And if the worst comes to the worst', his voice dropped a fraction, 'the Palace still knows how to tidy things up quietly. You and your squad do the rest'.

On the phone from his cruise, Lord Richard's voice rumbled with approval. 'Well judged. Strike fast, keep the pressure on, and never give them time to regroup. Now let's get to work'.

The patrol bent forward, pens scratching, voices low but purposeful. The Prime Minister listened without interruption, his presence both shield and endorsement.

Later, as the others dispersed, the Prime Minister lingered. He caught Richard's eye. 'Library?'

Behind closed doors, among the oak shelves and leather bindings, his tone grew harder. 'You've set out a sound plan, but don't mistake Alpha for a man who will wait patiently while you pull his house down around him. When you hit his supports, he'll feel it, and he'll strike back. Not at you directly, not first, but he'll go for your flanks. Friends. Family. He'll test whether you can protect them while keeping the pressure on him'.

Richard's jaw tightened. 'He's already tried'.

'Yes, I've heard', the Prime Minister said. 'But he'll try again, only more inventive. You need to be ready. I'll cover what I can in Westminster, but outside it? That's yours'.

Richard gave a single, firm nod. 'Then let him come'.

The Prime Minister allowed the ghost of a smile. 'His weakness is that he still thinks you're just the spoilt Australian heir. You can use that, hiding in plain sight until you're ready to spring the trap'.

He shrugged on his coat. 'Keep me in the picture, and when the cards start falling, I'll make sure the house doesn't collapse on you, too'.

Outside, the steady chop of rotor blades was already building again across the fields. The Prime Minister's protection team moved with quiet efficiency, shepherding him out through the side doors. A few minutes later, the helicopter lifted away into the sky, and Richard watched its navigation lights dwindling to a pinprick before returning to the hall.

Lydia stood there, coat over her arm, ready to leave for the station, the others having gone ahead to catch the train back to London.

'Heading back already?' he asked.

She nodded. 'Yeah, I have an early start on Monday, and I need to do some prep tomorrow, ready for then. You've given me a lot to think about. Wolves don't sleep'.

He hesitated a fraction, then smiled. 'Before you go to the station, will you join me for an early supper? Nothing formal. Just a local pub down the lane, and afterwards I can run you to the station'.

For the first time all weekend, her composure softened. 'OK, but don't expect me to go easy on you at the next board session', she said with a smile.

'I wouldn't dare', he said.

She climbed into the Defender beside him, eyeing the utilitarian dash and banks of concealed switches with a raised brow.

'Good grief, Richard, is this Gerald's alter ego, or just yours?'

The Defender crunched down the gravel drive.

He allowed himself a grin. 'Let's just say it does the job'.

From the dash came a soft chime, followed by a dry, neutral voice:

'Seat belts, please'.

Lydia blinked, then laughed. 'It talks?'

'Only when it thinks I need reminding', Richard said, easing the Defender onto the lane.

The Tickled Trout was warm with woodsmoke and the usual chatter. Over simple food and a single glass of wine apiece, the talk was lighter fragments of families, half-remembered campaigns on his side, half-forgotten battles of bureaucracy on hers, and how little either of them trusted the word retirement.

Richard swirled the glass. 'A local wine', he said. 'One of the few making a serious go of it'.

The landlord, passing by their table, overheard Richard and paused, amused. 'Brave souls, over in Tenterden', he said with a wry smile. 'Not much money in English wine yet — more hobby than business, if you ask me'.

'Maybe', Richard said, tasting again. 'But sometimes the hobbyists are the ones who change the ground beneath your feet'.

'Not bad', she said at last. 'Almost as good as your Gran's. Almost'.

Richard smiled faintly. 'High praise. Though Gran would probably tell you exactly what they did wrong in the barrel'.

Lydia glanced at the label again, her brows lifting. 'English wine in a country pub. Kent really is changing with the times'.

Richard raised his glass, eyes amused. 'Stranger still that it isn't half bad. Even I'm surprised'.

Her laugh came easily, the edge of formality slipping.

Afterwards, Richard drove her to the station, the Defender growling through narrow lanes. At the platform, she pulled on her coat and gave him a measured look. 'Next time, I'm buying'.

'Gladly', he said.

She boarded the train, sliding away into the dusk. Richard stood for a moment, the Defender's keys cold in his hand, before turning back for the drive to the manor.

The patrol was formed, and the campaign had begun. And perhaps, beyond the fight, there was room for something more.

In London, Alpha poured himself a late whisky in the study of his Westminster townhouse. The reports from the day were spread across the desk: markets, ministers, whispers from the City. But one sheet lay apart, brought in by his most trusted courier only an hour before.

Chequers. The Prime Minister's weekend residence. His man inside had sent a brief note: The PM arrived Friday evening, family in tow. Meetings scheduled with union leaders on Saturday. Little of interest.

Alpha read it twice, frowning. 'Little of interest', he muttered. The Prime Minister was careful, yes, but rarely invisible. No leaks of calls, no chatter from the civil service. Just silence.

He swirled the whisky in his glass, the amber catching the lamplight. 'Where did you go, old fox?' he murmured. 'And who did you see?'

The informer at Chequers would keep his ear open, of course. But for the first time in months, Alpha felt the faintest itch of unease. The Prime Minister had effectively vanished into a blind spot.

And Alpha hated blind spots.

Chapter 24: Cleaning House

It was a Monday morning. The rain had cleared, leaving pale light on the tall windows of the chairman's office. Richard sat behind the desk, Mary's list folded neatly before him. To anyone watching, it looked like an heir pressed into duty, carrying out his grandfather's will. The fiction was deliberate.

Anna slipped in first, crisp in a dark suit, a stack of envelopes in her arms. Each bore a name, severance pay enclosed, already signed under the crest of Aldridge Bank. She set them neatly on the desk, then glanced back towards the door where Mac's men stood waiting, silent and watchful.

'You'll want to know', she said quietly, 'the staff are already whispering. Not just about Mac's people. About you. Half the building saw you in *The Sunday Times Magazine* yesterday. It's all over the canteen this morning'.

The Sunday Times Magazine – Weekend Edition

Richard Aldridge: Soldier, Banker, Survivor

By Michael Denning, Political & Business Correspondent

He is the City's most eligible bachelor, the heir of an old dynasty, and a soldier who has swapped jungle fatigues for pinstripes. But can Richard Aldridge really bring battlefield grit to the boardroom of Aldridge Bank? Michael Denning meets the man behind the myth.

Inside the Aldridge townhouse, Richard Aldridge poured me a glass of Margaret River wine from his grandmother's own vineyard, he explained, with a flash of pride. It was a telling choice: tradition and family, but with roots reaching far beyond Britain's shores.

'I'm used to making decisions with half the information and none of the time', he said evenly. 'The City is hardly more dangerous than Dili or Pristina. The stakes are just... measured differently'.

His CV in finance may be sparse, but his record in uniform is not. Tours with Australia's Special Air Service Regiment included East Timor and Sierra Leone, with what he drily calls 'a little holiday in the Balkans' alongside the UK's own SAS during the Kosovo campaign.

The Aldridge family is no stranger to fracture: scandal, rivalry, and inheritance disputes have all tested the line. Yet the institution endured. 'Families fracture', he admitted. 'But they also endure. We're proof of that. The bank outlasted the Great Depression, the Blitz, and every attempted takeover since. I intend it to outlast me, too'.

Society pages have dubbed him the City's most eligible bachelor. He grimaced at the label: 'The tabloids will write what they like. My job is to keep the bank standing and my family safe. Anything else will have to wait'.

Downstairs, a knot of junior analysts and clerks crowded round a table, the glossy spread flattened between their coffee cups.

'Listen to this bit', one of them read aloud, tapping the page:

'I'm used to making decisions with half the information and none of the time', Aldridge told me. 'The City is hardly more dangerous than Dili or Pristina. The stakes are just... measured differently'.

Another snorted. 'Measured differently? Sounds like he thinks running a bank is like running a war'.

'Maybe it is', said a third, nodding at the pull-quote splashed in bold across the margin:

'For centuries, the Aldridge Bank has resisted influence, even when it meant standing alone. That will not change while I am here'.

They bent closer, pointing at the photo of Richard in the townhouse drawing room, wineglass in hand beneath the gaze of a long-dead Marquess.

'Eligible bachelor, soldier, banker', one of them murmured. 'Depending on who you ask, he's either our saviour or our undoing'.

The article ran across two glossy pages, photo left, profile right, a bold pull-quote cutting through the centre.

Upstairs, Anna gave Richard a measured look.

'It's the talk of the bank. The younger analysts think you're a hero. The old guard thinks you're reckless. Everyone else just wants to know if the wine in that photograph was really your grandmother's'.

Richard leaned back in the chairman's chair, unreadable. 'Good', he said at last. 'Then the article did its work'.

He inclined his head to Anna. 'Thank you. Exactly why I rely on you. Draft an all-hands in my name. Something simple, steadying'.

Within the hour, the message was in every inbox:

From the Chairman

Subject: Security & Resilience Review

In the coming weeks, you will notice new faces in and around the building. They are part of a comprehensive security and resilience review commissioned by the board.

Their remit is straightforward: to ensure Aldridge Bank is fit for purpose in an uncertain world, safeguarding both our people and our clients.

Please extend them the same courtesy you would to any colleague. Any questions should be directed to my office.

– R.A.

Richard scanned the final draft on his laptop before it went out and allowed himself a faint smile.

'That will settle the nerves. Professional. Calm. No one will look twice at Mac now'.

He inclined his head to Anna.

'Precisely. And thank you, you saw the gap before it became a problem. I can see now why my grandfather leaned on you'.

He tapped the folded list once with his forefinger, then set it aside.

'Grandfather's instructions are clear', he said evenly, voice pitched for the corners of the room. 'Each name will be called in turn. They'll be given their notice and escorted from the building, mainly for the benefit of anybody listening in. No delays, no discussions. Their personal effects will be boxed and delivered this afternoon'.

He didn't elaborate. He didn't need to.

The first purge had been a shock and spectacle, Richard reflected: a statement that no one was untouchable. This was different. This was housekeeping. No speeches, no theatrics. Just names on a list, each ticked off until the rot was gone.

The first name was called. A senior manager entered, face tight with suspicion. Anna handed him the envelope without a word. Mac's men stood ready, flanking the doorway.

'What's this?' the man demanded, tearing it open. His voice rose as he scanned the papers. 'Suspension? On full pay? You can't just... what about my things?'

Richard didn't even look up.

'They'll be sent to your home. Gross misconduct requires investigation. That's what this is. You're suspended until the process concludes. HR is here to ensure it's done correctly'. He gestured faintly to the quiet woman seated by the wall, clipboard in hand.

The manager's voice broke into anger.

'After twenty years, this is it? A piece of paper and two goons?'

Richard slid the next envelope across the desk as though the man were already gone. The dismissal was total. Mac's men moved in, firm but calm, guiding him out. His protests echoed down the hall, fading quickly.

The second name was called. This one left in silence, white as chalk, the envelope clutched in trembling hands.

By the third, the rhythm was set. No drama now, only inevitability. One by one, the list shortened, the absences accumulating. In under an hour, the office was quiet again, a row of empty desks marking the fall of those who had thought themselves untouchable.

Richard closed the folder, slid it into a drawer, and leaned back. Outwardly, he looked every inch the reluctant heir forced to act in his grandfather's shadow. Inwardly, he knew the purge had gone exactly to plan: fast, clean, absolute.

He straightened, glanced at Anna, and nodded once. 'Would you mind patching me through to the all-hands line?'

A few minutes later, the tinny chime of the conference bridge echoed through the room. Green lights blinked as departments joined: managers and staff, all waiting to hear the new chairman speak.

Richard's voice was calm, measured, pitched for trust.

'Ladies and gentlemen, you've seen today that certain individuals have been suspended pending investigation. That was not a decision taken lightly, but it was necessary. Unfortunately, there may be more to come. Bad apples cannot be allowed to spoil the whole harvest'.

He let the words settle before continuing.

'For the good of the Bank, we will be thorough, and we will be fair. My door is open to anyone who has concerns or information that may help us protect what we've built. This is your Bank as much as mine, and I will not see it compromised'.

There was a beat of silence on the line. Somewhere in the background, a cough was heard, the shuffle of papers. Then the conference system clicked off, leaving only the hush of the office once more.

Richard exhaled, his expression unreadable. If anyone in the Syndicate ranks had heard the invitation, they would know exactly what it meant.

The silence after the purge was sharp enough to hear a paper clip drop. Richard let it settle, then pushed back from the desk.

'That's done', he said clearly, for the bugs' benefit. 'Now we talk about what isn't'.

A knock at the door. Lydia stepped in, Anna rising to meet her, both carrying fresh files. Mary followed a moment later, pale from the morning's work. They took their seats.

Richard gestured toward the table, then—without hurry—opened his drawer and flicked on the scrambler. A faint hiss filled the corners of the room, swallowing the walls; a reminder they were now speaking in a register the Syndicate couldn't overhear.

'We've a gap to fill: Comms and IT. Someone who can go deeper than policy and paperwork—who can think like the threats we face. Anyone come to mind?'

Anna exchanged a glance with Mary before speaking carefully. 'There is someone. Graham Foster. Head of IT—systems man to his bones. He's probably forgotten more than most people ever knew. On a good day, he could trade notes with the best, and he's written the odd piece for *Computer Weekly*'.

Richard's brow lifted a fraction. 'And on a bad day?'

Anna hesitated. 'That's the problem. His wife walked out six months ago. Since then, he's been drinking. Sometimes late in, sometimes still smelling of it. He tries to hide it, mostly. But not well enough'.

Richard regarded her, compassion flickering behind the control. 'You're reluctant to put him forward—which means you still think he's worth it'.

Anna nodded. 'Because underneath the mess, the brilliance is still there. If we don't use him, someone else will. And we can't afford to ignore that weakness'.

Richard leaned back, eyes on the empty chair opposite him. He thought of field patrols—the one post you never left uncovered was signals, no matter how rough the operator looked after weeks in the bush.

'He's got baggage', Richard said at last. 'But if he can walk through the door sober and stay that way, we'll take him. Lydia, you'll judge if he's fit. Anna, get him up here this afternoon. And if he stumbles again, I want you to say it straight. No shielding him'.

Each gave a short nod, the decision settling like a weight over the empty chair.

Richard leaned back, considering. 'Anna, one more thing, can you have the French directors brought up? Together, please'.

When they entered half an hour later, Richard was alone behind his desk. Their resignation letters lay open before him; his grandfather's heavy fountain pen balanced idly between his fingers.

He didn't bother with pleasantries. 'You know as well as I do that a man can't serve two masters. At this table, there's no room for divided loyalties'. He tapped the nib lightly against the paper. 'So, your decision. Do I date these today, or do I put the pen away?'

The elder of the two bristled. 'Monsieur Aldridge, we have always served the interests of the Bank'.

'Spare me', Richard cut in. 'I've seen the Syndicate's fingerprints all over your numbers. Brussels, Paris, Luxembourg— useful doors, yes. But those doors swing both ways. You'll either hold them open for me… or I'll shut them in your faces permanently'.

A silence, taut as wire. The younger man glanced at his colleague, then back at the pen hovering over his own resignation. 'And if we choose you?'

'Then you stay in your seats. You carry weight in Europe, and I'll use it. But understand me that one whisper to Alpha, one hesitation when I call, and you're gone. No warning, no second chance'.

They exchanged a look, pride warring with calculation. At last, the elder inclined his head. 'We will serve'.

Richard let the pen hover a moment longer, then set it down with deliberate care. 'Good. You've chosen wisely. Go back downstairs. Look steady, look loyal. No one else needs to know what was decided in this room'.

They left in silence, and Richard closed the folder. Pieces shifting, one layer at a time. He reached for his phone and, from his grandfather's little black book, ensuring that the scrambler was still active, dialled a number.

'Buster, they're leaving now. Can you put some discreet eyes on them for me? I want to know just how steady their loyalties are. One misstep, and they'll have written their own resignations'.

They did not disappoint. By noon, Buster's cousins had the elder in their sights, already in St James's, shaking hands with a Syndicate intermediary whose face was well known from the Hereford files. The younger played it cooler, retreating home to Knightsbridge. But a quiet watcher on a motorbike caught him making an overseas call, bouncing through Paris to numbers that reeked of Syndicate shell companies.

Richard tapped the desk once with a fingernail, his grandfather's pen in his hand. The resignation letters were dated. All but one.

Adrien's envelope lay untouched at the bottom of the stack. His manner, his contacts, the faint stink of Syndicate clung to him, but there was no proof. Not yet. To date, it is now clean and decisive. To leave it undated was dangerous.

Richard set the pen down, decision deferred. 'One more piece', he murmured. 'One more move, then we'll see where you really stand, Adrien'.

No sooner had he put the phone down to Buster than it rang again. Mary's voice was crisp in his ear.

'I've just spotted unusual shorts against a transport firm out in Billericay. Medium-sized, not HGV, seven-and-a-half tonne trucks, mostly high-value secure contracts with the London auction houses. The timing stinks; whoever's betting against them knows something is about to go wrong'.

Richard's jaw tightened. He called Mac immediately.

'Looks like there's a firm in Essex that could do with somebody riding shotgun for them. Quiet presence, nothing flashy. Make sure whatever 'bad luck' was lined up doesn't land'.

That afternoon, Anna tapped lightly at the door. 'Foster's outside', she said. 'Looks like he's about to be shot at dawn'.

Richard gave a dry smile. 'Send him in'.

Graham Foster entered stiffly, shoulders hunched, tie crooked, a battered notebook clutched in one hand. Its pages bristled with half-sketched diagrams and notes in a crabbed scrawl. He adjusted his glasses nervously as the door shut behind him. That morning, colleagues had been called into this office and never seen again. Was this his turn?

'Sit down, Mr Foster', Richard said, not unkindly.

Foster obeyed, perched on the edge of the chair like it might collapse.

Richard let the silence stretch just long enough to see the nerves twist, then leaned forward. 'You know why you're here?'

Foster swallowed. 'I—assume it's the same as the others. If so, I'll go quietly. I won't make trouble'.

Richard shook his head. 'That's not why you're here. You're not being shown the door. You're being asked to step up'.

Foster blinked, uncertain.

'I know about your problems', Richard continued. 'Your marriage. The drinking. The mornings when you come in half-drowned. Don't bother to deny it. Anna vouched for your mind and, more importantly, vouched for your skill and you personally. Because of that, you've still got a place at this Bank if you're willing to stand'.

Foster's posture shifted, slowly, like a man remembering he had a spine. He tugged his tie straight, colour returning to his face.

'I... I don't know what to say', he murmured.

'Say yes', Richard told him. 'And mean it. Because from this moment, you're part of my team. There are bad apples in this Bank, and I am determined to root them out. We need you sharp, steady, and sober. And remember, my door is always open. If you need help in any way, I'm here. And if you need any external specialist help with your problems, you've only to ask'.

Foster nodded, more firmly now. 'Yes. I can do that'.

Richard stood, meeting his eyes. 'Good. Then do it. But listen carefully: out there, you keep the mask on. Let them think you're still the office drunk, a liability nobody notices. But in here, with me, we know different'.

For the first time in months, Graham Foster smiled. Not a wide grin, but enough that it carried weight. 'Understood'.

Richard extended his hand. Foster shook it, grip firm, shoulders squared. When he left the office, he no longer looked like a ghost of himself, but a man returning to the fight.

When the door clicked shut, Anna arched a brow. 'Well, he didn't look like a man on his way to the gallows anymore'.

Anna allowed herself the faintest smile. 'Beneath the hangovers and the nicotine stains, he's got more raw talent than anybody in the IT world. He just needed someone to give him a reason to stand up straight again'.

Mary was less convinced, arms folded tight. 'I hope you're right. If he stumbles, it won't just be his reputation on the line'.

Richard closed the file in front of him and tapped it once with the flat of his hand. 'He won't stumble. Not now. Out there, he's still the office drunk. Let them underestimate him. But in here, he's one of us. And he knows it. But just to be sure, I'll get a discreet eye on him for a couple of days'.

The room fell quiet. Another piece of the patrol had slotted into place.

That evening, Richard shrugged on his coat as he prepared to leave for a meeting with Fiona that she had called earlier to make. Down in the marble lobby, the cleaners were at work, and the usual hum of after-hours chatter was absent.

Carter was waiting by the doors, outwardly the same unflappable security man he'd always been. But now he was Richard's eyes as much as the Bank's.

'Sir', Carter said quietly, falling in step as Richard crossed the lobby. 'We've got company. Across the street. Same man, same patch of rail, since morning. He doesn't appear to be a tourist, nor is he waiting for anyone. He's just watching too much, mostly at the Bank and moving too little'.

Richard adjusted his coat, glancing idly at his reflection in the glass doors. 'You're sure?'

'Certain', Carter replied. 'Old habits, sir. I know a loiterer when I see one'.

Richard let his gaze slide past the revolving door. A man in a cheap raincoat leaned under a lamppost, cigarette burning down slow. Too still. Too patient.

'Good eye', Richard murmured. 'If he's there tomorrow, log it. If he's joined by friends, let me know before they've had time to light a second cigarette'.

'Yes, sir'.

Richard gave him a brief nod and stepped out into the dusk. His stride was easy, unhurried, but his mind was already plotting alternate routes to Fiona and three ways to flush a tail if one was on him.

The yard at Billericay was all corrugated sheds and diesel smell, floodlights throwing hard pools of light across the gravel. Mac found the owner in a cramped office above the weighbridge, jacket off, tie loosened, the ledger still open on his desk.

'Mr Ellis?' Mac said, stepping in. 'Name's Mac. I look after certain interests in the City. Thought we should talk'.

Ellis sized him up in a glance, then leaned back in his chair. 'If you're another one telling me to sell, save your breath. I've had enough suits in here the last six months, all with the same bloody offer'.

Mac shook his head. 'Not here to buy you out. Here to keep you standing. I hear you've had pressure. Maybe more than pressure'.

Ellis gave a short, bitter laugh. 'Pressure's one word. First, it was hints at how a man my age should think of retirement, how easy it'd be to cash out. Then it was offers, generous ones. When I said no, it turned sour. The brakes cut on one of my trucks. Anonymous calls at night. Bloke in a pub telling me accidents happen'. His jaw tightened. 'I built this firm from two vans. I'm damned if I'll hand it over'.

Mac nodded once, expression unreadable. 'Then we understand each other. You've got a contract coming up. Sotheby's run?'

Ellis blinked, surprised. 'That's right. We've got three loads next week: paintings, jewellery, the kind of stuff people kill for. High value, tight schedule. I've already told the client we'd deliver, but truth be told...' He spread his hands. 'I've been losing sleep'.

'That's where we come in', Mac said simply. 'You run your trucks as normal. But for that job, you'll have a couple of quiet lads riding shotgun. Nothing flashy, nothing in the papers. Just enough to make sure your lorries don't run into any more bad luck'.

For the first time that night, Ellis let out a breath that wasn't anger. Relief softened his face. 'Then you've got yourself a deal. About bloody time someone was on my side'.

Elsewhere, Alpha stood by the window of his Westminster townhouse, phone pressed to his ear, the Thames glittering darkly beyond.

A voice on the line was hesitant. 'There's movement at Aldridge Bank, sir. A senior staff member has gone this morning. No reason given. No fanfare. Just... gone'.

Alpha's jaw tightened, though his tone remained silken. 'I see. And the boy?'

'No sign he was involved. Still just the chairman's puppet'.

'Perhaps'. Alpha ended the call, staring out at the river. Something in his gut itched. A silence where there should have been whispers.

The boy was still in his blind spot. And Alpha hated blind spots.

Chapter 25: The Savoy

The American Bar was low-lit and murmurous, polished brass and leather gleaming under discreet lamps. Richard paused at the entrance, letting his eyes adjust. He spotted Fiona immediately — not alone.

She sat in a corner booth, composed as ever, a glass already before her. Beside her was another woman: dark blazer, sharp eyes, posture that spoke of command even out of uniform.

Fiona rose slightly. 'Richard, thank you for coming'. Her hand brushed the other woman's arm. 'This is Clare, my partner'.

Clare extended a hand — firm grip, steady gaze. 'Detective Inspector, Metropolitan Police', she said, then added with a faint smile, 'Economic Crime Command — a long way of saying financial fraud, money laundering, and the sort of white-collar parasites who think they're untouchable'.

Her tone was dry, but her eyes were sharp, measuring the room as much as the people in it.

Richard inclined his head, amused and impressed in equal measure. 'You don't do half measures, Fiona'.

'Never', she said, settling back. 'Which is why I asked you here. There's something you need to know'.

The drinks arrived: gin and tonic for Fiona, scotch for Richard, something neat and untouched for Clare. Silence held a moment before Fiona broke it, her voice lower, edged with something like relief.

'I lied about Lord Richard's test results. He isn't dying. He isn't even ill. For a man his age, he's in remarkable health. The truth is, he could have another decade'.

Richard's glass paused midway. He said nothing, waiting.

'They made me do it', Fiona pressed on. 'I was approached by some people who were polite enough at first, but somehow, they had found out about us — about Clare and me. They threatened to ruin her career, to turn our lives into public fodder, unless I gave them the report they wanted: the one that said your grandfather only had a few months to live.

'So I wrote it. A lie. And I've carried it like a stone ever since. I still don't know why they wanted it, only that they left me no choice'.

Clare's jaw tightened, but she reached for Fiona's hand under the table. Richard saw it, and in that moment, the whole story needed no further explanation.

He set his glass down gently. 'So my grandfather isn't out of time?'

Fiona shook her head. 'No. He's sharper than half the men I see — twenty years younger. And I had to tell you before the lie swallowed us all'.

Richard leaned back, studying the two of them. He thought of the Syndicate, of the cruelty of their leverage, and of the man in Margaret River who had carried his secrets this long.

'Then we adjust', he said simply. 'We play them at their own game. If they think he's dying, fine — we let them keep thinking it. But you never carry that stone alone again, Fiona. Not while I'm here'.

For the first time that evening, Fiona's shoulders eased. Clare squeezed her hand.

The waiter hovered, discreet as the walls themselves. Richard raised his glass. 'To the truth and to using their lies against them'.

They clinked, quiet and deliberate, the noise of the bar swelling around them.

Richard let the silence sit a moment longer, then turned his gaze to Clare. 'Since you're here, DI, there's something you should hear. My analysts have been tracking a pattern of short sales placed against small firms on the AIM. Always just before a 'stroke of bad luck' — fire, accident, compliance snag. The timing is too neat. Someone knows before it happens, and they're cashing in'.

Clare's brow furrowed, interest sharpening. 'Market abuse wrapped as a coincidence. That's not just fraud — that's organised crime with a balance sheet'.

'Exactly', Richard said. 'One of the targets is a transport firm in Billericay. Medium outfit, high-value secure contracts. They've got a Sotheby's run due — paintings, jewellery. High-profile enough to hurt if it goes wrong'.

Fiona exhaled softly. 'You think they'll hit it?'

'I know they'll try', Richard replied. 'I've got men lined up to ride shotgun, but if your unit were to take an interest...'

Clare leaned back, eyes narrowing in thought. 'A sting. Catch them in the act. My team could justify a protective deployment: financial crime, market manipulation, and potential armed robbery. It ticks every box'. She looked at him steadily. 'But this doesn't come cheap, Richard. If we do it, it's because we're all in. No shadows, no surprises'.

Richard gave her a faint smile. 'Then let's make it official. You bring the badge, I'll bring the muscle. Between us, we'll make sure Sotheby's doesn't make tomorrow's scandal sheets'.

Clare raised her glass again, this time with steel in her eyes. 'To stop parasites'.

'And to a clean operation', Richard said, touching his glass to hers. The sound was soft but decisive.

The streets outside were quiet, the lamps casting long reflections across the pavement. Richard pulled his coat tighter as he stepped out into the Strand with Fiona and Clare. The two women were laughing quietly at some remembered line from earlier, their heels clicking on the pavement.

The sound of footsteps fell in behind them, much too close, too deliberate. Richard's neck prickled.

Two men, thickset in leather jackets, closed the distance near the mouth of an alley. The lead man shoved forward, voice low and ugly. 'Wallets. Purses. Now'.

Fiona froze. Clare's arm tightened around hers. Richard stepped half a pace in front, hands raised. 'Easy, gentlemen. No need for'

The second heavy swung. Richard moved with it: elbow to wrist, twist and down. Bone cracked. The man howled, collapsing against the wall.

The first lunged at Fiona. Richard was faster. His knee drove up, sharp and efficient, into the man's gut. He folded, gasping, and Richard guided him down as if steadying a drunk. Seconds — that was all it had taken.

A couple across the street turned at the noise, saw two thugs groaning on the pavement and a well-dressed man dabbing a split lip with a handkerchief while the two women clutched each other, wide-eyed.

'Ugly business, a bit like being back in Sydney', Richard said, slipping the handkerchief away. 'That's what comes of taking an evening stroll without a big mate beside you'.

He ushered Fiona and Clare on, their footsteps quickening as they crossed toward the car park.

Clare gave him a sidelong glance, still keeping her voice low. 'That wasn't luck. That was training. Military, not police'.

She let the silence hang for a beat, then added with the faintest curl of a smile, 'And if the ones riding shotgun on those lorries are half as good as that, God help the poor sods who try to take them'.

Richard's faint smile didn't reach his eyes. 'Old habits'.

Behind them, the heavies wheezed on the pavement, their mission failed. Across the road, behind a tinted windscreen, a man lowered a compact digital camcorder and reached for his mobile.

Not far from the West End, in a discreet Westminster apartment, the watcher's call was answered. The footage was short and grainy, but clear enough: Aldridge with the doctor and a woman, intimate and trusting. Alpha listened without comment, a glass untouched at his elbow.

'Follow him home', he said finally. 'No theatre. A road rage, a mugging, a crash-for-cash gone wrong. Whatever's clean. Just make sure he doesn't get up'.

The line went dead.

Back in the West End, after saying goodnight to Fiona and Clare, Richard got into the Defender and set off for the drive to the London house not far from the Strand in Belgravia. The Defender growled through the streets, and the rain that had threatened earlier had finally started. Richard kept his eyes on the mirrors. Same car, three turns running. It made every deviation he made — left, right, detour round the square — never once pulling ahead or peeling off. Whoever was behind him knew the rules of a tail.

He checked the mirror again. 'Looks like we've got ourselves a tail', he said under his breath — half a joke to himself.

To his surprise, a calm female voice replied, 'Defensive systems armed'.

A soft hydraulic thump followed at the rear as the concealed spike deployed. Richard blinked, then gave a quiet huff of disbelief. So the prototype *did* listen after all.

He glanced toward the dashboard. 'What else have you got hidden under there?' he muttered.

What looked like an ordinary retractable tow bar dropped into place — in reality, a hardened spike angled just high enough to punch through a radiator, hidden until the tail came too close.

It did. Too eager, radiator high and hot. One lurch forward, one sharp hiss — then a plume of steam burst into the night. The car slewed sideways, hazard lights flaring.

Richard kept the Defender steady, slowing just enough to catch the moment in his rear-view mirror. Doors slammed. Three men spilled into the road, weapons glinting, their rage plain even through the mist of steam. They shouted, waving knives and bats at the night, but the Defender was already pulling away.

He shifted up a gear, the spike retracting with a muted click. The mirror showed the stranded attackers fading into the dark, furious and helpless.

Alpha's plan had failed before it even began.

The Defender nosed back into the townhouse garage just after midnight, its engine ticking as it cooled. Richard killed the lights and sat a moment longer in the driver's seat, the journey replaying in his head. The Syndicate wasn't hiding their hand anymore.

Inside, the house was silent, the city beyond muted. Richard poured a whisky, leaned against the window, and looked out across the darkened square, the trees below swaying faintly in the night breeze. The commute from Canary Wharf to here — twenty-odd minutes on a clear run, twice that in traffic — was almost killing him. Tonight, it very nearly had. He set the glass down, decision forming clean and sharp. An apartment near the bank, quiet and discreet. Somewhere he could vanish to when needed, without a tail catching him between worlds.

The patrol was in place. The Syndicate were moving. And now, Richard thought grimly, so would he.

Chapter 26: Close to Home

Richard stood at the window of his office, looking down at the shimmer of the dock. The attempted hit on the Strand was already buried under reports and chatter, but the decision it forced was sharp and clear.

'The commute nearly got me killed', he said flatly. 'That ends today'.

Anna looked up from her notepad, calm as ever. 'Leave it to me. I'll get onto Chestertons in Marsh Wall straight away. Rent or buy?'

'Whichever is quickest'.

Lydia, standing by the table, frowned. 'If you're moving closer, personnel will need to update your file and make the adjustments'.

Richard hesitated. He understood what she meant: he didn't want Mac tied down with paperwork or babysitting him. But the logic was solid.

'Anna, sorry. Can I dump this on you? Make sure the right people are informed about my change of address'.

Before Lydia could reply, the door opened without ceremony. Graham Foster hurried in, glasses slipping down his nose, notebook clutched tight. Before Graham could say anything, Richard's hand shot up, while he turned on the scrambler. Once done, he gave Graham the thumbs-up to continue.

'We've got a problem', he said, breathless but sharp. 'I found something buried deep in the system. Trojan horse. It's been copying everything: reports, mails, financials, and exfiltrating it out. It's been hidden for months'.

Richard's eyes narrowed. 'Where to?'

Graham flipped open his notebook, pages dense with scribbled diagrams. 'Not sure. But the information's leaving the Bank. Could be a competitor, or something a lot scarier'.

The silence that followed was heavy.

Lydia broke it first. 'So we kill it. Put it down before it leaks another byte'.

Graham shook his head. 'Not so fast. We don't have to go all or nothing. I can keep it alive, but cage it. That means everyone here watches their language on the system and assumes anything typed or saved might walk straight to Alpha.

'At the same time, I can build a kill switch. One command from me, and the horse drops dead without a trace. They'll think it burned out on its own.

'And while it's breathing?' He tapped the scrawled diagrams. 'I can trace it. Work backwards through the ISPs. If we're lucky, we won't just know who is listening; we'll know where they are listening from'.

Richard leaned back, weighing it. It wasn't without risk, but it was better than choosing between blindness and exposure. 'Do it. Keep it leashed, keep it quiet. And Graham', his tone softened just enough to register, 'that's bloody good work'.

Foster straightened, pushing his glasses back up, a flicker of pride breaking through the nervous energy.

Richard looked around the room. 'We cut the rot yesterday. Now we bait the hook. Let's see what Alpha swallows'.

That night, the evening news hummed in the background of the boardroom.

'...a new record price at Sotheby's today for an eighteenth-century portrait fetching over forty million pounds. The auction house confirmed several more high-value consignments scheduled for transport this week. Security, as ever, remains discreet'.

Richard didn't glance at the screen, but Mac caught his eye across the table. The hook was baited.

The A13 was shrouded in mist reflecting off the headlights. Three unmarked lorries rolled in convoy, each cab carrying one of

Mac's men, alongside the driver, quiet reassurance more than muscle. Shadowing them, two plain vans.

The ambush came suddenly: a broken-down estate car slewed across the road, hazard lights blinking. Figures emerged from the dark, faces masked, crowbars and bats in their hands.

But before they reached the first lorry, the vans braked hard. Doors slammed open, and half a dozen men and women in plain clothes spilled out, warrant cards flashing, voices sharp. 'Metropolitan Police! Armed officers down, now!'

The would-be hijackers froze, caught between the roar of authority and the quiet menace of the men in the cabs who hadn't moved a muscle. One tried to run; Clare's people had him face down in the wet tarmac before he reached the verge.

By the time the convoy rolled on, the estate car sat abandoned, its hazards still winking in the rain. Police lights washed the scene in blue, the suspects cuffed and silent, and taken to West End Central, just off Savile Row, for questioning.

Elsewhere, Alpha stood in his Westminster study, the phone pressed white-knuckled to his ear.

'They delivered?' His voice was silken, but the anger beneath it was unmistakable.

'Yes, sir. On time. And... there were arrests'.

Alpha turned to the darkened square beyond the window. Forty million gone and the short still open. Every hour the price held, his margin bled. He had forty-eight hours before the cover call landed.

'Find out who interfered', he said, voice low and cold. 'And make them regret it'.

Two days later, the lift doors opened onto the thirty-seventh floor of Pan Peninsula, Canary Wharf's gleaming twin towers. Lydia stepped out beside Richard, the glass walls revealing London sprawled below them, the river looping silver through the Docklands, the dome of St Paul's a faint curve against the horizon.

Mat Adams from Chestertons was waiting in the corridor, his smile professional, clipboard in hand. 'Mr Aldridge, Ms McCarthy. Thank you for coming. We've arranged for you to see one of our short-term rentals. It's fully furnished, it has gym and pool access included. We can have the keys in your hand almost immediately if you're satisfied'.

The apartment was modern, with sleek lines and pale oak floors, furniture chosen for style more than warmth. Richard walked slowly through each room, opening cupboards, testing the weight of the balcony doors, and noting angles and vantage points without speaking. Lydia trailed him in silence, watching him assess the space less like a tenant and more like a soldier establishing a fallback position.

On the balcony, wind tugging at his coat, Richard finally spoke. 'This will do, thank you, Mat. Not home but close enough to pass for one'.

Mat produced a slim folder, his Chestertons logo pen already uncapped. 'Normally, this would take a few days. But your assistant was... persuasive. Everything's already in motion. If you could sign here and here, the Tenancy Progression team at our Tower Bridge branch will walk through the paperwork this afternoon, and you will have the keys by tomorrow evening. You can move in immediately'.

Richard glanced at Lydia, who only lifted an eyebrow in faint amusement. He signed without hesitation, the nib scratching against the paper. Speed mattered more than ceremony.

Mat gathered the documents, slipping them neatly back into the folder. 'Congratulations, Mr Aldridge. You'll find Pan Peninsula a very safe place to live, and there is a concierge downstairs to look after all your needs'.

Richard gave him a short nod, then turned back toward the wall of glass, watching the city lights spark to life in the dusk. A new foothold in London — closer to the fight, closer to danger, and exactly where he needed to be.

When he had gone, Richard stepped out onto the balcony. The lights of Docklands glittered against the water, the towers a forest of glass and steel. West India Quay lay barely a mile across the bendy bridge, a jogable distance along the waterfront. He made a mental note: some mornings he'd take that route instead of the Defender.

Not just for fitness, but to see the city as others did, anonymous among the runners, eyes sharp beneath the disguise of routine.

The next evening, with the keys finally in his hand, the apartment smelled faintly of garlic and rosemary. Richard had surprised himself by cooking, nothing elaborate, just pan-fried lamb and vegetables, something he hadn't done since Perth. The ritual was grounding; a reminder he could still take care of himself in ways that didn't involve orders or operations.

A knock at the door broke the quiet. He checked the camera, then opened it to find Lydia, a bottle of Rioja in hand.

'Housewarming', she said dryly, stepping inside before he could protest. 'Don't say I never bring gifts'.

Richard arched a brow. 'I thought housewarmings involved parties and half a dozen people trampling the carpet'.

Her mouth twitched. 'Consider this the SAS version. Lean, discreet, no witnesses'.

He let out the faintest chuckle and gestured towards the counter. 'You've timed it well. Food's nearly done'.

Her eyes flicked towards the pans, then back to him, surprised. 'You cook?'

'When I have to'. He pulled two plates from the cupboard. 'Don't tell the analysts. They'd think it undermines the mystique'.

She smiled properly at that, setting the wine down. 'Don't worry. Your secret's safe with me. Besides', her tone softened, 'everyone needs something normal. Even you'.

They ate without hurry, the city glittering beyond the glass. Conversation stayed light — travel, food, fragments of stories neither of them had shared before. For once, no operations, no reports, no weight of the Aldridge name pressing down on the moment.

When she rose to leave, Lydia collected her coat from the back of the chair. Richard walked her to the door, wineglass still in hand.

'Thank you for dinner', she said lightly. 'Not bad for a soldier in disguise'.

He tilted his head. 'Don't tell anyone. They'd never believe it'.

For a heartbeat, they stood close in the doorway, the quiet hum of the city seeping in from the balcony beyond. Lydia leaned in first, brushing her lips against his cheek just enough to linger, not quite enough to be casual.

Richard didn't move, but his eyes caught hers, sharp and searching. 'That', he said softly, 'was unexpected'.

Her mouth curved, almost a smile. 'Then you'd better get used to it'.

And with that, she was gone, the echo of the kiss still warm against his skin as the door clicked shut.

Richard stood for a long moment in the silence, then set the glass down carefully on the counter. A soldier could ignore wounds, bury pain, carry on without flinching, but this? This was different. He caught himself almost smiling, then shook his head, muttering under his breath:

'Dangerous territory, O'Connell. Very dangerous indeed'.

Next that day, back at the Bank in Graham's office, the blinds were half-drawn against the late afternoon sun, the room thick with the hum of machines and the scent of burnt coffee. Graham hunched over the terminal, notebook open beside him, glasses sliding down his nose as his fingers danced across the keys.

Richard, Lydia, Anna, and Mary watched from the table, each waiting in silence. Graham muttered under his breath, tapped a final command, then turned in his chair.

'It isn't just information leaving the Bank', he said, voice tight. 'The Trojan's been used to send messages to us. Someone's trying to communicate in a way only we'd notice. A message came through this morning. Encrypted — but not beyond me'.

He slid a printed transcript across the desk. Richard picked it up. The first line stopped him cold.

Gerald, old friend…

Only Jonathan would be trying to reach Gerald.

The others leaned in as Richard read aloud. Jonathan's voice unfurled in every oily word: alive, smug, desperate. He wrote of how the Syndicate's 'HR men' had tried to retire him, how he had planned ahead, how he had insurance.

And then, the bombshell:

Here's the truth: Alpha isn't the king you think he is. He's a muscle. A blunt instrument. Dangerous, yes, but he takes orders like the rest of us. From above. From the ones who really run it. They call themselves the Partners.

Richard read on, each phrase heavier than the last. The banker in the City. The U.S. senator. The PLA general from Beijing. The Australian media baron. The Russian oligarch. Together, the Syndicate's true masters: global, untouchable, united. *I can tell you more, but it has to be face-to-face, and I want protection.*

When he finished, silence pressed in.

Lydia was first to speak, eyes flashing. 'He's lying. He has to be. Jonathan was Alpha's lapdog. Now he wants us to believe he's sitting on the keys to the kingdom?'

Mac, standing in the doorway with arms folded, gave a grunt. 'Lapdogs bite if you feed them scraps. Maybe he did squirrel something away. But trusting him? That's suicide'.

Mary's voice was quieter, but steady. 'The structure fits. We've all suspected Alpha wasn't the top. This confirms it, or at least gives us enough to test'.

Anna tapped the page with one finger. 'And it explains the Trojan. Jonathan wasn't just covering himself; he was listening in. This could be real'.

Richard laid the paper down, expression unreadable. 'Real or not, he's made his offer. Protection for information'.

'Protection?' Lydia snapped. 'From us? After everything?'

Richard's gaze cut across her, cool and deliberate. 'Sometimes the dirtiest sources give the cleanest intelligence. We don't have to like him. We just have to use him'.

Mac leaned forward, voice a growl. 'And when he sells us out the second, it suits him?'

Richard stood, folding the transcript into his pocket. 'Then we make sure he never gets the chance'.

He looked to Anna. 'Draft a reply. Tell him yes, he'll get full protection in exchange for everything. Not drips, not crumbs. The banquet'.

Anna hesitated. 'And when he takes you at your word?'

Richard's mouth curved into something that wasn't quite a smile. 'Then I brief Clare. Jonathan gets his protection, the kind that comes with a warrant and steel bars. Safe from the Syndicate, but not from the law'.

Anna began to type, but Richard lifted a hand. 'Add this. I want to see him face-to-face'.

That brought Lydia's head up. 'You can't be serious'.

'I am', Richard said flatly. 'I want to look him in the eye. Smell the fear, weigh the truth for myself'.

Minutes later, the encrypted channel flared again. Jonathan's reply was brief.

Not London. Not your manor. Paris. Neutral ground. Tomorrow afternoon.

Mary frowned. 'Neutral ground for him, maybe, but for you it's exposure'.

Richard pocketed the transcript with finality. 'Then Paris it is'.

'Where?' Mac asked.

Anna scrolled the thread, lips tightening. 'He's suggested the Hôtel Lutetia. It's central and public. Busy enough that neither side can risk a scene'.

Richard nodded once. 'Good, we'll use the crowd. He'll no doubt think it's a cover, but in fact it's our shield'.

He turned, his eyes finding Lydia. 'Would you like to come with me?'

She studied him for a long moment, as though weighing whether he meant it as an order or an invitation. Then she gave the faintest of smiles. 'Try and stop me'.

As he turned back to the window, Anna asked if he wanted her to make the travel arrangements and book a hotel in Paris.

Richard's response was simple. 'Please, Anna, that would be good, thank you. And could we not have the same hotel that we are meeting in?' Then, as an afterthought: 'Oh, and Anna, would you be so good as to pull together everything we've got on Jonathan. I know just the person to hand it to before I leave. That way, the protection he's after will be waiting for him when our meeting ends'.

He didn't elaborate, but Anna caught the meaning: the authorities would be ready to take Jonathan into custody.

His thoughts had already shifted to Alpha and Jonathan. Alpha thought he held the reins. Jonathan thought he was clever enough to play both sides.

They were both wrong.

'The Partners', Richard said quietly. 'Now we know who's really at war with us. But if we can take out a lieutenant along the way, so be it'.

Chapter 27: The Road South

They didn't take the Eurostar from Waterloo to Paris. Anna worked with her usual efficiency, no raised brows when she suggested they take the train from Ashford International for discretion and a discreet Left Bank hotel with 'double interconnecting rooms' already waiting in Paris. Richard didn't comment. Neither did Lydia. But when Anna handed him the envelope with the tickets and confirmation slips, there had been the faintest trace of a smile in her eyes.

The Defender nosed out of Canary Wharf just after dusk, Richard at the wheel, Lydia beside him. He had collected her from her flat, pausing while she stuffed a few things into a bag. The sight of her home photographs on the mantel, a half-read novel on the coffee table was a reminder of the life she put on hold every time the Syndicate intruded.

The city gave way to suburbs, then to open roads, the lights thinning as the miles slid past. Above them, the sky was clear, scattered with hard, bright stars, the kind that promised a frost by morning. The hum of tyres on tarmac filled the silence. Neither spoke much; there was no need. The mission ahead, Jonathan's name at the centre of it, carried enough weight in the quiet.

By the time the Defender turned between the stone pillars of West Farleigh Manor, the night had settled thick and still. The manor stood waiting, its long windows glowing against the dark. The butler was already on the steps to take their bags. Supper was simple, the fire in the library burning low, the air heavy with history and expectation.

Later, Richard walked Lydia up the wide oak staircase, their footsteps hushed on the carpet. The gallery portraits watched as they reached the landing, their rooms facing one another across the corridor.

For a moment, they stood in the lamplight, the quiet of the house wrapping around them.

'Tomorrow, then', Lydia said softly, a small smile flickering at her lips.

'Tomorrow', Richard replied, his own smile edged with resolve.

The kiss was unhurried, lingering just long enough to leave no doubt of what lay between them. When they parted, she gave him a final look before retreating into her room. The door clicked shut.

Richard lingered a moment in the silence, then turned into his own room. He lay awake a long while, staring at the ceiling, knowing Lydia was too, just across the landing.

At first light, the Bentley purred at the steps, Mason in the driver's seat, immaculate as ever. Richard handed Lydia into the rear, the cabin already warmed against the early morning chill, leather soft beneath her hand. He settled beside her as the countryside blurred past hedgerows silvered with frost, fields just beginning to show the pale light of dawn.

Richard slipped a phone from his pocket and scrolled through his grandfather's Black Book until he found Luc's number. Luc answered on the second ring, his voice carrying that easy Parisian drawl.

'Mon capitaine', Luc said. 'It has been too long. And tell me, how is your grandfather? The old lion still roaring?'

A faint smile touched Richard's lips. 'He's on a slow boat to Margaret River with my grandmother. Making up for the time they lost. I imagine he's giving the crew hell and drinking the cellar dry'.

Luc chuckled warmly. 'Bon. That is how it should be'. His tone sharpened a notch. 'And you? You do not call me at dawn without a reason'.

'Hôtel Lutetia. This afternoon. I want discreet eyes, nothing heavy, nothing Jonathan can smell. Just enough to keep the roof from falling in'.

'Considéré fait', Luc replied. 'You will not see us, but we will see everything'.

Richard ended the call, slipped the phone away, and leaned back into the leather. Paris awaited. So did Jonathan.

The silence was companionable, the hum of the engine steady beneath them. Somewhere along the M20, between Junctions 8 and 9, as the road swept through open fields, Richard felt Lydia's hand brush lightly against his on the armrest. Neither of them shifted. The contact remained quiet, deliberate, unacknowledged, a thread between them stronger than words.

Even in that closeness, Richard's gaze drifted to the rear window now and then, noting the cars behind them, never quite trusting that they weren't being followed.

They drove on like that, side by side, until the glass and steel of Ashford International rose ahead.

Mason pulled up at the barrier and stepped out, opening the rear door. 'Safe travels, sir. Ma'am'.

Richard gave him a nod, and together he and Lydia crossed into the terminal. Security was brisk, the staff unbothered. Soon they were descending the escalator to the platform, the waiting Eurostar humming with power.

Side by side, they boarded. The doors closed with a hiss, and moments later the train slid into motion, carrying them east through the tunnel and toward Paris and Jonathan.

The Eurostar pulled into Gare du Nord just after midday, the great glass canopy echoing with voices and rolling luggage. Richard and Lydia disembarked among the crowd, unremarkable in their coats, two travellers among hundreds. Outside, a clear winter light lay across Paris, the air crisp with the promise of frost.

A black Peugeot eased to the kerb. Luc stepped out, scarf wound loosely at his throat, smile quick but eyes already scanning the street.

'Bienvenue à Paris', he said, embracing Richard briefly before turning to Lydia with a courtly nod. 'And you must be Mademoiselle McCarthy. An honour'.

Richard kept it business. 'The Lutetia?'

Luc's smile thinned. 'My people are in place. You will not see them, but they will see everything'. He slid back into the driver's seat and took them through the traffic, the city flashing past cafés spilling warmth onto pavements, motorbikes darting between lanes, the grey dome of Les Invalides beneath a cold sky.

At the Hôtel Lutetia, discreet staff guided them through the marble lobby to a private lounge. Jonathan was already there, lounging with that air of self-satisfaction Richard remembered too well. His suit was sharp, but his eyes were hollowed by sleepless nights.

'Gerald', Jonathan drawled, using the name like a taunt. 'And you've brought company. Brave, or foolish'.

Richard ignored the jab, taking a seat opposite. Lydia settled at his side, cool as glass.

The conversation was taut, Jonathan offering scraps of intelligence, Richard pressing for the banquet. Names, dates, fragments, all confirming the Partners' shadow across continents. Jonathan played his part, hinting at leverage, at secrets that could burn them all.

When at last Richard rose, Jonathan's smirk faltered.

'Protection, remember. You promised'.

'You'll have it', Richard said evenly. 'The kind that comes with handcuffs'.

He crossed to the door. Two plainclothes officers were already in the corridor, Clare's magic at work, the French police ready with a European Arrest Warrant in hand. Richard gave the faintest nod as he stepped past.

They entered without a word. Jonathan's protest died as one officer recited the charges in brisk French while the other snapped the cuffs shut. Fraud. Laundering. Conspiracy. The list was long, the evidence longer.

Jonathan twisted in outrage, eyes blazing at Richard in the doorway. 'You set me up'.

Richard met his stare, voice flat. 'No. You set yourself up. We just made it official'.

He turned on his heel and walked away, leaving Jonathan to the law he had thought would never touch him.

Later, Luc rejoined them at their hotel, leaning on the desk as Richard collected the room keys. He glanced at the brass tags. 'Ah, the Saint-Jacques. Sensible choice. Close enough to walk, far enough from the noise'. His eyes warmed. 'There is a bistro two streets over, Le Petit Marché. Nothing grand, but real Paris. Good food, good wine, no tourists. Come, eat with me. You'll need it after Jonathan'.

An hour later, the three of them sat at a small table by the fogged window. The air smelled of garlic and butter; a chalkboard listed tonight's *plats du jour*. Luc ordered a carafe of Burgundy, and soon the table was filled with cassoulet, duck confit, and baskets of bread.

For a time, they let conversation drift from Paris to food, to memories of campaigns past. Then, over the rim of his glass, Luc said quietly, 'I have never met the man, but you know Jonathan is not finished. He plays to survive. But he fears you now. And that, mon capitaine, may be the best leverage of all'.

Richard said nothing, only raised his glass. Lydia's hand brushed his beneath the table, a small anchor against the storm gathering again beyond Paris.

The walk back to the hotel was short, the air sharp with frost, their breath clouding in the lamplight. Paris glimmered around them with shuttered shops, the glow of a late café, the faint echo of laughter spilling from a bar.

At the Saint-Jacques, Luc parted from them at the entrance with a quick embrace and a promise of eyes on the street until dawn. Richard and Lydia crossed the lobby in silence, the hush of carpeted corridors wrapping around them as they climbed to the third floor.

The receptionist had been discreet: adjoining rooms, keys handed over without comment.

Richard unlocked his door and waited as Lydia did the same next door. For a moment, they lingered in their separate thresholds, the quiet of the hotel pressing close, the city muffled outside.

Their eyes met. No words, no declaration, just the weight of everything shared, and everything waiting ahead. Lydia's smile was small but certain, the kind that closed the distance without a step.

Richard's hand shifted in his pocket, brushing against the folded slip he'd been given at reception. A single line in the receptionist's tidy script: *Message from Detective Inspector Clare Bennett — Call me. He's already bargaining.*

The warmth of Lydia's smile lingered, but in Richard's mind the game was already moving again. Jonathan wasn't finished. Not yet.

Richard inclined his head, almost a bow. 'Goodnight, Lydia'.

'Goodnight, Richard'.

The doors closed, almost in unison. But the pause that lingered, the thin sliver of light under the adjoining door, told a different story.

By morning, only one bed had been slept in. They ate breakfast together in the room, coffee and croissants balanced on the side table, sunlight spilling through the shutters. No words were needed. From that night, their relationship was changed forever.

By day, they were comrades; in private, they were now something more, partners, bound by trust and desire as much as by the mission.

Outside, morning broke clear and cold over Paris, the rooftops glazed with frost, chimney smoke curling into a pale sky. After breakfast, Richard stood at the window, watching the city slowly come to life: street sweepers brushing pavements, the first delivery vans rattling through narrow streets. Behind him, Lydia appeared, already dressed, coat buttoned, eyes bright though she had slept little.

Neither spoke of the night. Something had shifted, and the silence between them was no longer the old silence of comradeship but a newer, closer thing, dangerous in its own way because the mission had not ended.

By mid-morning, they were back at Gare du Nord, the Eurostar platform crowded with travellers, coffee steaming in paper cups. Richard kept a watchful eye on the concourse, but Luc's quiet nod from a distance was reassurance enough: they had not been followed.

The train slid out beneath the city, carrying them west. Frost still clung to the fields of northern France, the land flat and wide beneath the hard winter sun. Lydia read a file without really turning the pages; Richard stared at the blur of hedgerows, already planning the next moves against the syndicate and the Partners.

Hours later, the Eurostar slid into Ashford International, brakes sighing as the train came to rest. Outside, Mason was already waiting, the Bentley drawn up by the kerb, its engine humming gently against the winter chill. He bowed his head in greeting as Richard and Lydia stepped out from the station.

'Sir. Ma'am'. His tone was clipped but warm. He relieved Richard of the bags, opened the rear door, and ushered them into the warmth of the cabin. The leather was already heated; the glass misted faintly from the difference in temperature.

The drive through Kent was brisk, the countryside dipped in winter light, hedgerows rimed with frost. Conversation was spare, the comfort of silence more than the absence of words. By the time they turned into the long approach of West Farleigh Manor, dusk was gathering again.

The butler was at the door before the engine stilled, immaculate in a tailored black suit with a crisp white shirt and dark silk tie, gloves folded neatly in his hands. He opened Lydia's door first, offering a steady hand as she stepped out.

'Safe journey, ma'am?' he asked politely.

'Very', Lydia said, her smile warming the winter air.

Richard followed her up the steps, but Mason lingered a moment, setting his driver's gloves on the hall table as the staff glanced towards him expectantly. He allowed himself the faintest of smiles.

'I've just met the next Lady Aldridge', he said simply.

The words settled among them like a benediction: quiet, certain, and true.

The evening passed quietly. Dinner was simple but well prepared, served in the smaller dining room by staff who, though discreet, could not hide their curiosity at the woman seated at Richard's side. Later, the house settled into silence, leaving only the crackle of the fire and the unspoken sense that Paris had changed everything between them.

Morning broke clear and sharp, frost whitening the gravel drive. Mason had brought the Defender round to the steps, engine warming in the cold air. He stood by the open door as Richard and Lydia approached, handing it over for their drive back to London and whatever waited for them.

Paris had redrawn the lines; there was no going back now.

Chapter 28: Retaliation

The news reached him in clipped phrases, delivered with eyes downcast.

The ambush on the Strand had failed. Aldridge had walked away without a scratch.

The hijack on the convoy had failed, and millions were potentially lost. They couldn't prove Aldridge's hand in it, but Alpha didn't care. In his mind, that Australian popinjay was behind it all. How was he doing it?

Worse, men were in custody with stories they couldn't be allowed to tell.

Alpha stood in the darkened room, hands clasped behind his back, jaw tight enough to crack. First Jonathan. Now this. Every failure was a wound to his authority, and Jonathan's ghost only made it bleed deeper.

He turned slowly, the shadows carving hard lines across his face. If fear slipped from his grasp, respect would follow.

No one dared speak.

A single cough broke the silence. One of his lieutenants shifted his weight, eyes fixed on the floor.

Alpha's head turned, slow as a blade. 'Do you know what happens when dogs forget their master?'

The man froze, colour draining from his face.

Alpha stepped forward, his boots deliberate against the concrete floor. 'They start to believe they can choose which orders to follow, which battles to win. Which masters to serve?' His voice dropped, soft and poisonous. 'And then they are put down'.

He let the words hang, then snapped his fingers. Two guards moved without hesitation. The lieutenant was dragged from the room; his protests smothered against the echo of slamming doors.

Alpha turned back to the others, the faintest smile cutting across his face. 'Retaliation', he said simply. 'Something public. Something loud. Remind London who owns the shadows'.

Every man in the room nodded. None dared meet his eyes.

Alpha clasped his hands behind his back once more, gaze fixed on the city skyline beyond the window. 'Aldridge thinks he's clever. He thinks he's untouchable. Let's show him how wrong he is'.

At West End Central, the Police and Criminal Evidence Act compliant interview suite was sterile: pale walls, strip lighting, the faint smell of disinfectant and stale coffee. One by one, those arrested at the attempted hijack were brought in, each carrying the marks of their failed ambush.

The first had his arm in a sling, collar stretched awkwardly around the strap. The second eye was swollen near shut, and dried blood crusted on his nose. The third moved stiffly, wincing every time he sat, the bruises beneath his jacket plain enough.

Clare didn't comment. She set a slim folder on the desk, opening it with deliberate care so the forms inside were visible.

'Here's the reality', she said evenly. 'We've got enough to charge all three of you. But the Crown Prosecution Service won't take the whole lot. They'll take the ones who don't cooperate. One of you walks out. The other two don't'.

The heavy in the sling tried bravado. 'You're bluffing'.

Clare's eyes didn't flicker. 'You think they won't sell you out? I'm telling each of you the same thing: whoever talks first walks. The rest are going down. The Crown Prosecution Service likes it neat and tidy'.

Silence stretched. She leaned in, her voice dropping to a whisper.

'And if you don't cooperate, I'll see to it that the others think you did — that you sold them out'.

She left the first to stew, and by the time she'd finished with the second, the man with the black eye had already cracked names, drop points, and a burner number. By the third interview, all three had betrayed one another, each convinced the others had already sold them out.

Clare gathered her folder and stepped into the corridor, stripping off the latex gloves she hadn't really needed. Through the glass, she caught Richard watching, arms folded, expression unreadable.

'You didn't lay a hand on them', he said at last. 'But you broke them'.

Clare shrugged. 'Parasites like that, they'll always turn on each other. All you have to do is give them the choice'.

Richard's gaze shifted to the notes she carried. 'And did they give us what we need?'

She hesitated, then tapped the folder. 'A name. Not one of theirs, though, but someone who pays the bills. A contact in Knightsbridge referred to as Adrien. They didn't know the surname, but they all swore the same first name'.

Richard's expression hardened. 'Adrien', he repeated, almost to himself. He let the silence hang; the syllables sour in his mouth.

Richard's eyes narrowed, the name bitter in his mouth. 'I might have a surname to go with that. Aldridge'.

Clare's brow furrowed. 'Do you want to explain?'

Richard leaned back, voice low. 'Adrien's a distant cousin — and a board member at the bank. He sought me out on my first day and went out of his way to make the introduction. I've suspected him from the start. His rise through the bank was a little too smooth, a little too well-greased. He has Syndicate written all over him. But it's circumstantial. No proof. Not yet'.

Her eyes hardened, the blackmail still raw in her mind. 'Then he's on my radar as well as yours'.

He gave the smallest of nods. 'Good. Just don't let him see it'. Then, more evenly, for the room at large: 'It wasn't just a hijack. It was a message'.

Clare closed the folder, watching him carefully. Richard gave nothing away, but the flicker in his eyes said enough. Adrien was on borrowed time.

He exchanged a glance with Mac, who had been standing quietly by Richard's side. He raised his brows in grudging respect. Richard allowed himself the faintest smile.

'Remind me never to end up across the table from you'.

Across town, Alpha turned from the window, voice low and deliberate.

'If the head cannot be taken cleanly, then we cut out the heart. Aldridge has a sister in Margaret River. Remove her'.

Adrien shifted uneasily at his side. 'Do you want it handled from here?'

Alpha shook his head. 'No. Push it through Melbourne. The Australian Alpha owes me; let him earn his keep'.

No one dared question him. Orders moved, men dispatched. Across oceans, another trap was set, not from London but from Melbourne, where another Alpha waited to prove his worth.

And back at West End Central, Richard sat in silence a moment longer, Adrien's name still bitter on his tongue. He didn't have proof yet, but the shadows were tightening, and he knew the mask would slip soon.

The blinds were half-drawn against the glare of a Melbourne afternoon, the air thick with espresso and cigarette smoke. On the top floor of a Collins Street office block, the Australian Alpha leaned back in his chair, phone pressed to his ear.

The instruction from London was short, cold, and final: 'Margaret O'Connell Junior, Margaret River. Remove her and anybody that gets in the way'.

He smiled thin, deliberate, and then stubbed out his cigarette in a crystal ashtray.

'Consider it handled'.

The call ended. He swivelled toward the window, watching the trams rattle past below, bells clanging in the heat. Margaret River was a long way from Collins Street, but it wasn't untouchable. Not anymore.

He reached for a file already waiting on his desk. Photos paper-clipped together: the O'Connell Estate, young Maggie outside the homestead, rows of vines glinting under the Australian sun. The dossier had come from a local fixer with aerial shots, vehicle logs, and even staff rosters.

'Beautiful place', he murmured, flipping the photos one by one. 'Shame about the inhabitants'.

His enforcer appeared in the doorway. 'We've got the Perth boys on it who can move quietly. A couple of days and they're down there. Car accident. Fire, just nothing to tie it back'.

Alpha considered, then shook his head. 'Not just an accident. Make it theatre. Something that rattles Aldridge when the news reaches London. The message is the point'.

The enforcer nodded once, then left.

Alone again, the Australian Alpha picked up his espresso, swirling the dregs. In Margaret River, under the shade of a jacaranda tree, the last of the O'Connell line was living in peace.

Soon, she wouldn't be.

Margaret River's main street was quiet, most shopfronts shuttered, the night breeze carrying the smell of eucalyptus and woodsmoke. Maggie O'Connell Junior walked arm in arm with Sergeant Davies, laughing softly as they left the wine bar. To anyone watching, it looked like a young couple ending a night out.

They crossed toward the car park, headlights glinting off the big Holden Ute that Sergeant Davies insisted on driving when he was off duty. Maggie reached for the passenger door when movement flickered at the edge of her vision.

Two men peeled away from a parked sedan, coming fast.

Davies saw them first. He caught Maggie by the arm, pushing her behind him with calm, clipped authority.

'Stay down'.

The first man lunged with a blade. Davies stepped into the arc, drove an elbow across his jaw, and dropped him to the tarmac. The second swung a length of pipe; Davies ducked, swept his legs out, and slammed him hard against the kerb.

Silence crashed back in. Maggie's breath came ragged, but she kicked the knife away with the toe of her shoe before it could be snatched up again. Davies was already hauling the conscious one upright, dragging him into the shadow of the alley beside the bakery.

The interrogation was swift, merciless, but measured: no wasted blows, no theatrics, just pressure until the words spilled out.

'Melbourne', the man gasped. 'Safehouse. St Kilda Road. Alpha's there. He's been running ops from the inside'.

Davies released him, letting him crumple. His phone was already out, thumbing the secure line Campbell Barracks had drilled into every man on the team.

'Target confirmed', he said into the line. 'Passing to command'.

Maggie gripped the Holden's door handle, knuckles white. A flash of her grandmother's jacaranda tree cut through her thoughts, sharp as glass. The date was over. The danger was all too real.

Before dawn, ASAS operators moved like shadows through the quiet streets of St Kilda. The nightlife strip was dark now, its neon signs blinking out one by one, the trams silent on their tracks. To the north, the first light of morning caught the glass towers of

Melbourne's CBD, turning their upper floors gold while the streets below still lay in shadow.

The safehouse sat among a row of weathered apartments, curtains drawn, anonymous in a street that had seen a hundred just like it.

Then the breach came fast, violent, overwhelming.

Flash-bang grenade. Doors splintering. A two-man stack clearing each room with brutal precision.

Alpha reached for a weapon, but it never cleared the drawer. He was dragged to the floor, cuffed, hooded, and lifted bodily from his chair. No glory, no dignity, just a man revealed for what he was.

By the time the sun was fully over the bay, he was in custody, bound for a blacked-out transport. His empire was reduced to ash in the span of a heartbeat.

Half a world away, in London, Richard set the fresh report on the table. The words were stark, final:

TOP SECRET – AUS/UK EYES ONLY ASAS OPSUM // ST KILDA RAID // 041530Z TARGET SECURED. ALPHA IN CUSTODY.

- 041507Z: Entry Team Bravo breached the target safe house, St Kilda.
- Resistance: minimal. One weapon recovered (unfired).
- Subject detained, hooded, transferred to black transport.
- Forensic sweep ongoing.

MATERIALS SEIZED:

- Ledgers (shell corporations, offshore structures).
- Encrypted hard drives (initial scan: Aldridge Bank account numbers identified).
- Comms equipment (burners, scramblers).

INTERROGATION – INITIAL CONTACT:

Subject provided limited verbal before non-cooperation. Direct quote (verbatim):

'Not just me'.

STATUS: Subject in secure holding, location undisclosed. Materials to be transferred to the AUS/UK Joint Task Group within 72 hrs.

END REPORT

[Distribution: PMO / MOD / SIS / ASAS Command / Aldridge Liaison]

Richard read the cable twice, the weight of it pressing into the quiet. Jonathan's message was no longer conjecture. The Partners were real. One Alpha was gone, but the name itself was a misdirection. There were more chairs at that table, more hands on the strings.

He closed the folder, eyes narrowing. One Alpha had fallen, but the table was still set. Too many chairs, too many hands on the strings.

This was only the beginning...

Chapter 29: Operation Sweep

Cabinet Office Briefing Room A (COBRA)

The secure sub-basement of the Cabinet Office was windowless, its oak panelling lending an illusion of comfort. The air was cool, the silence heavy. Outside, traffic murmured across Downing Street, but in here no signal could leak, no ear could intrude.

Anna set a folder on the polished table, neat tabs bristling from its edges.

In the week since Paris, the task group had worked without pause, cross-referencing Clare's arrests, Graham's network maps, and Mary's offshore data until every thread pointed to the same people.

'Two dozen names. Nine fronts. Four primary nodes. Hit them together and the Syndicate's blind and broke before lunch'.

The Prime Minister sat opposite, jacket off, shirt sleeves rolled, looking more like a staff officer than a statesman. His private secretary, kept to the shadows at the edge of the room, pen scratching across a notebook but saying nothing.

Clare leaned forward. 'Hit them all at once, and they don't have time to recover. We've seen this before: snip a few threads, and the rest just rewires itself. You want the whole net down'.

The PM tapped the table, thoughtful. 'And you can do this?'

Richard glanced at the squad: Anna's cool precision, Lydia's steady fire, Foster's nervous energy still bristling from his discovery. Then he looked the Prime Minister square in the eye.

'With the right backing, yes. But let's not dress it up. It won't be clean. It won't be quiet'.

For a long moment, the Prime Minister held his gaze. Then he gave the smallest nod.

'Then let's get to work'.

Mary turned her tablet toward the others. 'The French directors folded. Brussels contacts are already cautious. Here', she tapped a cluster of dots on the screen, 'these are the money pipelines. They match perfectly with the warehouse flows Mac traced from Carter's observations at the bank'.

Mac gave a grunt of satisfaction. 'Trafficking hub in Manchester, counterfeit depot in Birmingham, a corporate nest at Canary Wharf, and a laird in Scotland. We can lift them all. But it must be early, before anyone spooks'.

Clare added her own folder to the stack. 'Warrants are ready. Economic Crime Command will take Canary Wharf. NCA, the UK equivalent of the FBI, will handle Birmingham, Greater Manchester Police will cover the north, with Lothian and Borders looking to Scotland. All at once, no leaks, no hesitation'.

The Prime Minister had been silent until now, elbows on the table, fingers steepled. He opened the red folder at his side, glanced at the signature page, then looked across to Richard. 'This is what you wanted? Clean, coordinated, decisive?'

Richard met his gaze. 'No half-measures. We cut every artery at once'.

The PM uncapped his pen and signed with a heavy stroke. The sound seemed loud in the quiet room. He slid the folder across. 'Then it's official. At dawn, we move'.

The squad exchanged glances, tired, grim, united. Lydia gave a single nod, already running the timings in her head. Anna closed her folder with quiet finality. Mac and Clare reached for their phones.

Richard leaned back, arms folded. 'Then we execute'.

A cough sounded from a shadow in the corner. Michael Denning rose awkwardly from a chair, notebook tucked under his arm. His expression was careful, caught between curiosity and caution.

The Prime Minister stiffened. 'What the devil—?'

Richard raised a hand. 'Relax. He's not here for the details. He's here so that tomorrow morning, the right story is told'.

Denning managed a faint smile. 'Off the record until you say otherwise'.

The PM regarded him for a long moment. 'You trust him?'

'I do', Richard said simply. 'And more importantly, he owes me'.

The PM considered that, then gave a slow nod. 'Fine. But he gets the line we give him. Nothing more'.

Richard's voice was calm. 'Tomorrow he gets his scoop: the largest coordinated anti-crime operation in decades. A Prime Minister who signed the order. The public sees a clean strike. Alpha sees his empire burn'.

Denning jotted a note, then looked up. 'And who takes the bow?'

The PM allowed himself the faintest smile. 'I do, of course. But you'll write it as history being made, not politics. That way, everyone believes it'.

Denning nodded once. 'Understood'.

By first light the next day, the orders had moved from Whitehall to the field. Across the country, teams stood ready. Grey vans braked hard outside Canary Wharf's Aldwych House, spilling officers in stab vests into the marble lobby. Clare strode at their head, helmet strapped, warrant folder raised.

'Metropolitan Police. This building is under warrant. Step away from your desks'.

On the fifteenth floor, Syndicate 'consultants' in pinstripes barely had time to look up before they were face down on the carpet, cuffed. Servers and ledgers were wheeled out past junior analysts staring in shock. Clare allowed herself the faintest smile. Months of threats and pressure, and now, floor by floor, the kingdom was falling.

In Manchester, the steel shutter screamed as Greater Manchester Police stormed the warehouse, boots hammering concrete. Partitioned cubicles lined the floor, each one holding a girl, some no older than sixteen, wrists chained.

'Cut them loose', a Bronze commander barked. Bolt-cutters snapped, medics swarmed with blankets and water bottles. A trafficker in a silk shirt and gold watch shouted curses until a constable's baton silenced him.

Mac watched from the observation point, comms crackling in his ear. This raid wasn't about ledgers. It was about lives. And the Syndicate had just lost them.

In Edinburgh, dawn mist curled across manicured lawns. Police Land Rovers lined the drive of a stately home, officers carrying out family silver and evidence boxes. A silver-haired laird in a dressing gown watched from the steps, unnervingly calm.

'Very well', he said, almost amused. 'Do what you must. Please… be careful with the family silver'. Cameras flashed as he was led back inside.

An hour later, when the search turned up a revolver hidden in his study, the tone shifted. The laird stepped forward, eyes bright, hand closing on the weapon. Shouts rang out, 'Armed police!' before the crack of gunfire ended it.

The papers called it a tragic end for a respected landowner. The Syndicate knew better. They had lost a Partner.

In Birmingham, a battering ram punched a shutter from its track. Floodlights swept across crates of counterfeit goods, smuggled cigarettes, and unlicensed pistols. Within minutes, the depot was sealed, suspects herded into vans as the press swarmed the cordon.

In London, Graham hunched over monitors. One by one, glowing nodes on his network map winked out. 'That's four down', he muttered. 'Alpha's blind'.

Anna ticked boxes on her clipboard, voice clipped. 'Targets secured. Detainees processed. Evidence in transit'.

Lydia stood beside Richard, eyes on the feeds. 'The battlefield's clearing. He's running out of cover'.

Richard folded his arms. 'Then it's time to finish this'.

The first shaky footage appeared before breakfast: vans outside Canary Wharf, men in suits led away in cuffs. By 7 a.m., the morning bulletins were looping it, presenters talking of 'coordinated dawn raids' and 'a major strike against organised crime'.

By midday, *The Times* carried the banner headline:

EXCLUSIVE: Prime Minister personally authorised dawn raids from the Whitehall war council

By Michael Denning, Political Correspondent

The article laid out the scale in measured prose: numerous arrested, millions seized, simultaneous strikes in four cities. The scoop was clear: this had not been a routine police action but a personally sanctioned assault on Alpha's empire.

By evening, the story dominated the *BBC News at Ten*. Arrests in Manchester, crates in Birmingham, and in Edinburgh, the fatal shooting of a laird during a police search, all neatly packaged. The Prime Minister appeared outside Number Ten, delivering a clipped line to the camera:

'This government promised to take action. Today we have. No one is above the law, no matter how powerful they believe themselves to be'.

In the studio, Michael Denning sat on the panel, introduced as Political Correspondent, *The Times*.

'Following on from the strides against organised crime highlighted earlier this year', he said, 'today's raids show the government moving from rhetoric to decisive action. The Prime Minister's personal involvement is unusual, but it sends a clear message'.

Richard watched from his office without a word. The public saw a police triumph, a Prime Minister strong on crime. He saw Alpha's empire crumbling, piece by piece, and knew Denning had played his part perfectly.

Beside the screen, the Prime Minister set down his coffee and allowed himself a thin smile. 'Good man, Denning. He's made it sound like I've been planning this for months'.

Alpha stood at the window of his ministerial office, watching the drizzle smear across Whitehall. His phone lay on the desk beside a half-drunk glass of whisky, still vibrating with fresh reports.

Raids in Canary Wharf... Manchester... Edinburgh... Birmingham.

Each alert was another artery cut: arrests, assets frozen, ledgers seized.

He poured another drink and let it sit untouched.

They had struck everywhere at once. No warning. No leaks. The machine that had carried him for decades, the web of shell companies, traffickers, fixers, and launderers, all reduced to rubble in a single morning.

And still worse, the whispers. The playboy Aldridge. The grandson. His face, his name, appearing in the edges of these reports. The impossible thought that somehow, he was the hand behind it all.

Jonathan's treachery had stung. But this... this was humiliation.

An hour later, the encrypted WebEx call connected. A half-dozen faces flickered across Alpha's laptop screen: the Syndicate's 'Partners'.

The chairman, a thin man in rimless glasses, spoke first, voice cold as steel. 'Alpha UK region, your report'.

Alpha forced himself upright. 'We have suffered losses. Coordinated raids across four nodes. Police moved without warning, supported by intelligence I cannot account for'.

Murmurs rippled across the screens. One partner leaned in. 'Losses? You call these losses? Your region is gone. Accounts frozen. Properties seized. Personnel arrested'.

Another, older, and smoother raised a hand. 'Performance metrics are clear. Every quarter, we review. Every quarter, you are measured against the curve. You know what happens to those who fall below'.

Alpha's mouth was dry. He'd sat on this side of reviews before, watching other regional heads being edged out, and what 'edged out' meant in Syndicate terms. He opened his mouth to argue, but the chairman cut him off.

'You have not met your targets. You are on the wrong side of the curve'.

The words hung in the air more final than any sentence a court could deliver.

The chairman adjusted his glasses. 'We will assign an interim overseer until the region is stabilised. Further instructions will follow'.

One by one, the screens winked dark, leaving Alpha alone with the drizzle outside, the untouched whisky, and the knowledge that his empire, and his life, were now running out of time.

Chapter 30: The Resignation

The black car drew up to Downing Street, headlights cutting across the cobbles. The Deputy Leader of the Government stepped out slowly, a slim folder in his hand. To the cameras clustered across Whitehall, it appeared to be routine business, nothing more.

Inside the folder: his resignation. Ill health. Exhaustion. A neat lie for a dirty truth.

He was ushered past the Cabinet Room, along the corridor, and into the Prime Minister's office. The PM stood behind his desk, expression grave. Beside him, seated in a leather chair, was Richard.

For a heartbeat, the Deputy froze. His eyes narrowed, and then the penny dropped. The Australian playboy heir, the spoiled grandson with the wine cellar and the easy smile, not a mask but a cover. The real Richard, the one Alpha had dismissed, had been there all along. Watching and stripping everything away.

The Deputy laid the folder on the desk, his fingers lingering on it. 'I wanted to hand this to you personally. After all these years'. His voice was steady, but his eyes flicked once more to Richard. 'I see I've been misinformed'.

The Prime Minister opened the folder, scanned the single sheet, and closed it again without a word. 'Your resignation is accepted. Take whatever time you need to recover'.

The Deputy nodded stiffly. He turned to leave, but his gaze locked on Richard's one last time. No words passed, but the message was clear: he knew who had undone him. And Richard's silence confirmed it.

The door closed. The sound of footsteps retreated down the hall.

The Prime Minister exhaled, then glanced at Richard. 'One down'.

Richard's reply was cold and certain. 'Four to go'.

Later that evening, in Richard's study in the townhouse, the phone rang. He lifted the receiver.

'Michael Dunning', the voice said without preamble. 'You'll see it on the wires by morning, but I wanted you to hear it first. Alpha's dead. Found last night at his private residence in the constituency'.

Richard leaned back, saying nothing.

'Officially', Dunning went on, 'natural causes. A quiet heart attack, nothing to see. Unofficially…' he paused, as though even wondering whether to go on. 'There's been a leak from inside government. Some are whispering it was Five – MI5, the Security Service. Others that the Syndicate couldn't let him walk away'.

Richard let the silence stretch. Finally: 'And you, Michael? Which story do you believe?'

Dunning exhaled. 'That's why I'm calling. I'd value your view as much as you value mine'.

Richard's eyes flicked to the window, the winter sky beyond. 'Alpha never believed in retirement. He made too many enemies. I'd say the truth hardly matters now'.

'Perhaps not', Dunning allowed. 'But someone thought it did. And that should give us pause'.

The line clicked dead, leaving Richard staring at his reflection in the glass.

'For now, the war receded. In its place came quieter battles— the kind fought not in offices or back rooms, but in hearts and families'.

Part III

The Light Endures

*From the ashes of shadowed legacies, a new generation rises —
and the fight for the Aldridge name becomes a fight for the future
itself.*

Chapter 31: The Flight Out
and the Wedding

The months that followed brought no peace, only a colder kind of order. The Syndicate reeled, then regrouped; probes were launched, watchers unmasked, new fronts opened in Westminster and beyond. Richard's team hardened with each passing week, learning the rhythm of pressure and counter-pressure.

And yet, beneath the grind of strategy, a quieter pulse began to steady — one that spoke not of war, but of renewal. A year later, when the next set of envelopes appeared, their weight carried not the shadow of resignation but the promise of beginning.

The invitations were sent on heavy cream card, the Aldridge crest embossed in gold, with the O'Connell vine motif subtly twined around its edges. The lettering was formal, almost regal:

By command of The Most Honourable, The Marquess of Hunton and Lady Aldridge, request the pleasure of your company at the marriage of their grandson, Captain Richard Aldridge, to Miss Lydia McCarthy at the O'Connell Estate, Margaret River, Western Australia.

In a Brixton flat thousands of miles from Margaret River, a postman's knock broke the morning quiet. When James Carter slit his envelope open, he whistled low. His wife, Sarah, leaned in, brow furrowed. 'Sarah', James muttered, tapping the gilt crest with his thumb, 'you'd better start thinking about a new dress. And a hat'.

She frowned at him. 'It's a vineyard wedding, James, not Ascot'.

He shook his head slowly, eyes still on the grand script. 'This isn't just a vineyard wedding. Look at it — 'By command of the Marquess of Hunton'. We're not just going to a family party, love. We're meeting royalty — or near enough'.

Sarah laughed, swatting his arm. 'Sometimes I wonder if we are'.

James folded the card carefully back into its envelope, his grin sly. 'Well then, you'd better make sure that hat's good enough for the Queen'.

Two weeks later, Heathrow's private Concorde Room had been cleared. With Anna's trademark unflappable efficiency, together with more than a little help from Mason, plus the Aldridge name opening every door, an entire first-class cabin on the Perth-bound 747 had been bought out without fuss. Family, friends, and allies had managed to clear their calendars; few would dare decline such an invitation. The Aldridge–O'Connell wedding party now had the skies to themselves.

With Mason as her backup, Anna marshalled it all with her usual precision, her headset in one ear and her tablet in hand. For years, she had been Lord Richard's personal assistant, running his life with impeccable efficiency. Now she served his grandson, Captain Richard, with the same loyalty and fierce protectiveness.

'Boarding in twenty', she announced crisply, scanning the room. 'Passports, visas, health certificates, all in order. And yes, James, that includes yours'.

James Carter grinned from his seat, passport already in hand. Sarah reached for the hatbox that contained the hat she had chosen for the occasion, just to make sure it was still there.

Lydia's parents sat apart, polite but subdued, murmuring over coffee. Her father's gaze tracked Richard as he stood by the window, Lydia's hand entwined with his. 'A soldier turned banker', he said quietly. 'And now splashed across the papers as the City's most eligible bachelor. Tell me, do we truly know this man?'

Her mother's reply was soft but edged. 'We know he has a title and a fortune. Whether that makes him a husband…' She left the thought unfinished, watching as Richard bent his head to whisper something that made Lydia giggle. 'I only hope she sees past the shine and knows what she's letting herself in for'.

Clare rustled the newspaper she was reading, drawing Lydia's glance. 'What is it?' she asked.

She tapped the byline with her thumb. 'Michael Denning again. He's got you in print, Richard'.

Richard looked up from his notes. 'What now?'

Clare read aloud, his tone dry. "The City's most eligible bachelor has finally surrendered his liberty. Captain Richard Aldridge, grandson of the Marquess of Hunton, known until recently for a cellar of fine claret and a flair for the discreet exit, is reported en route to Western Australia. There, at the O'Connell Estate, he is to be married in a union that promises to entwine old blood, new money, and no small measure of intrigue. London's social calendar will look poorer for the loss, though bookmakers will be relieved to close a long and lucrative market'.

She folded the paper with exaggerated care. 'Well, that'll set tongues wagging'.

Lydia arched a brow at Richard. 'Off the market, hmm?'

Richard's smile was rueful but warm. 'Took them long enough to notice'.

Lydia's parents murmured politely to Fiona. Mac's men, broad-shouldered and calm, lingered near the walls, indistinguishable from ordinary travellers save for the way their eyes swept every corner.

Richard stood by the window, Lydia at his side. She leaned against him, her smile warm, her fingers laced through his. On her hand, the sapphire ring caught the light — the heirloom his grandfather had once pressed into Maggie's palm in a wartime apartment, when he asked her to marry him. Its deep blue stone seemed to glow with its own fire, a quiet reminder of the love and resilience that had carried their family this far. Her dress, carefully tailored for the flight, could not quite disguise the gentle curve of her belly. It made Richard more protective than ever — and prouder, too.

Twenty hours, three continents, and a dozen time zones later, the scent of eucalyptus cut through recycled air. Perth International shimmered in the morning sun. As the 747 taxied to its stand, the wedding party gathered their bags. A head stewardess guided them out of first class ahead of the other passengers, down a side airbridge, and into a service corridor.

There, a waiting officer in khaki slacks and short sleeves snapped to attention. Colonel Jameson's grin was as dry as ever.

'Couldn't let you sneak in without a fuss, O'Connell', he said, clapping Richard on the shoulder. 'You're on my home turf now. We'll see you through'.

They were escorted into a private arrivals room, where immigration officials were already briefed. Stamps came down in a neat rhythm; forms were signed, and baggage was discreetly lifted aside. Within minutes, the party was free to walk out into the warm Perth air.

And waiting for them at the barriers stood Lord Richard and Lady Aldridge—Maggie to her kin, but here and now every inch the Dowager Lady Aldridge—with Maggie Junior at their side.

Lord Richard's frame was thinner now, but his eyes were alight with pride as he clasped his grandson's hand and kissed Lydia on the cheek, his gaze softening when it fell on her swelling form. 'The future, standing before me', he murmured.

Then his breath caught. On Lydia's hand, the sapphire ring gleamed with the same heavy gold and deep blue stone he had once carried into France against orders—the ring he had slipped onto Maggie's finger in the dim light of their French apartment all those years ago. His eyes flicked to Maggie's, and in that instant, she saw it too. A lifetime's worth of memory passed between them, unspoken—their past, now carried forward into the next generation.

The murmur of conversation swelled again around them, the spell quietly breaking. Beside him, Lady Aldridge's eyes found

Anna lingering just behind Richard. She reached for her hand briefly, surprising her with the gesture. 'And you, my dear, thank you. You've kept him safe all these years, seen him through storms none of us could calm. That's no small thing'.

Anna blinked, caught off guard, and inclined her head. 'It was an honour, my Lady. It always has been'.

Maggie's smile held a glint of mischief. 'Some honours weigh more on the heart than on the schedule'.

Lord Richard turned at that, puzzled, but Anna had already slipped back into her professional mask, tablet in hand, directing the luggage handlers as if nothing had passed between them.

As the party made its way toward the waiting transport, Mason came up beside her, having discreetly overheard the exchange between Lady Aldridge and Anna.

'He's been very lucky to have you by his side all these years', he said quietly.

Anna glanced at him, a small smile softening her usual composure.

'Likewise with you'.

For a moment, a quiet respect passed between them — two of Lord Richard's most trusted **confidants**, bound by years of service and shared understanding.

The convoy rolled south, eucalyptus crowding the highways, the dry tang of dust and sea salt on the breeze. As the coaches eventually turned down the familiar drive, the vines stretched ahead, green and heavy in the late sun. The homestead rose beyond, the O'Connell crest fluttering from its veranda.

Behind the main house, the wedding guests found a different kind of luxury awaiting them. The vineyard community had worked tirelessly for weeks, erecting rows of elegant canvas lodges beneath the gums—camping in the luxurious accommodation only normally seen on African safaris. Each tent boasted a proper bed dressed in white linen, a woven rug underfoot, and a lantern at the door. Hampers of vineyard produce — cheeses, breads, bottles of O'Connell vintage — awaited each couple.

James stared at his tent, eyebrows climbing. 'I was braced for the Ritz', he muttered to Sarah. 'Turns out we've got canvas walls and a billy by the door. Love, this is more Boy Scouts than Buckingham Palace'. Sarah laughed, ducking inside to inspect the linen. 'It's still better than our honeymoon hotel'.

That evening, the homestead came alive. Long trestle tables were carried out beneath the gums, lanterns hung from the branches, and great grills were stoked until the air shimmered with the smell of steaks, garlic, and woodsmoke. Barrels of O'Connell vintage were rolled out and tapped, glasses filled faster than they could be emptied.

It was no London banquet. The descendants of the men and women who had first broken this soil came too—neighbours and cousins and vineyard hands, their families woven into the place as surely as the vines themselves. They mingled with the guests from England and Ireland, aristocrats laughing awkwardly at bush stories, Mac's men quietly demolishing plate after plate of delicious barbecue steaks and salad, and Lydia's bridesmaids barefoot in the grass by the firepits and, standing quietly in the wings, Mason and Anna.

Lady Aldridge moved among them with ease—no title here, just Maggie—greeted with hugs and backslaps, old stories of the early years spilling out in rough country voices. Richard slipped easily into the rhythm of the vineyard; he had grown up here after all, pitching in, doing his bit—turning meat on the grill beside one of the vineyard hands, cradling a borrowed guitar to strum a half-remembered tune, lifting a child onto his shoulders so she could see the fire-dancers better, even trading words with the Aboriginal children in their own tongue.

Lady Aldridge, Maggie, appeared at Lydia's side, her hand warm on the younger woman's arm. 'There's someone you should 'meet', she said, guiding her towards the edge of the gathering where an elder sat watching the firelight with calm authority.

'Lydia, this is Elder Miran, Richard's grandfather on his mother's side. It was his wisdom that helped us build this place, his people who taught us how to read the land'.

The old man's gaze was steady, his nod solemn. 'Welcome, child', he said. 'You marry into more than a family; you marry into a country. Remember that, and you will never walk alone'.

Lydia bowed her head, feeling the weight of both family and history settle over her. 'Then I'll honour it', she promised quietly.

Her parents watched, at first reserved, the scepticism they had carried across oceans still close to the surface. They had feared their daughter was being swept into a dynasty, married to a soldier who had become a banker by name and little more. But here, under firelight and starlight, they saw something different: a man at ease in the dust, laughing without calculation, as much O'Connell as Aldridge.

Her father leaned closer to her mother, voice low. 'He's not just the playboy the papers made of him'.

Her mother's eyes softened as Richard knelt to hand the borrowed guitar back to a grinning vineyard lad. 'No. He's a man who knows where he belongs. And maybe Lydia does too'.

As the night wore on, and embers settled to ash, songs rose over the vines, some Irish, some Australian folk, one or two hymns carried in harmony until the stars themselves seemed to lean closer. Richard and Lydia slipped away before midnight, their hands twined, the firelight behind them, and the future ahead.

The wedding was held three days later, beneath a wide marquee pitched among the vines. The air was thick with the scent of sun-warmed vines, wild lavender, and the sea carried in on the breeze. Guests gathered in linen and lace, their laughter mingling with the birdsong.

Richard stood straight in his dress uniform, the medals on his chest catching the morning light. Beside him, Lydia was radiant in ivory — not the sleek satin of a modern gown, but something older, finer. The lace at the cuffs had been carefully mended, the silk cleaned and pressed back to life. It was Maggie's dress, worn once in wartime France, now restored for peace.

When Lord Richard saw Lydia standing there with his grandson, it caught him unguarded. He could almost see Maggie standing there again in that same light — laughter in her eyes, defiance in her smile. And now Lydia, carrying that legacy forward, made the past feel less like loss and more like home.

Her pregnancy was evident to all, and somehow that made her glow brighter still — the promise of the next generation carried both in her arms and in the fabric of the past.

Some guests stole glances; others politely ignored it. Lady Aldridge, ever blunt, leaned over to Lord Richard and whispered, 'Well, nothing like efficiency. Vineyard folk don't waste time'. He chuckled, squeezing her hand.

When the vows were spoken, his eyes shone with tears. He had not only lived to see his grandson wed, but to glimpse the continuation of the line in Lydia's form.

After the priest's blessing, silence fell as Elder Miran stepped forward, leaning on his carved stick. He carried the weight of years like a mantle, his presence as old as the land itself. The air seemed to hold its breath as he lifted his gaze over the couple.

'The land remembers', he said, his voice low and resonant. 'It has seen your joining, and it will see the child you carry. Walk with truth in your steps and respect in your hearts, and the spirits will walk with you. May your vines bear fruit in season, may your fire never burn low, and may your children rise strong beneath these skies'.

For a moment, no one moved. Then Richard bowed his head, and Lydia did the same. The guests followed, a ripple of reverence spreading across the gathering. The moment lingered, fragile and sacred.

Lord Richard exhaled slowly, his hand tightening around Maggie's. His voice was pitched low, meant for her alone. 'I feel it, you know. That blessing wasn't only for them. The land remembers us too, all that we've carried, all we've lost'.

Maggie's eyes glistened, though her smile stayed steady. 'Yes. And it sees what we've given back. That's enough, Richard. More than enough'.

He nodded, the weight of history pressing on his shoulders even as pride shone in his gaze.

The reception followed with long tables under the marquee, lanterns swinging, O'Connell vintages flowing. Anna kept the schedule in hand, ticking off speeches as though it were another board meeting.

Lydia's father spoke first, warm and slightly pompous, welcoming Richard into the family. He cleared his throat, then added with a smile, 'And it seems the next generation is already impatient to join us'. Laughter rippled, glasses raised.

Lady Aldridge followed, her words brisk but full of pride. 'He can track a 'roo across half the state and build a fire in the rain, but it's Lydia who'll keep him honest in the ledger. Between the two of them, they'll manage just fine'.

Then Anna stepped forward, a small velvet box and a sealed envelope in her hands. 'Delivered by courier', she said crisply. 'From Downing Street'.

A hush fell. Richard broke the wax seal and unfolded the letter. His voice carried steady across the marquee.

'Captain O'Connell, known also as Aldridge. Today, you stand not only as husband and heir, but as a servant of the Commonwealth. May this union give you strength for the battles yet to come. The nation owes you a debt. Enjoy this day, for when it is done, your work begins. Prime Minister'.

He set the letter down and opened the box. Inside lay an old antique silver compass, its back engraved simply with the initials R.A.

Richard drew in a sharp breath. His fingers trembled as he lifted it free, the metal cool in his hand. 'This… this was yours', he said softly, looking at his grandfather.

Lord Richard reached out, his fingers brushing the worn metal. 'I lost it in France, on my last mission', Lord Richard said. 'I thought it had gone forever'.

Silence held for a moment. Then Lord Richard raised his glass high, voice rough but clear.

'To the future Aldridge, O'Connell, McCarthy. One family, one bloodline'.

Glasses clinked, music struck up.

For the first time in a long time, joy outweighed shadows.

And far beyond the vines, unseen, the Syndicate took note, not in blessing but in calculation.

Chapter 32: New Generations

The vineyard glowed in late afternoon light, the vines heavy with fruit, the homestead verandas strung with lanterns left over from the wedding.

Fiona had been the first to notice, a quick glance at Lydia's swollen ankles, the way she shifted her weight as she stood. She drew her quietly aside, her doctor's eye missing nothing.

'Your blood pressure's too high', she murmured. 'It's nothing dangerous yet, but the long flight back would be a strain. My advice? Stay here, rest. Let the baby grow strong'.

Richard had overheard enough to know there would be no debate. He had seen what came of ignoring such warnings in the field, and he would not risk Lydia – or their child – for anything.

Lydia had tried to argue, but Maggie Senior was already at her side, slipping an arm around her shoulders. 'You're O'Connell now as much as Aldridge', she said firmly. 'This land has a way of holding its own. We'll see you safe, child. You and the little one'.

Maggie Junior joined them, slipping her hand into Lydia's. 'You're family', she said softly. 'The sister I never had. That means you're not alone here, not for a minute. We'll make sure you feel at home until Richard returns'.

The words—so plain, so certain—eased something in Lydia's chest. For all her courage, she had feared being seen as an outsider in this sunlit corner of the world. But in their voices, she heard not politeness, but welcome.

She stood now on the homestead steps, one hand resting on her growing belly, the other clasped firmly in her husband's.

Captain Richard's bags sat at his feet — a soldier's instinct for readiness at odds with the husband who didn't want to leave. His car was waiting to take him to the airport.

'You don't have to go so soon', Lydia murmured.

He touched her cheek gently. 'The Syndicate won't wait. The Bank won't wait. But I'll be back. Before the harvest, before she arrives'.

She smiled faintly. 'You say 'she' as though you already know'.

'I do', he said with certainty. 'And she'll need me to build a world worth living in'.

Lord Richard came forward, his frame thin but his voice steady. He clasped his grandson's arm. 'Go. Do your duty. We will keep Lydia safe until you return. She is more than just your wife now; she is part of our family'.

Outside, Anna and Mason waited with the car — her tablet already open, the timetable managed to the minute. Mason stood beside her, scanning the horizon with the same composed focus she showed the screen. As Lydia approached, Anna gave her a reassuring nod. 'We'll make sure he comes back, Lydia', she said quietly. 'You have our word on that'.

London was warm and sunlit, the kind of pleasant day that softened even the sharp edges of the city. Richard moved through Aldridge Bank's marble foyer, his presence enough to silence the whispers that had dogged the family for years. The Syndicate had not stopped circling, but the name Aldridge now had a spine again, as though a touch of Margaret River sunshine had followed him back across the world.

There were other matters waiting too: a stack of messages demanding his attention, decisions to be made. The Pan Peninsular apartment still held his clothes, his habits, the life of a man who had lived half in shadow. But the London townhouse – Aldridge stone, family ground – was calling him back. He would have to choose which would be home, and soon. Next time he spoke with Lydia, he would ask her to choose: the apartment was perfect for the Bank, but no place to raise a child. The London house would be perfect for that.

Richard had left Margaret River in late summer, the vines heavy with fruit and Lydia only beginning to show. The weeks became months. Reports, briefings, and board meetings filled his London days, while telephone calls and coded messages carried his voice back to the vineyard each night. Lydia would laugh at his fussing, assure him she was walking the verandas with Maggie Senior, and tease that their daughter was already impatient to arrive.

But as the pregnancy advanced, so did the strain. Fiona's early warning had proved right: Lydia's ankles swelled, her blood pressure climbed, and rest was no longer enough. By the time autumn shadows lengthened over the rows of vines, the family watched her with worried eyes.

In London, winter gave way to spring. At Chequers, away from prying eyes, the Prime Minister poured two whiskies and gestured Richard to a chair.

'In your grandfather's day', he began without preamble, 'Churchill had the Special Operations Executive, men and women who worked in the shadows but carried the weight of the nation on their shoulders. What I'm asking is not to rebuild the SOE, but to carry their spirit forward. British, deniable, sharp enough to cut where our official services cannot – terrorism, syndicates, state-sponsored crime'.

He sipped once before continuing. 'When I served in the Territorials, I learned that small teams can change the balance. Today's threats—syndicates, shadow economies, alliances struck in quiet rooms—demand that same precision. MI5 is bound by oversight, Interpol is too slow, and the police can only swat at symptoms. I need something cleaner. Something faster'.

Richard's eyes narrowed. 'And you believe I can provide it'.

'I believe', the Prime Minister replied carefully, 'that you already have. The team you trust, the reach you've built, the channels that never appear on Whitehall ledgers – all of it. I will not bankroll you, nor will I carve out some new branch of government. But I can quietly broaden your Special Adviser remit. Certain doors opened, certain files unlocked. You'll remain who you are. The State will simply look the other way when you move'.

Richard sat back, the weight of it settling over him. The Regiment had taught him how to fight. His grandfather had taught him why. And now the State itself was conceding what the Syndicate had always known — that the Aldridge name could still be a weapon.

As he considered his answer, thousands of miles away, another battle was already being fought.

At the vineyard, Lydia had been restless through the night, her swelling ankles and pounding head refusing to ease. By dawn, Lady Aldridge had insisted that she go to the hospital. The doctors confirmed it: pre-eclampsia. Lydia was admitted immediately and placed under close observation. Lady Aldridge sat by her bedside, wiping her brow, while Maggie Junior hurried back and forth with cool water and fresh cloths. Elder Miran stood at the foot of the bed, leaning on his stick, his voice calm amid the worry.

'The land remembers', he said softly, placing a hand on Lydia's shoulder. 'It has seen your joining, and now it sees the child you carry. She will be called Kalla — in our tongue, it means fire — the spark that will not be put out. And in the city, they will call her Callie. Two names, one spirit'.

Back in London, the Prime Minister was still watching him closely.

Before Richard could answer, the door burst open. An aide, phone in hand, murmured apologies, but there was an urgent message for him.

He took the handset, dread tightening his chest. Anna would never have interrupted unless it was critical.

'Sir, it's Lydia. She's in the hospital. Pre-eclampsia. They're monitoring closely, but the doctors think they may have to deliver early', Anna's voice came brisk but steady. Then softer: 'You go. I'll cover everything here'.

Richard's face drained.

The Prime Minister didn't hesitate. 'Take my helicopter to Brize Norton. I'll have a jet waiting for you'.

The PM moved fast. By the time Richard reached the lawn, rotor blades were already clawing at the air. Within minutes, the helicopter skimmed low over the Chilterns, racing west towards Brize Norton, where a waiting jet crouched on the tarmac, crew standing by.

The pilot gave Richard a brief nod. 'We'll put you down at Busselton. Closer than Perth. You'll make it'.

The flight was a blur. Richard stared out into the darkness, fists clenched on his knees, his mind already in Margaret River.

When dawn broke, the jet touched down on the coastal strip. At the edge of the tarmac, a dark WA Police–spec Holden Commodore SS idled, exhaust rumbling like a caged animal. Sunlight caught the lightbar recessed into the roof, half-concealed under plainclothes fittings.

A senior constable in short sleeves and aviators waited at the wheel, seconded quietly through contacts in London. 'Busselton Hospital', was all he said as Richard slid into the back.

The Commodore launched forward, V8 snarling, tyres spitting grit before finding the smooth asphalt. The road into town was short, but the driver treated it like Bathurst, the racetrack of the legendary 1000, gears snapping clean, engine climbing hard. Within minutes, the hospital came into view. The Commodore braked hard at the doors, nose dipping, engine still ticking hot. Richard was out before it stopped rolling, a nurse already waiting to lead him inside.

Boots hammered the linoleum as he followed a nurse who had recognised the urgency in his face and the name he gave. The corridor blurred, the sound of monitors and voices muffled by the thud of his pulse.

'She's stable, but her blood pressure's climbing', the nurse told him as they ran. 'Pre-eclampsia. The doctors have decided it has to be a Caesarean. They're prepping her now. You'll need to scrub in'.

They thrust a bundle of pale-blue hospital scrubs into his hands. With fingers that wanted to shake but refused, Richard stripped out of his jacket, tugged the paper gown over his shoulders, mask and gloves following. He caught his reflection in a glass panel – not the soldier, not the heir, just a man about to become a father.

They led him into the theatre where Lydia lay on the table, pale but calm, monitors flickering at her side. The anaesthetist was preparing to administer an epidural so she would remain conscious during the delivery. As Richard took her hand, she gripped his with surprising strength — enough to make his fingers ache — and he held on all the tighter, grateful simply to be there.

'I'm here', he whispered, his voice breaking. 'I'm here'.

The surgeons worked with swift precision, voices low and steady. A final command, a cry, and then their daughter's voice, sharp, strong, defiant, filling the room.

The midwife lifted the tiny bundle, swaddled and perfect. 'Would you like to cut the cord, sir?'

Richard's hands trembled as he took the offered scissors, snipping the tie between womb and world. The nurse placed the child into Lydia's waiting arms.

Richard bent close, eyes wet, kissing them both.

'She's beautiful', Lydia murmured.

'She's ours', Richard said, voice breaking. His lips brushed the child's brow as he whispered the name Elder Miran had given: 'Kalla. Callie. Our fire'.

For a long moment, he simply held them both, the blur of the theatre lights giving way to the warmth of the setting sun filtering through the blinds. Outside, the day that had begun with his arrival in Busselton was drawing to a close and with it, the first chapter of their new life together.

A few days later, the family gathered on the wide veranda of the homestead. Lydia, much against the doctors' advice, having only just undergone major abdominal surgery, had insisted on leaving the hospital at the first opportunity. She wanted Callie to meet her family, especially her great-grandfather, Lord Richard, whose health was failing.

The vines shimmered in the late afternoon sun, the scent of eucalyptus drifting on the breeze. Lord Richard had been brought out in a chair, a blanket over his knees, his breathing shallow, his hands trembling. Yet when they placed the infant in his arms, strength seemed to return. His eyes shone as he gazed down at the child.

'Kalla', he whispered. 'Callie. Our fire… and the promise of all we have fought for'.

He looked up at his grandson one final time. 'Richard… she is your duty now. Guard her. Guard them all'.

His eyes closed, his breath stilled. And with his family around him, his wife's hand on his, and his great-granddaughter cradled in his arms, the Fifth Marquess of Hunton slipped away in peace, the spirits of his son and daughter-in-law waiting for him beneath the jacaranda.

Days later, the jacaranda's leaves drifted down in the autumn breeze, a slow, rustling fall that carpeted the ground around the mourners. The family stood in silence as the coffin was lowered into the earth, the air heavy with the scent of earth and vine.

Elder Miran leaned on his carved stick at the foot of the grave, his voice deep, carrying with a weight older than the tree itself.

'A warrior returns to the spirits', he intoned. 'The land remembers his courage, his scars, and his love. He has kept faith with his people, and now he walks the Dreaming paths. May the roots of this tree guard his rest, and may the sky welcome him home'.

Richard lowered his head, Lydia's hand firm in his. Lady Aldridge laid a sprig of vine upon the coffin, her touch tender, her eyes barely holding back the tears that she knew would come later when she was on her own.

Richard's thoughts echoed the Elder's words: the land remembers. It had witnessed a wedding, welcomed a birth, and now bore this farewell. The cycle held, and the bloodline endured.

Richard leaned closer, his voice barely more than a breath. 'I'll guard them, Grandfather. All of them. I swear it'.

The days that followed blurred — arrangements made, goodbyes spoken, the long flight home heavy with silence and unspilled tears. Duty, as ever, waited.

Weeks later, West Farleigh Manor stood hushed in early spring sunlight. The great hall was stripped of grandeur, its portraits shrouded, its long windows opened to the gardens. The staff had gathered—butlers, housekeepers, gardeners, kitchen maids, and Mason, Lord Richard's driver for more than two decades—the quiet army who had kept the estate alive through good times and bad alike.

At the front of the room, a chaplain spoke the words of remembrance, his voice low but steady. A portrait of Lord Richard rested on an easel draped with black ribbon, a single candle burning before it.

When the prayers were done, Richard stepped forward with Lydia at his side. In her arms, swaddled in white, was the infant girl. He lifted her gently so all could see.

'Kalla', he said simply. 'Callie, in your tongue. The fire that endures. She carries both names, both lands. And she is the future of this house'.

The staff bowed their heads, some with tears in their eyes, others smiling faintly at the sight of the child. In that moment, the weight of service shifted from the grandfather they had honoured to the great-granddaughter they would now protect.

As the gathering began to break, Mason stepped forward, his cap in his hand. 'He would be proud, sir. The Manor is in good hands'.

Richard inclined his head; his gaze fixed on the child in Lydia's arms. 'Then we will honour him by keeping it so'.

West Farleigh Manor lay hushed, its shutters drawn against the damp grey drizzle that clung to the Kent countryside, a stark contrast to the brightness of the day before, as though the house itself were mourning the passing of the Fifth Marquess. The remembrance service was held yesterday. Now he was gone, and the Manor felt emptier for it, its silence deeper than ever.

In the Library, the fire crackled, casting steady warmth against the dark oak shelves. Richard sat at the long table with Lydia beside him, their infant daughter cradled in her arms. The baby's tiny breaths came soft and steady, her fist curled tight around her mother's finger.

By the hearth, the old wingback chair stood empty, the flames painting its worn leather in gold. Richard's gaze lingered on it, memory carrying him back to the night his grandfather had sat there with a glass of O'Connell red, listening as he laid out his resolve to take up the fight. It was there that Lord Richard had given his blessing, his counsel, his loyalty, his promise that Richard would never carry the war alone.

Now the chair was vacant, the promise passed on. Richard bowed his head slightly; the vow renewed in silence: *I'll guard them all.*

Opposite them, Michael O'Shea adjusted his spectacles and cleared his throat. Age had stooped his back, but his voice carried the authority of long habit. For decades, he had been the Aldridge family's solicitor, his Irish burr as much a fixture of the estate as the portraits on the walls.

'Thank you for keeping this private, my lord', O'Shea said, bowing his head slightly. 'Your grandfather would have wanted it so. No audience, no pomp, just family'.

Richard inclined his head, though he still found the title strange to his ears.

O'Shea opened a leather folio; parchment yellowed at the edges. 'As expected, the marquisate passes to you. But your inheritance is not simply titles and lands. It is bound, protected by the Hunton family trust. It was your ancestor, Albert Aldridge — the First Marquess, who first established it to shield the estate from the reach of inheritance tax. Each successor since has strengthened it, your grandfather most of all'.

He tapped the page with a bony finger. 'Because of that foresight, West Farleigh, the lands, and all assets tied to the Aldridge name remain intact. They cannot be broken up or sold to satisfy the Treasury. They belong, in perpetuity, to the bloodline'.

Lydia looked up from the baby. 'So the trust holds everything, not Richard personally?'

'Precisely', O'Shea replied. 'Your husband is a trustee, not an owner. He stewards it until the next generation takes his place'.

Richard's gaze dropped to the child in Lydia's arms. The weight of it settled on him more heavily than any battlefield order.

O'Shea continued, turning a page. 'There is one other matter. Aldridge Bank. As you know, it is not a public concern. All shares are held within the trust, and have been since the First Marquess's time. The directors are appointed by the family, but authority rests with the trustee, now yourself. In plain terms, my lord, you control the Bank. It cannot be sold, nor divided. Its fate is tied to yours'.

Richard sat very still. 'So the Bank lives or dies with us'.

'Exactly so', O'Shea said. 'And your grandfather never forgot it. He often warned that the Syndicate would seek their purchase there, if anywhere. You must not allow it'.

He closed the folio and reached inside his jacket, producing a sealed envelope stamped with the Aldridge crest. He placed it gently on the table.

'Your grandfather left this in my keeping. He wrote it only days before your daughter was born and sent it by special delivery from Western Australia. He asked that it be read in your presence, with your wife and child beside you'.

Richard broke the wax, unfolded the letter, and read aloud in a voice thick with restraint.

The handwriting was firm but trembled faintly at the edges, each line unmistakably his grandfather's hand. Richard drew a breath and began:

My Dear Boy,

If you are reading this, then my time has run its course. Do not grieve too long, for I have had the rare fortune of seeing the circle close, to live long enough to know my grandson, and through you, to glimpse the future—your child yet to be born.

I cannot tell you the regret I feel that fate kept us apart for so many years. That is a wound I will carry into the next life. But the time we were granted together has been beyond price to me. Every conversation, every shared glass, every memory of you and your sister—they will go with me, and I will keep them always.

You inherit a burden heavier than titles. You are Aldridge, O'Connell, and now McCarthy as well. Three names, one bloodline. Guard it well. Guard them all. The Bank is your shield, but it will also be the Syndicate's prize if you falter. Stand firm. Do not give them what they crave.

And remember this: honour is not in medals or marble, but in those who sit at your table and call you family and friend. Protect them, Richard, as I tried to protect you—though from afar, and too late. In the end, love endures longer than any title, any vault, or any stone.

I go now to rest beside my son and his wife, where the jacaranda blooms. My body will lie in Australia, but my heart will remain here with you, with Lydia, and with the little one who will carry our name forward.

Make me proud, my boy. But more than that, make her proud.

R.A., Fifth Marquess of Hunton

Richard lowered the page slowly. His voice had held steady, but his hand trembled as he folded the letter once more.

Michael O'Shea cleared his throat gently. 'That letter reached me only a day or two before the news of his passing. He told me, in the covering note, that it was the last duty he would perform. He meant for you to hear his words with your wife and child beside you. Nothing else would do'.

For a moment, the room was silent, save for the crackle of the fire. Lydia drew Callie closer to her chest, her eyes shining.

'He knew', she whispered. 'He knew she'd be here… the land remembers'.

Richard's hand closed gently over hers, the weight of two legacies binding them together in the firelight. Callie stirred in her mother's arms, her tiny fist brushing against Lydia's hand— nothing more than a newborn's reflex, yet it felt like an answer.

He hesitated, then added softly, 'He left you the Bank, my lord. But more than that, he left you his peace'.

The Times – Obituary

Lord Richard Aldridge, Fifth Marquess of Hunton

Lord Aldridge, who has died aged ninety-three in Western Australia, was for decades a fixture of the House of Lords, known for his trenchant speeches on defence and his unwavering commitment to public service. A decorated veteran of the Second World War, he later devoted himself to the stewardship of Aldridge Bank and to the quiet restoration of the Hunton estates.

In the Lords, he was often described as a 'conscience of the chamber', sharp when needed, generous in victory, and relentless in his belief that public duty outweighed personal gain. Many considered him close to becoming Father of the House.

A private burial was held in Margaret River, Australia, beside his son and daughter-in-law. He is survived by his wife, Maggie Senior, his grandchildren, Captain Richard Aldridge and Maggie Junior, and his great-granddaughter, Callie.

House of Lords – Tribute

The chamber rose in silence as the Lord Speaker paid tribute. 'My Lords, we have lost a warrior, a statesman, and a voice of uncommon clarity. The House is quieter without him'.

Peers bowed their heads. For a moment, the ancient chamber felt emptier, its marble and oak unable to mask the absence of one who had shaped so many debates.

Chapter 33: The Briefing

Grief had its place, but duty waited in the wings. The house that had buried one Aldridge now called another to arms.

The morning sun broke clean and bright over the lawns of West Farleigh, the kind of hard light early spring sometimes brought after weeks of gloom. The Manor's stone walls caught the glow, every mullion and gable picked out in sharp relief. From the trees along the drive came a scatter of birdsong, sharp and insistent in the stillness.

Inside, the drawing-room fire burned more for comfort than necessity, its warmth balancing the lingering chill of the old stone floors. The house felt quieter than Richard liked; his grandfather's absence still pressed in from every corridor, an echo that sunlight could not quite dispel.

But the room was not empty. His squad was gathered: Anna, precise with her tablet in hand; James on the sofa with Mary by his side; Fiona and Clare side by side, perched in the window seat, sharp-eyed as always; and Mac's men standing in the shadows at the back, steady as a wall.

Lydia was there too; Callie was cradled in her arms. She moved among them with quiet pride, letting each see the child before kissing her daughter's brow. James leaned forward, a rare grin flickering across his face. 'A fighter's lungs on that one'.

Fiona, sharp-eyed even now, softened for a heartbeat. 'She has your beauty, Lydia, and by the looks of her, the strength of her father. Don't let her lose that'. Clare nodded beside her, the hint of a smile playing at her lips.

Even Mac's men stirred, one murmuring, 'Little warrior', before lapsing back into silence.

Lydia only smiled, kissed her daughter's brow again, and carried her upstairs. 'Bedtime', she murmured, the soft creak of the stairs fading into silence. Moments later, she returned, the

266

Chief of Staff once more, shoulders squared, eyes clear, ready to take her place at Richard's side as the meeting began.

Richard cleared his throat. 'Thank you all for coming down on short notice. We have laid my grandfather to rest in Western Australia. Today we begin something new'.

He went on. 'The Syndicate is not finished. Jonathan was only their mask. The Alphas are still out there, and power abhors a vacuum. With the Deputy Leader of the Government's chair suddenly empty, from their top table, it won't be long before somebody slips in to fill that gap. I suspect my cousin Adrien is already being circled; he's perfect for them: an Aldridge name, in line for the title, if a little further down the order. If they succeed, this family, the Bank, and the bloodline itself are back in their grip'.

He let that sink in before continuing. 'Before my grandfather died, the Prime Minister made me an offer. He wants what Churchill once had: a Special Operations Executive. Deniable, off the books, able to fight in ways the police and MI5 cannot. His words were clear: he can't fund us, he can't admit we exist, but he'll cover us when we need it'.

James Carter raised an eyebrow. 'So… ghosts with a government blessing. Lovely'.

A ripple of grim amusement passed through the room.

Richard nodded. 'Which brings us to money. You can't fight shadows on empty pockets. The Aldridge trust secures the estate. The Bank is private, family-held. Between them, we have resources—enough to keep this team alive'.

Anna spoke crisply, stepping forward. 'We'll handle funding as consultancy contracts and overseas retainers, dressed up as legal and banking services. Plausible on paper, invisible in practice'.

Richard inclined his head. 'But there is another option. Syndicate money. Every time we seize an account or break a laundering channel, it doesn't have to vanish into Treasury coffers. With your skill between us, it can be redirected here'.

Fiona gave a dry laugh. 'So we're mercenaries now'.

Anna's expression didn't flicker. 'No. Justice. We use their own money to fund the fight against them. And not just for us. Some of it can be channelled towards the people they've hurt— shelters, safe houses, legal aid for children trafficked by their rings. Call it restitution'.

That stilled the room. Even Mac's men shifted, nodding faintly.

James rubbed the back of his neck. 'My wife already thinks I work for the Queen. Now I'll have to tell her I'm paying for charities with gangster money. She'll think I've gone mad'.

Richard let the humour settle before speaking again, voice low but firm. 'If we do this, we do it right. No greed, no slush funds. Every penny traced and accounted for — routed through lawful vehicles and forensic audits. What can't be used on operations will be returned to those the Syndicate harmed. We fight them — and we repair what they broke'. He straightened, letting his eyes meet each of theirs.

'First principles. Three fronts. Finance—we cut their funding lines. Anna, that's yours. Influence—they're grooming Adrien already. Mac, James, we need eyes in Westminster and Fleet Street. Every move, every whisper. Muscle—their enforcers are still out there. Mac, can you cover security as well? Watch our backs, nothing gets past'.

He paused, then turned to Clare. 'And you. You've got a badge, clearances, and a network the rest of us can't touch. What support can the Met give us, off the books if it has to be?'

Clare's expression was steady, professional. 'I can pull quiet checks through the system—vehicles, names, addresses. Get an early warning if they move people or cash through London. If I push harder, I can lean on a few friends in Counter-Terror and Organised Crime. Nothing that puts a spotlight on us, but enough to keep you ahead of their play'.

Richard gave a single nod. 'That's exactly what we need. We fight them in the shadows, but we don't fight blind'.

The fire popped in the grate. No one moved.

Richard's voice hardened. 'And Adrien, I'll take him. Wherever he hides, whatever mask he wears, he's mine. Cut him out, and the Syndicate dies'.

Silence stretched, heavy with unspoken resolve. Then Clare reached for Fiona, who gave a crooked smile; Mac's men gave a single, sharp nod.

Richard felt the shift—the same pulse he'd known in ambush zones and jungle patrols. His regiment, reborn in another form.

He drew a breath. 'From this moment, we are what the Prime Minister asked for—a modern SOE. No name, no flag, no record. Just results. And family. That's what we fight for'.

No one argued. No one walked away.

In the quiet of West Farleigh, with the afternoon sun dipping towards the trees and the fire burning steadily, the fight shifted up a gear.

Chapter 34: Adrien's Elevation

Adrien Aldridge was not a man who rattled easily. Yet when the encrypted email appeared in his private inbox, his hand hovered over the trackpad longer than he would ever admit.

Subject: *Invitation. Syndicate Council – UK.*

Body: *Log in at 2200. Follow protocol. You will be observed.*

He had heard stories; everyone had. The Council. The 'Partners'. The faceless circle that pulled the Syndicate's strings worldwide. No photographs. No names. Just shadows behind fortunes, ex-spymasters, and something darker still. Adrien had laughed at the tales before. Alone in his Mayfair flat with the blinds drawn, he wasn't laughing now.

He opened the laptop and entered the access code and the screen flared. Silhouettes congealed into black shapes; voices were flattened until they sounded less human than threat.

'Adrien Aldridge', a clipped male voice intoned. 'We acknowledge you'.

He inclined his head, careful to mask the thrill surging in his chest. Acknowledged.

Another voice, female, precise: 'Jonathan failed. The Deputy Leader of the Government is gone. The Laird in Scotland has fallen. The Syndicate's British arm is leaderless'.

A pause followed, the kind designed to tighten a man's stomach.

'You will rebuild it'.

Adrien let the words hang as though weighing them, though inside he burned with vindication. After years overshadowed by Alpha and his cousin, here at last was acknowledgement. Here was power, and with it, the title he had long craved.

Still, the whispers echoed in his mind: those who faltered after hearing such words were never seen again.

'And if I succeed?' he asked evenly.

The first voice returned, iron behind the distortion. 'Then you will take a seat at this table. Fail, and the chair you occupy will be your coffin'.

The silhouettes shifted. Adrien noticed one empty seat, its outline blurred yet undeniable. The Laird's chair. Failure made visible.

He drew a slow breath. 'Then I will not fail'.

The screen went black. No farewells. No signatures. As though they had never been there at all.

Adrien sat back in the silence of his flat, the city humming faintly beyond the glass. For the first time, he was no longer a bystander.

In that moment, he was the Syndicate's Alpha for the UK.

And if he played his cards right, one day he would sit at the Partners' table itself.

Miles away in Kent, the BBC ticker rolled across the bottom of the muted television in the manor study, its pale light washing over the leather-bound files on the desk.

British businessman killed in Alpine skiing accident. Survived by wife and two children.

Richard stood with his arms folded, gaze locked on the scrolling text. Lydia sat nearby, Callie nestled against her shoulder, the baby's breathing soft and steady. For a moment, Richard let his eyes linger on them, then forced himself back to the screen.

'It isn't an accident', he said at last. His voice was calm, but his jaw was set like stone. 'Not with this family. Not now'.

Lydia looked up, exhaustion in her eyes but steel in her voice. 'Who?'

'A fourth cousin', Richard replied. 'Barely on the radar. But technically still in the line of succession'.

Lydia shifted Callie gently, protective arms tightening. 'And Adrien has the family tree'.

Richard nodded once. 'He's pruning'.

The baby stirred, a small cry breaking the silence. Lydia soothed her, rocking gently. 'She isn't even eligible', she whispered, eyes on her daughter. 'Not yet. Not under the law as it currently stands'.

Richard reached out, brushing Callie's tiny hand with his finger. 'That won't matter to him. Eligibility is irrelevant. She's my child. Our line. As long as she exists, she represents a future he can't control'.

Lydia's gaze hardened. 'Then she's in danger, just like the rest of us'.

Richard's jaw tightened. 'More than that. She's the future. And he'll know it'.

The room was quiet but heavy, the weight of their unspoken vow filling the air: Callie would be protected, whatever it cost.

Richard lingered a moment longer, watching Lydia settle the child into her cradle. He bent, kissed Callie's brow, then brushed his lips against Lydia's temple. 'I'll be in the library', he murmured. She nodded, her eyes fierce even through the exhaustion. He left them there, safe for now, and stepped into the corridor.

Adrien Aldridge's Mayfair flat was immaculate, minimalist. Tonight, the polished table in the dining room served as a boardroom. Three men and one woman sat around it, expressions tight.

The banker, pale and heavyset, wiped his glasses nervously. The Westminster fixer, a former lobbyist, lit another cigarette, hands trembling. The enforcer, all scar tissue and watchful eyes, said nothing. The woman, an investment consultant with Syndicate ties, tapped a pen against her notepad, calm but wary.

Adrien let the silence stretch before he spoke.

'Jonathan is gone. The Deputy Leader of the Government has resigned. The Laird in Scotland is dead. The Syndicate's British arm is fractured. But it will not stay that way'.

The fixer scoffed. 'And you'll rebuild it? With what? Half our contacts are burned, accounts frozen, assets seized'.

Adrien's mouth curved in a thin smile. 'Then we start again. We rebuild on three fronts. Finance. Politics. Enforcement. The same pillars we've always used, but stronger, leaner, disciplined'.

The enforcer finally spoke, his voice gravelly. 'And who commands?'

Adrien's gaze swept the table, cold and unyielding. 'I do. I am Alpha (UK). The Partners Council has confirmed it'.

A flicker of fear ran through them. They had all heard of the Council. None had ever spoken to it directly.

Adrien leaned forward, voice lower now, each word deliberate. 'Richard Aldridge thinks he's inherited a legacy. He's building a squad, a cause, a family. Let him. What he builds in daylight, we will take back in shadow. The Bank, Parliament, the streets, they will all be ours again'.

The banker cleared his throat. 'And the title? The marquisate?'

Adrien's smile tightened. 'One step at a time. First, we secure the Syndicate's ground. Then...' He let the pause linger. 'Then we prune the family tree until only Richard stands in my way'.

The woman lifted her glass, eyes steady. 'And after that?'

Adrien raised his own, the Bordeaux catching the lamplight. 'After that, the marquisate comes home to me'.

The glasses clinked.

Chapter 35: The Manor: Orders

While Adrien was being promoted to Alpha, the squad at West Farleigh was already in motion.

Richard's voice stayed even. 'Adrien won't wait for us to regroup—and neither should we. Every decision we make, he'll try to anticipate; every step, he'll seek to turn against us. If we let him shape the game, he'll take the title and the Bank by default'.

Fiona leaned forward, voice clipped. 'So this isn't just about the Syndicate anymore. This is family against family'.

Richard met her gaze. 'It always has been. Which is why we don't match him blow for blow—we out-think him. The day we start fighting on his terms, we've already lost'.

Clare spoke next, calm but firm. 'Then we treat this like a major investigation. Evidence review, the way I'd run it in the Met — pull every scrap together and see what connects, accidents, donations, phone calls, names. Lay it all out and see what's missing. Somewhere in there is the thread we haven't pulled'.

Richard nodded. 'Agreed. What do you need?'

Graham stirred at last, eyes glinting behind his glasses. 'One place to put it all. Call it a library, call it a pool, a data lake. Every document, call log, account, and witness note goes in. Once it's there, I can run the patterns — who connects to who, what repeats, what doesn't fit. But it'll take more than a laptop. Serious kit, which means serious money'.

Richard's mouth curved faintly. 'So instead of chasing trees, we finally see the forest'.

'Exactly', Graham said.

Fiona frowned. 'But where do we get the kit, and where do we set it up? We can't use the Bank. And if you try filling a serviced flat with servers, the neighbours will complain'.

Clare tapped her pen. 'Then we do what Docklands does best — disappear in plain sight. We lease office space; there's empty office space all over the Wharf. There's that ground-floor area right next to the Bank in West India Dock that they've been trying to let for over a year. We front as a consultancy, take a lease, and set up the kit. No concierge peering over clipboards, no awkward questions. Just another brass plate no one cares about'.

Anna added quietly, 'We can also house a small Family Centre in the spare reception wing — a Bank-funded community initiative. It gives us a public presence, charitable goodwill, and explains why staff and visitors come and go. The charity will use the front offices and some public rooms; our servers and the Library will be tucked away in an unused suite off the service corridor'.

Graham's eyes lit faintly. 'Perfect. Canary Wharf is full of ghosts — the Family Centre will make us invisible ghosts'. Everyone will assume I'm crunching derivatives for a hedge fund. Which, in a way, I am'.

Richard nodded, decision made. 'So be it. West Farleigh remains where we meet, where we decide. The office in West India Quay becomes a satellite of the Bank and is our front office. Graham, the Friends can ghost in the hardware overnight. You build the Library there'.

The squad nodded — two homes, one purpose.

Anna broke the silence. 'All right, but who's paying for it? Office leases, racks of servers, ghosted hardware drops — none of it's cheap. Even the Friends don't work for free'.

The others exchanged glances.

Mary set down her notebook, voice quiet but steady. 'Then maybe this is the moment I come clean. In the archives, I found a dormant trust account. Supposedly wound up decades ago, but the ledgers didn't match the microfiche. The money was moved into shells offshore, and it's been sitting ever since. Nearly five million, untouched. The trail runs straight back to the Syndicate'.

Mac gave a low whistle. 'And you can reach it?'

Mary slid a slip of paper across. 'I already have the keys'.

Graham scanned it once and nodded. 'I can make it move. Half a million at a time, disguised as consultancy retainers. Bankers in Docklands see that every day. Enough to stand up in the office and the Library. The rest goes where Adrien least expects it'.

'Where?' Fiona asked.

Mary's voice was calm but fierce. 'The charities working with the women we freed. If his money heals what he broke, that's justice'.

Richard allowed himself the faintest smile. 'Then we fight him with his own fortune. Graham, draw up your shopping list. Mary, see that the rest reaches the victims'.

He lifted his glass. 'And if Gerald were here, he'd probably call it poetic finance'.

The others raised theirs in answer. The fire cracked. Outside, the night deepened over West Farleigh. For the first time since Adrien's rise, the squad felt less like survivors and more like hunters.

Chapter 36: The Library

Weeks later, the sign over the vacant offices changed from To Let to Just Let.

A lease signed. A brass plate fixed: *Aldridge Consulting Ltd.*

From the outside, it was just another anonymous firm among hundreds, which was precisely the point.

Inside, the work began. Rows of cardboard boxes and bare desks made the floor look like a company still settling in. Only the whisper-quiet server racks behind a locked door hinted otherwise.

Anna paused by the reception desk, tablet under her arm. 'One thing, Richard. What about our day jobs? The Bank will notice if three of us vanish'.

Richard's answer was steady. 'On paper, Aldridge Consulting is wholly owned by the Bank. We can even have the Bank refer customers to us. You're all on secondment — compliance, IT security, executive protection — building up this capability for the Bank. Perfectly respectable, perfectly boring. You'll still draw Bank salaries, and the board will see this as my pet project'.

James gave a dry grunt. 'So to the City, we're chasing paperwork. To Adrien, we've disappeared'.

Richard's smile was faint but cold. 'Exactly. We hide in plain sight'.

The transformation unfolded in quiet stages:

- **Furniture:** unmarked vans brought in desks, chairs, and filing cabinets. A flat-pack boardroom table was assembled under fluorescent lights, and forgettable prints hung on the walls. Bland, anonymous camouflage for the City.

Security passes: Clare set up a grey backdrop and photographed each squad member. She laminated the cards herself, clipping out IDs stamped with the Aldridge logo. A receptionist's desk took shape near the lifts.

• **Server room:** behind a door marked *Storage*, racks hummed softly. The Friends had ghosted them in at three in the morning, crates stencilled *archival systems*, slid through the loading bay with no one the wiser.

• **CCTV:** discreet domes dotted the ceiling, ordinary to building management, but all tied into Graham's network. From his workstation, he could see every corridor, every exit.

Richard walked the floor, pausing as James took up station at the reception desk, suit pressed, clipboard in hand — a receptionist to the world; a soldier's eyes for them. Beneath the desk, taped out of sight, sat a slim panic button wired straight to their security system — Richard's quiet approval of layers no visitor would ever see.

Graham emerged from the server room with a small stack of fresh passes, each with the pictures Anna had taken. He set one down in front of Richard.

'Not just plastic', he said.

Richard turned it in his hand. 'Go on'.

'Looks like a standard magstripe card. Opens doors, logs swipes. But the Friends built an upgrade. Inside is a wafer-thin GSM beacon. The battery lasts about thirty-six hours. Dock it here every night to recharge'.

'And outside the building?' Fiona asked.

Graham nodded. 'Still whispers. Triangulation, not GPS. If one of us gets lifted, I'll see movement east, west, and north. Not a red dot, but enough to know where to start looking'.

Gerald's echo seemed to flicker through Richard's thoughts, and his mouth curved faintly. 'Breadcrumbs in our pockets'.

'Exactly', Graham said. 'And if they ditch the card, the trail ends. So keep it on you'.

Richard weighed the pass as though it were heavier than it looked. 'All right. Everyone carries one. But you don't dock them overnight; you hand them to James on the way in, and he puts them on charge. He gives them back when you leave. That way, we know exactly who's in the building and who isn't. If someone vanishes, it gives us a thread to pull. But remember it's a thread, not a miracle'.

Anna clipped hers to her jacket. 'Front office open for business'.

Richard looked out through the windows. Canary Wharf stretched away in glittering steel and mirrored panes, every window reflecting another.

'Good', he said quietly. 'From here we fight him. And no one outside will ever know'.

Later that evening in the Aldridge London residence, the six o'clock news flickered across the sitting room, sunlight slanting through tall windows onto polished oak floors. On screen, Canary Wharf gleamed. The anchor's voice was bright and professional.

'Aldridge Bank today announced the opening of a new Family Centre at its Docklands offices. Chairman Richard Aldridge, himself a new father, said the initiative reflects the Bank's commitment to supporting employees and their families in an era of rising City pressures'.

The footage cut to Richard at a modest podium, Lydia beside him with Callie in her arms. His voice carried the weight of duty, softened by pride.

'If we claim Aldridge Bank has a future, then we must show we believe in one. Families matter. Our staff give us their best every day — they deserve nothing less in return'.

Applause rose faintly from the television. The camera lingered a moment on Lydia smiling down at their daughter before fading back to the anchor.

'Industry analysts have praised the move as progressive, though critics call it a publicity exercise. Either way, it marks another bold step by a chairman intent on reshaping the Aldridge legacy'.

Richard muted the set. In the quiet that followed, Callie stirred, fussing softly before Lydia soothed her with a touch. Richard watched them both, his expression unreadable — equal parts pride and the faint shadow of foreboding.

Lydia glanced up, her smile tired but certain. 'She'll grow up knowing you built this for her too'.

Across town, Adrien was also watching the news without expression as two enforcers dragged one of his underlings into the back room — a punishment for a minor infraction, and a warning to everyone else present. The door closed, muffling the man's protests. Adrien swirled the Bordeaux in his glass, letting the silence press down on the room before finally turning to face them.

The banker, pale and sweating, dabbed at his forehead. The investment consultant kept her eyes on her notes, careful not to meet his gaze. The scarred enforcer by the window stood very still, jaw tight. Adrien's tone, when it came, was measured, almost reasonable. 'Five million does not simply vanish. It was taken. Which means one of you has grown greedy... or careless'.

No one spoke.

He set the glass down with surgical precision. 'From tonight, every account, every transaction, every shell company is to be audited. Quietly. Thoroughly. If there is rot in this circle, I will cut it out'.

The banker found his voice at last, brittle. 'That... that will take weeks'.

Adrien's smile was thin as a blade. 'Then I suggest you move faster'.

He stood, smoothing his cuff, letting his gaze linger on each of them in turn. 'Consider this your chance to prove your loyalty. Fail, and you will join the man in the back room — and nothing about your disappearance will be spoken of kindly'.

At the door, he paused. His voice was ice. 'He parades his wife, his child, his family values. Let's see how those values hold when the family is gone. Start with the child'.

No one at the table dared argue. Orders went out. Canary Wharf. Strike the family. How — that was for them to decide. But it had to send a message.

Adrien's footsteps echoed down the corridor. A muffled thud carried faintly through the closed door, followed by silence.

The Syndicate lieutenants sat in brittle stillness. Suspicion coiled between them like smoke, heavy and choking. Each knew Adrien had cast the die — and in his world, innocence was no shield.

Chapter 37: The Shield

Late next afternoon, just before families would be collecting their children, the nursery door burst open.

The first shout came seconds before the crash of glass. Two masked men stormed through, weapons raised.

'Everyone down!' one barked. Children screamed. A carer froze, hands over her mouth.

James stumbled in behind them from the reception area next door, dragging his right leg as if it weighed a ton. His face was all panic.

'Please', he gasped, hamming the limp, leaning on the wall. 'There are kids—don't—'

The nearer gunman sneered and shoved him aside. James went down hard, his prosthesis clattering on the tiles. Laughter followed.

That was the mistake.

James's hand snapped up, steel-trap fast. He hooked the man's wrist, twisted, and wrenched the weapon free in a brutal, practised motion. Bone cracked. The gunman howled and crumpled.

James pivoted on the prosthesis, drove his shoulder into the second man's gut, and sent him staggering into the wall. In the same movement, he ripped free the fallen Uzi — instantly recognising it for what it was: an ex–Eastern Bloc, black-market vintage weapon. He checked the safety and magazine in a blur, then snapped it up into firing position.

'Storeroom! Now!' he barked.

The carers herded the children inside. James passed Richard's infant to them one-handed, then dragged desks against the door, bracing himself, the weapon rock-steady.

The corridor outside echoed with shouts. More Syndicate men. Boots pounding.

James wasn't moving. They would have to go through him to reach those children.

The first muzzle flashed in the hall. James returned fire — short, disciplined bursts. Plaster dust filled the air. One gunman went down hard, dragging another with him. James's eyes never left the sightline. Old drills. Different war, same duty.

Behind him, in the storeroom, children whimpered, but quieter now; they sensed the authority in his voice, the unyielding calm.

Minutes stretched. Sirens wailed faintly outside. Alarms shrieked throughout the building — Graham's hand on the systems.

Boots thundered, then: 'Police! Armed police!' The corridor filled with the roar of authority and the bark of commands.

James sagged against the frame; Uzi still raised until the Met team swept through. The last Syndicate man dropped his weapon and was pinned to the tiles.

Only then did James lower his own, chest heaving. He stepped back into the storeroom, knelt among the children, and gathered Richard's daughter into his arms.

When Richard arrived minutes later, escorted by Clare, he found James sitting on the floor, blood on his sleeve, eyes steady.

'Your daughter's safe, sir', James said simply, voice gravel. 'They're all safe'.

Richard crouched and met his gaze. For a long moment, nothing passed between them but the unspoken weight of what had nearly been lost.

Then Richard said quietly, 'Not just a desk sergeant, James. You're the shield'.

James looked down at the children clutching him. 'Not on my watch'.

Chapter 38: First Blood/Counterplay

The next day, Graham sat down at a terminal and let decades of paper become a map.

The machines hummed as algorithms traced patterns through old crimes. Around him, hard-copy files lay open: raids, scandals, disappearances, pulled together for the first time.

Mary adjusted her glasses, finger marking a line.

'Brink's-Mat, Heathrow, 1983. Six thousand gold bars, twenty-six million pounds. Half the gold was never recovered. It didn't just vanish; it was laundered through property, front companies, and the very banks meant to guard against it. Brink's-Mat wasn't their first job, but it was their breakthrough — the moment they proved they could move mountains of illicit wealth without leaving a trace. That model underpins everything since'.

She opened another file. 'Knightsbridge Security Deposit, 1987. Inside job. Sixty million in cash, jewels, and gold. Guards bought off. Vault compromised from within. A refinement of the same pattern — control through bribery, access through influence'.

Graham leaned back, the reflections of a dozen charts flickering across his glasses. 'Two robberies, two different years, same DNA. Corruption, laundering, violence. Brink's-Mat and Knightsbridge aren't isolated crimes. They're milestones in the Syndicate's evolution'.

Clare frowned, tapping the table. 'And now they're planning something new. We can feel it. Chatter about bullion, movements in shell companies, and purchases of heavy kit. They're setting up another strike'.

James rubbed his jaw. 'The Bank of England's always the dream target. Gold reserves, prestige. But no one can clear out Threadneedle Street. Not anymore'.

'Exactly', Mary said. 'That's what makes it the perfect distraction. If everyone's looking at the gold, what aren't they looking at? My bet's De La Rue — the note-printing works. Move the cash before it even hits circulation'.

The room went quiet.

Richard broke the silence. 'Speculation's one thing. Evidence is another. We need proof. Small wins first, then we build the case'.

Clare nodded. 'The Met's circling a people-smuggling hub in Southall. We know it's real: forged passports, human cargo. If Graham can tie their accounts to Syndicate shells...'

'I already can', Graham said. 'Van rental in Hayes, cash deposits flagged as remittances, and a burner phone pinging off the same mast as a known courier. I'll drop this in a digest by morning'.

'Do it', Richard said. 'Clare, pass it where it needs to go. No fingerprints on us'.

Within days, the raid went in. Southall's lock-up was stormed at dawn, plainclothes officers hauling out boxes of forged IDs, SIM cards, and ledgers. Eight arrests, forty migrants freed. CPS signed off within the week.

Headlines rolled across the Library's screens:

MET SMASHES LONDON PEOPLE-SMUGGLING HUB

The squad gathered to watch the ticker crawl. Clare allowed herself a small smile. 'One nest down. And clean enough no one can trace it here'.

'First blood', Richard said.

He leaned forward, palms on the table. 'Proof of concept: the Library works. Anna, would you mind drafting a briefing paper — Brink's-Mat, Knightsbridge, Mary's archive, tie it to Southall. Clean and clinical. I'll take it to the Prime Minister for sign-off'.

Anna tapped her tablet. 'It'll read like a Treasury red-team assessment. Cold facts, clear connections. No trace to us'.

Richard's gaze drifted to the wall of screens, timelines glowing gold and red. The Syndicate's past bled into their present.

'They built their empire on stolen gold', he said softly. 'Now we'll bury them under the weight of it'.

Across town, in rooms where the blinds were always drawn, plans were being made to answer that raid with terror of their own.

Crystal light from a chandelier fell across a table scattered with files and half-drunk glasses. The room smelled of cigar smoke and nerves.

Adrien Aldridge moved behind his lieutenants like a panther in a cage, every step deliberate, every pause calculated to remind them who held the leash.

He stopped, palms flat on the table, gaze hard. 'Two strikes: the Bank of England first — prestige, theatre, distraction'.

The fixer tapped ash into a tumbler, hands shaking. 'Debden's printing line is tight. You'll need insiders'.

Adrien's smile was thin as a blade. 'Already in place. Security rotas rewritten, lorries booked under clean fronts, police patrols quietly redirected. All paid for with money the Partners trusted me to spend. That missing five million? Consider it an investment'.

The money man dabbed his forehead. 'And if the Bank hit collapses? Even an attempt will draw fire, we don't need'.

Adrien leaned back, swirling his Bordeaux. 'It doesn't matter. Success or failure, the Bank hit dominates the narrative. Panic is profit. By the time Whitehall finishes arguing, Debden will already be stripped to the bone'.

Silence stretched. The enforcer by the window shifted; the consultant stared at her notes, pen tapping an anxious rhythm.

Adrien let the pause linger, then spoke softly, daring them to contradict him. 'The Council has sanctioned this. Deliver, or you're finished. Live on their payroll — or in their graveyard'.

One by one, they nodded. Fear was as binding as loyalty.

Adrien raised his glass in a toast that tasted like a threat.

'To Friday midnight — the night Britain remembers fear still has a name'.

Chapter 39: The COBRA Briefing

The Cabinet Office Briefing Room was never built for comfort. Windowless, wood-panelled, the air recycled until it tasted of dust and stress. Around the oval table, the full cast of Whitehall was assembled: MI5, MI6, the Met Commissioner, the Treasury, the Home Secretary, and Defence. Each with aides, files, and doubts.

At the head sat the Prime Minister, flanked by his Private Secretary and Richard Aldridge.

The PM began without ceremony. 'You've all seen the paper. Everything points to the Syndicate hitting at the heart of our financial system and in the foreseeable future. No speculation, Not gossip. Not smoke. Fact'.

The MI5 Director cleared his throat. 'With respect, Prime Minister, freelance operators collecting this intelligence raises questions of legality, evidential chain of custody. If we rely on it, convictions risk collapsing on appeal'.

The Treasury representative joined in, sharp. 'And freezing accounts, seizing assets on partial intelligence? We risk spooking the markets. The cure could be worse than the disease'.

Richard let the objections gather, then leaned forward, voice level.

'You all see the elephant in the room. We know what they're planning. We know where. What we don't know is when. The Syndicate will strike, but we can't say if it's tomorrow, a month, or a year. That's the gap. And you've got two choices.

You can wait. And when the raids come, you can roll out the same old statement: 'lessons will be learned, an inquiry will be launched, and we'll investigate how this slipped through the net'. Or', he let the pause sharpen, eyes sweeping the table, 'you can act. You can have a statement ready that says you stopped it before it happened. That this government broke up an organised crime syndicate before they touched the Bank of England or the note works. That you were ahead of the threat, not chasing it'.

The silence stretched. Even the MI5 Director's pen stopped moving.

The PM leaned back, folding his hands. 'You've heard him. And let me remind you: every success we've had in the last six months has come from this channel. The Kent raids. The Docklands smuggling ring. Even the traces back to Brink's-Mat. Without it, we'd have been blind. Results speak louder than process'.

The Home Secretary shifted awkwardly. 'But if we act and miss?'

The PM's Private Secretary spoke smoothly. 'Then the Attorney General knows how to misplace a file when it serves the national interest. Problems can... be lost'.

A ripple of dark humour ran around the table, quickly swallowed.

The PM snapped his folder shut. 'Enough. The Syndicate thinks they can touch the crown jewels of this country's economy. They are wrong. Resources are committed. Authorisations cleared. We strike first. And when the press statement goes out, it will be the second kind Richard mentioned'.

No one dissented.

Richard sat back, his expression unreadable. They had admitted it. The when was unknowable. But the if was certain.

The answer came from a lieutenant Adrien had leaned on too hard, too often. He wanted out. 'Got something', Graham muttered, tapping the keyboard. 'Accountant type in Adrien's circle. He's cracked'.

Clare frowned. 'Cracked how?'

'An indiscreet phone call, picked up by GCHQ. Spoke of the old lady in Threadneedle Street and Friday. Midnight. That's when the biggest money movements land'. Graham pulled up another overlay: payments, transfers, shell-company shuffles.

'New accounts in Luxembourg, Zurich, Gibraltar. Big sums. Greased palms. Hire contracts. Everything pointing to one window'.

Clare leaned forward, eyes sharp. 'So... Friday midnight, something goes down. But what?'

Mary tapped her pen against the folder in front of her. 'Let's put it against precedent. Every time the Syndicate's moved like this, it's been to grease access. Remember Knightsbridge, '87? They bought off guards and staff in the weeks before'.

'Same with Brink's-Mat', James added. 'Corruption, not brute force. Always cheaper to open the door than blow it off'.

Richard folded his arms. 'So what doors are they buying now?'

Graham switched screens. A new dataset filled the wall: logistics schedules, overtime rosters, night-shift patterns. 'I've cross-checked the payroll anomalies against transport. The spike lines up with high-security night work. Not banks, not ATMs. Bigger'.

Mary looked up from her notes. 'Printing'.

Everyone turned to her.

She slid a file across the table. 'De La Rue, Debden. They handle note production for the Bank of England. Midnight runs are when uncut sheets are moved between presses and secure vaults. If you're going to hit it, that's when you do it'.

A silence fell, heavy, as the scale of it sank in.

'But why the Bank of England too?' Clare asked. 'The hint was the Old Lady...'

Richard's expression hardened. 'Diversion. You make every paper and every copper in the country watch Threadneedle Street while you strip Debden bare'.

Clare gave a low whistle. 'Goldfinger without the fantasy'.

'Not all of it', Anna said, cool as ever. 'They don't need everything. Just enough that laundering it destabilises markets and makes them rich twice over: first on the haul, then on the panic'.

The fire in Richard's eyes was unmistakable. 'So we know the window. Friday. Midnight. The Syndicate's sanctioned it, Adrien's bankrolled it. If we move fast, we can make this their last throw'.

Just before midnight, the heart of the City was unusually quiet. Rain glazed the cobbles, the great bulk of the Bank of England looming in floodlight.

A van rolled up to the east service gate, its markings bland: facilities maintenance. The guard on duty checked the clipboard thrust into his hands: signatures, permits, all appearing genuine. He waved them through.

Inside, the crew moved with mechanical precision. Overalls, toolkits, radio silence. But when the lead man lifted a false panel and reached for the vault sensor wiring, the lights flared bright.

'Armed police! Down, now!'

The van doors behind them slammed open. SCO19 officers stormed in, carbines raised. The 'maintenance' crew froze, one man reaching instinctively for a concealed weapon. A red dot blossomed on his chest. He dropped it.

From a balcony above, Clare gave the nod to her team. 'All units secure. Zero casualties. Package contained'.

The suspects were herded into vans under the glare of news cameras. Clare allowed herself a rare smile; the journalists had been tipped. Tomorrow's headlines would carry a single story: another Syndicate plot smashed.

'Package delivered', she said quietly.

The real storm was thirty miles north.

At the perimeter fence of the sprawling facility, a lorry idled, its tarpaulin concealing a squad of masked Syndicate contractors. Their inside man had already looped the cameras, the gate code entered clean. Within minutes, they were inside, moving for the secure loading bays where fresh-printed banknotes sat in sealed pallets, ready for distribution.

But the bays were not empty.

Floodlights snapped on. Dozens of figures emerged from the shadows: Special Forces troopers in black kit, faces masked, weapons steady. A voice thundered through the tannoy:

'Armed response! Drop your weapons and lie face down. Now!'

The Syndicate gunmen hesitated, then opened fire. The night erupted.

Automatic bursts rattled against ballistic shields. Flashbangs cracked, white light searing the yard. The contractors went down hard, stunned and disoriented. Within two minutes, it was over, half a dozen men cuffed, two dead, the lorry immobilised, pallets untouched.

Richard crouched beside one of the captured Syndicate men, a bruised lieutenant still spitting defiance.

'You thought you were taking the country's money', Richard said evenly. 'Instead, you've just lost the Syndicate half its army'.

The man snarled. 'Adrien will make you pay'.

Richard rose, his expression unreadable. 'Adrien just lost. He doesn't know it yet, but the Partners won't forgive this'.

Hours later, Adrien hurled a glass against the wall. It shattered, Bordeaux spraying across the parquet. His lieutenants flinched but said nothing.

'Both. Both at once!' Adrien raged. 'How did they know?'

No one answered. The truth was written in their silence. The Alpha of London had presided over catastrophe. His credibility with the Council was collapsing by the hour.

Adrien stared out at the dark London skyline, his jaw clenched.

If victory was denied him, then fear would serve. And fear was a currency he still owned in full.

Chapter 40: Homecoming

Perth International was alive with the hum of arriving flights, the long-haul passengers moving in bleary silence as they queued at immigration. But in one corner of the terminal, things were different. A discreet set of airbridge doors opened, and the Aldridge–McCarthy party stepped through into the brightness of the Western Australian sun.

On the terminal forecourt, a line of black Henderson limousines waited, polished to a mirror gleam, each bearing the unmistakable plates: HENDERSON 1, HENDERSON 2. The drivers stood at attention in dark suits, caps squared, the efficiency of an old Perth institution.

Lydia's parents looked around, jet-lagged but impressed. Her father muttered, 'Not exactly a taxi rank, is it?' Her mother swatted his arm, though her eyes betrayed the same awe.

Richard said nothing, but as he slid into the back of the lead car, he allowed himself a flicker of a smile. The Burswood loomed in his memory, a place where Gerald, his other skin, had once made his first appearance. Lydia caught the smile.

'What's funny?' she asked.

'Nothing', he said, brushing it away. 'Just a reminder'.

By the time the limousines pulled up at the Crown complex, the sun was dropping. The McCarthys were shepherded inside to check in, suitcases trundling over polished marble floors. Lydia leaned close to her husband. 'They'll be fine here. One night's rest before we head south'.

Richard nodded, though his eyes were already elsewhere. Tomorrow was the real homecoming.

The following day dawned clean and sharp, the kind of Perth morning that felt scrubbed by the Indian Ocean breeze. The convoy of Henderson cars headed south along the highway, the landscape shifting mile by mile, eucalyptus pressing in, the sea flashing to the west, vineyards beginning to mark the hillsides.

At last, they turned down the road leading to the vineyard. The O'Connell crest fluttered on the veranda, and the homestead stood proud against the wide sky. Vines stretched heavy with fruit, and the air was rich with lavender and dust.

Two figures were waiting at the steps. Maggie Senior, straight-backed despite her years, her sun-browned face set in a look that was at once fierce and tender. Beside her, Maggie Junior waved warmly.

Richard felt something ease in him as he climbed from the car. This was home as much as any stone manor in Kent or the London townhouse could ever be.

Maggie Senior clasped him hard, then Lydia, before her gaze fell to the bundle in Lydia's arms. She reached without hesitation, and Lydia let her take the baby.

For a long moment, Maggie said nothing. She studied Callie's face, her silence deep enough to make the others shift awkwardly. At last, she spoke.

'She carries the look', she murmured.

Richard frowned. 'The look?'

'The Miran line', Maggie said firmly. 'I've seen it before, in her great-grandfather's people. It's there in her bones; in the way her eyes fix on yours. Elder Miran's blood runs strong in this one'.

Lydia glanced down at the baby, unsure how to respond. Maggie's eyes softened as she rocked the child.

'Aboriginal children carry the land with them', she said, voice low, almost reverent. 'Callie will too. Stronger than she looks'. She handed the baby back to Lydia, then added in a quieter tone, meant for Richard's ears as much as hers: 'In time, you'll take her to meet her great-grandfather. Elder Miran will want to see her.

And she will need to know where that part of her spirit comes from'.

Her briskness returned in a snap, as though she'd said nothing unusual at all. 'Now then, get yourselves inside. You've come a long way, and tomorrow's a day that will test us all'.

Richard looked back at the convoy, at Lydia's parents still blinking in the sun, at the homestead standing proud among the vines. He felt the weight of the past and the promise of the future meet in that moment and knew Maggie was right.

The wedding would be tomorrow. But today, the family had come home.

The next day dawned clear and sharp, the kind of Western Australian morning that made the air taste of salt and eucalyptus. The homestead buzzed with preparation. Richard's sister was to be married to Sergeant Peter Davies — the same man who had once guarded the vineyard when they first met and, over time, fell in love. Steady, respected, forged in the same fires Richard knew too well, he was as much a part of their story now as the land itself.

Guests filled the vineyard grounds: family, vineyard folk, and half a troop's worth of Swanbourne comrades, their posture betraying discipline even in linen shirts. Many knew Richard by reputation, a few by sight. They watched him now with quiet respect, the mythical 'Captain Aldridge' who had walked out of shadows most men never entered.

Lydia's parents moved among the guests, still wide-eyed at the scale of it all, and surprised that they had been included on the invites. They had seen this once before, on the day of their daughter's wedding – that strange sense that Richard was two men at once. In London, he had been the polished banker and heir; here, he was something different: soldiers saluting him, comrades clasping his hand, Elder Miran greeting him like kin. The contrast was stark, yet undeniable. He belonged to both worlds, yet only one seemed to anchor him. As they watched him among his own, rooted in these surroundings and this ancestry, they both knew which Richard they hoped was the real one.

The ceremony was held under a wide marquee pitched among the vines, reminiscent of Richard and Lydia's own wedding, Elder Miran offering his blessing beside the chaplain. Laughter carried on the breeze, wine glasses caught the sun, and for a moment it seemed nothing could intrude on the joy.

Then the Syndicate arrived.

Four Utes rolled down the track, engines snarling, men spilling from the trays with rifles and machetes. Adrien led them, his face twisted with arrogance and rage. Shouts cut the air. Guests screamed. The Syndicate heavies surged towards the marquee, intent on hostages, plunder, humiliation.

For a few terrible moments, they had the momentum. Guests dropped under tables, children clutched close. Adrien's voice rang out, triumphant:

'This is ours now! You belong to me, Aldridge!'

And then the first spear flew.

It struck one of Adrien's men square in the chest, dropping him mid-charge. Another whistled through the air, grazing the ear of a second intruder. From the tree line, Elder Miran's kin emerged, faces painted, spears balanced with deadly precision, eyes like flint.

The Syndicate faltered. And in that heartbeat, the ASAS veterans moved.

Chairs toppled, champagne bottles shattered, and suddenly the marquee was a battlefield. The soldiers fought with brutal efficiency, years of discipline snapping into place. Every guest was shielded, every Syndicate heavy met with unrelenting force. One by one, the intruders fell, their bravado collapsing into panic as they found themselves outnumbered and outmatched.

Richard himself cut a path through the chaos, his movements measured, controlled. He met Adrien near the head table, and the music stand was knocked aside between them. Adrien swung wildly, desperation etched on his face. Richard caught the blow, twisted, and drove him to the ground with a precision born of training and fury.

'Enough', Richard growled, his knee in Adrien's chest, his forearm across his throat. 'This ends'.

The last Syndicate man dropped, felled by a veteran's elbow and a waiting spear. Silence descended, broken only by the heavy breathing of those who remained standing.

Adrien struggled once, then stilled, pinned under Richard's weight. The arrogance had gone, leaving only fear.

Around them, guests slowly rose from their hiding places. Lydia clutched Callie to her chest, her eyes shining with relief and pride. Her parents stood beside her, their faces pale but resolute. They had seen the man their daughter married – not a banker, not a title, but a protector, a leader, a warrior.

Elder Miran stepped forward, his staff thudding against the ground. 'The land has judged', he said. 'This storm is broken'.

Adrien was dragged away in cuffs. The wedding resumed, shaken but unbroken, laughter returning in cautious waves as wine flowed again. The Syndicate had tried to desecrate the day. Instead, they had handed Richard his greatest victory yet: the capture of Alpha, who was head of the UK region, reporting directly to the Partners.

The UK tactical unit of the Syndicate was no more.

Chapter 41: The Webex

The vineyard office was silent but for the low hum of a single terminal, its uplink threaded halfway around the world. Richard sat at the head of the table, Adrien cuffed and bound to a chair in the corner, bruised and beaten but still breathing. Lydia had taken Callie back to the homestead. This part was not for her eyes.

In Richard's ear, Graham's voice came calm and steady, the faint clatter of London keyboards behind him.

'Their system's good. Hardened, multi-layer, triple-hop relay. But not good enough. I've seeded the entry point with a mirror.

They'll think it's one of their own chairs logging in. Once they're inside, I'll hold the line. They won't be able to cut you off'.

Richard flexed his hands once, then nodded to the screen. 'Do it'.

The monitor flickered. One by one, shadowed silhouettes resolved against a grey background. Distorted voices rolled through the speakers.

'Connection established. Who called this session?'

'This wasn't scheduled'.

'Identify yourself'.

In their view, the identifier was blank: just **UNAUTHORISED CONNECTION.**

Static rippled. Someone barked, 'Cut the link'.

Another voice, low and hard: 'No. Let him speak'.

But nothing cut. One of the silhouettes shifted as though trying to terminate the call. The connection didn't drop. Another tried the same failure. Icons flickered uselessly, frozen in place.

Richard leaned forward into the camera. Calm. Cold.

'Don't bother. You can't end this. Not tonight'.

In his ear, Graham's voice was casual, almost amused. 'They can pull cables, reboot servers. Won't matter. Until I release it, they're locked in here with you'.

A ripple of unease crossed the shadowed panel. Distorted whispers bled into the feed.

Richard's voice cut through them. 'You know who I am. And you know what I've already done. The Laird in Scotland—gone. Jonathan—gone. The UK region closed down, and their Alpha...'

He jerked his thumb towards Adrien, slumped in the corner. 'In chains'.

One of the filtered voices tried to sound contemptuous. 'You've made enemies you can't even name'.

Richard smiled without humour. 'I don't need your names. I've got your patterns. And I will take you apart one by one. Don't think your mansions, your guards, or your shadows will save you. Don't think your island fortress or your villas will protect you. I'll come there too. None of you is beyond reach'.

For the first time, a note of panic leaked into the distortion.

Someone hissed, 'How does he know that?'

Another snarled, 'Trace him! Trace the call!'

Graham's voice slid silk over steel. 'Go ahead. Trace away. All you'll find is yourselves chasing your own tail'.

Richard leaned closer, eyes hard. 'You've lived for decades on fear. Tonight, you get a taste of your own medicine. You will hear footsteps in your halls. You will check shadows twice. You will wonder, every time a door opens, if it's me'.

The silence stretched, taut and electric. Even through the distortion, he could hear their breathing shift.

Finally, Richard straightened, his tone dropping to something like a vow. 'Your time is over. The Syndicate ends here, in my lifetime. That's the only certainty you can take from this call'.

Richard's expression hardened. 'End it'.

The screen went black, leaving the room in sudden silence.

Adrien let out a bitter laugh from the corner, blood in his teeth. 'You think you scared them?'

Richard turned, meeting his gaze with quiet fury. 'No. I reminded them what fear feels like'.

He walked out into the night, leaving Adrien to the guards.

Richard left the glow of the homestead and walked into the cool air. The vines whispered in the breeze, the scent of eucalyptus sharp in the air. In his arms, Callie stirred, a small sound against his chest, her warmth grounding him in the present.

The jacaranda loomed ahead, its branches etched silver in the moonlight. Beneath it lay his father, his mother, and now his grandfather—the line he carried forward.

He paused, shifted Callie so her tiny hand curled against his collar, and stood in silence.

'We took one of them tonight', he said softly. 'Adrien's in chains. The rest... they know I'm coming. And I will come, one by one, until there's nothing left of them'.

The baby sighed, her breath a whisper against him. Richard's voice gentled. 'I'll keep her safe. I'll keep them all safe. That's my duty now. Yours is done. Rest easy'.

He bowed his head, just once, then turned back towards the homestead. As he walked away, the night seemed to thicken with presence.

From the shadowed boughs of the jacaranda, unseen but felt, the spirits of his ancestors watched him go—warrior, heir, and father—carrying their bloodline and their fight into the dawn.

Book 2 Coming January 2026

The Inheritance of Shadows

A story of family, power, and the price of legacy.

Five years have passed since Richard and Lydia's wedding in Margaret River.

Callie, their bright bilingual daughter, grows between two homelands — London's winter bells and the red earth of Western Australia. Her laughter carries the cadence of both worlds, her innocence a living thread between past and future. Yet to some, that thread is dangerous.

In Whitehall, a new generation of the Prime Minister's covert unit — Richard's own *shadow squad* — moves quietly beneath the surface, facing an enemy that now wears respectability like a mask. The Syndicate has not vanished. It has evolved.

For Nicholas Aldridge-Orlov, distant cousin and ruthless heir to the old order, the family name is no longer heritage — it's a weapon. From his super-yacht moored under Richard's very nose in Canary Wharf, he reaches for influence that could bend Westminster itself to his will.

And as the world turns toward a new century, Richard and Lydia must protect not only their daughter, but the fragile peace they've built — a peace shadowed by old debts, buried secrets, and a coming reckoning that will test the loyalties of family, nation, and blood itself.

A Note from the Author

Thank you for reading *The Heir and the Shadows,* my debut novel.

I hope you've enjoyed the journey as much as I enjoyed bringing Lord Aldridge and his world to life.

Your thoughts mean a great deal to me; they help shape future stories and keep the characters alive long after the last page is turned.

I'd love to hear from you!

Scan the QR code below or message me on WhatsApp to share your feedback and let me know what you thought of the book.

With warm regards,

Nic Smurthwaite

Author of The Heir and the Shadows

Printed in Great Britain
by Amazon

.